The Old Buzzard Had It Coming

The Old Buzzard Had It Coming

An Alafair Tucker Mystery

Donis Casey

Poisoned Pen Press

Copyright © 2005 by Donis A. Casey

First Edition 2005

10 9 8 7 6 5 4 3 2 1

Library of Congress Catalog Card Number: 2005921160

ISBN: 1-59058-149-0   Hardcover

Poisoned Pen Press
6962 E. First Ave., Ste. 103
Scottsdale, AZ 85251
www.poisonedpenpress.com
info@poisonedpenpress.com

Printed in the United States of America

In memory of my mother, Anna Beth Casey
Phoebe's girl

Love and thanks to my siblings, Carol DeWelt, Marti Casey, and Chris Casey, and their spouses and children, for whom I wanted to write our family's stories. Thanks also to my friend Suzanne Kiddy, for forty years of encouragement, to my sisters-in-law Lorraine Kinkg and Dolores Lukenbaugh for some great stories, and especially to my husband, Donald Koozer, my true partner in life and most loving critic.

Chapter One

It was just after dinner on that January day in 1912, and very cold with a threat of snow, when Harley Day began the journey to his eternal reward.

He made it to the outhouse, though he didn't remember if he actually managed to do his business inside or not. He did remember that there was a good sized stash of moonshine in the barn, and he navigated that fifty or so yards with only a couple of stops to rest and regroup. He got somewhat turned around in the barn, and after he had retrieved a jar, he realized that he had gone out the back and was headed for the woods instead of the house.

This fact in itself put him in a bad mood, for he couldn't quite get his feet headed back in the right direction. But as he drew near the trees, he could hear voices murmuring. Having to think about this quite put him out.

When he drew near enough to recognize the voice of his nineteen-year-old son, John Lee, Harley's irritation turned to anger. Something about that boy made Harley mad, especially since the boy had become so contrary. John Lee was supposed to be slopping the hogs now, and it occurred to Harley that he hadn't seen the boy in the barn. Indignant, he staggered toward the voices, then stopped, swaying in his tracks, when he realized who John Lee was talking to.

It was that Tucker girl.

It seemed like there were hundreds of Tuckers in Muskogee County, and Okmulgee County, and they were married to everybody and held every third office and owned every other business in the area. Harley hated the Tuckers, with their highfaluting ways, and he hated the fact that John Lee was talking with Phoebe Tucker, whose father's large property nearly wrapped around Harley's ratty little eighty-acre farm.

Harley's anger turned to rage. He could see them through the trees, sitting with their heads together on a little hillock, so engrossed in their conversation that a mule could have sat on them and they wouldn't have known it. Harley dropped his jar and lunged at the pair, feeling murderous.

The young people saw him at the last minute and scrambled apart, he with a yelp and she with a shriek of terror. Harley took a swipe at John Lee with his right hand and missed, but he managed to grab Phoebe's arm with his left.

Phoebe was a small girl, but her alarm gave her strength, and she almost twisted away. Harley managed to hold on and jerked her toward him, and she stumbled and fell to her knees. Harley was aware that John Lee was yelling at him. John Lee often yelled at him, lately. But there was something new in the tone of John Lee's voice that penetrated the fog of Harley's thinking.

John Lee sounded angry. Not afraid, like he usually did, or desperate, but angry. A righteous anger, like the preacher at a revival. For a second, Harley's curiosity got the better of his fury and he looked at his son.

John Lee's eyes, big and black and usually as mild as a deer's, were snapping. "You let her go, Daddy," he ordered.

The fury was back as suddenly as it had abated. "Boy, you should have listened to me when I told you never to see this gal again," Harley yelled.

"Let her go," John Lee repeated. His voice had dropped a register, and was as taut as a barbed wire fence.

"Don't you be talking to me like that," Harley warned. "I'll skin you alive. You get on back up to the house. I'm going teach this little piece of baggage to stay at home…." Harley had planned to say a lot more, but he didn't get the chance. John Lee punched him in the jaw.

For an instant, the wonder of this inexplicable event knocked every thought out of Harley's head. For nineteen years Harley had been abusing John Lee at his pleasure, and never before had the boy retaliated. At most, he would try to escape, or sometimes he'd run off and not be seen for the entire day. For the last year or two, he had been objecting when Harley hit the boy's mother, though sensibly she always told John Lee to mind his own business when he tried to intervene. In fact, there had been an incident with the boy recently, Harley remembered. Was it this morning? But this was the first time he had actually struck his own father.

Harley's befuddlement only lasted for an instant, and then the fury returned, doubly intensified by John Lee's unforgivable outrage.

Harley let go of Phoebe's arm and grabbed something off the ground. It may have been a stubby tree branch, or a clod, or a rock, Harley wasn't sure. He swung, aiming as well as he could through the red haze that glazed his view, and connected. There was an odd crunching sound and John Lee was flung face down into the leaf litter and lay still.

Phoebe screamed, but did not run away as any sensible girl would have. She tried to reach John Lee's prone form, but Harley seized her by the shoulders, and she turned toward him. He was vaguely aware that she was making a high-pitched sound, part fear and part outrage. She was fighting him. She attempted to jerk out of his grasp. Harley wasn't steady enough to keep his feet, and they went down together. Harley fell on the girl like a sack of potatoes, and her breath whooshed out past his ear.

Harley thought that Phoebe was struggling and crying under him. He thought that he saw John Lee sit up, then brace himself unsteadily with his hand on the ground. The boy said something that Harley didn't understand. He turned his head enough to look at his son, who was coming at him. John Lee reached into the bib pocket of his overalls.

Chapter Two

Alafair Tucker was standing on the porch, clutching a dishtowel, watching the two young people come up the tree-lined drive toward the house, and she shaded her eyes with her free hand in order to see them better against the pale gray afternoon sky. They were walking slowly, perfectly decorous, at least a yard apart, but Alafair was not fooled. Phoebe's face may have been serene as an angel's, but it was also beet red. The white house sat on a gentle rise facing the long drive that ran the quarter-mile from the road to the barn and stables so it was easy for Alafair to observe the couple for a considerable time before they reached her.

Alafair had not seen John Lee Day much since he had gotten so well grown, but there was no mistaking who he was. He still had the same stunning, big-eyed face that he had had when he was a ten-year-old and used to hang around the farm with all the other kids in the vicinity. He looked like a man, now, Alafair thought with a pang. A young man, to be sure, downy-cheeked still, but those cheeks were surely more gaunt than when she had last seen him. He looked to be a little less than middle height, but that still made him taller than Alafair's little Phoebe.

"Well, look what Phoebe has drug in," said the girl in the porch swing to Alafair's left. "It's John Lee Day as I live and breathe."

"Don't you have something to do, Alice?" Alafair asked, without taking her eyes off the advancing couple.

"Sure I do, Mama," Alice answered in that light, sassy way of hers. "But this here is much more interesting."

Alafair had long ago learned to school her pleasant features to look all business, but her mouth often betrayed her with unbidden smiles, as it did now as she looked over at Alice. Alice and Phoebe were twins, both seventeen and beautiful, but so unlike that it was hard to believe that they were even sisters. Alice was tall and incorrigible, blond as wheat and blue-eyed as the sky. Phoebe was like the little bird she was named for, small and neat, with an abundance of waving dark russet hair and fine, deep-set hazel eyes that could be either green or gold depending on the light and her mood. She was brave, Phoebe was, and could stand up for herself when she had to, and with Alice for a twin, she often had to. But left to her own devices, Phoebe was by far the sweetest of all of Alafair's children, and a real dreamer. "I can't remember the last time I saw John Lee," Alafair observed to Alice. "He used to be around a lot to play with you kids when he was a youngster."

Alice shrugged. "Ever since he's gotten old enough to walk behind a plow his daddy's kept him as a slave, I think. You know how we've got to walk by their place on the way to town? Seems like he was always there by the road, at the gate in front of their farm, watching us go by when we went to school."

"Didn't he go with you?"

"He left school when he was about thirteen, if I remember right. He still shows up at that gate, though. Especially when Phoebe walks by. I think he's sweet on her."

Alafair looked back out at the advancing pair and rubbed her arms, wishing that she had thought to throw on a shawl before she stepped outside. Her breath clouded the air as she sighed. "Now, why haven't I heard about this?" she wondered aloud.

"Why, you know how Phoebe is, Ma."

"I know you'd never let her hear the end of it if she got her a beau."

"True enough," Alice said with a laugh. "And you know what? Now that I think on it, Phoebe sure has taken a liking to strolling up and down the road lately."

Alafair shot Alice a stern look. "You just go inside, now, and help your sisters with supper, or find something else useful to do. It's too cold to be sitting around doing nothing, anyway."

Alice looked as though she might say something else annoying, but apparently thought better of it and stood up. "Want me to make the cornbread tonight?"

"Ask Martha. She's in charge of supper this evening. Now hurry up. Your daddy and the boys will be in directly."

The screen creaked and the door clumped closed behind her when Alice went inside. Alafair walked down the porch steps to meet Phoebe and John Lee as they came in the gate.

A white fence defined the front yard where in summer Alafair grew herbs in small plots along the stone walk, and sometimes flowers, when she had the inclination. Native elms dotted the yard, and a large hackberry tree shaded the side of the house. A square stone well graced one corner of the yard, though it was covered and seldom used, now that a pump had been installed next to the back door. There was no back yard, only a fire break of twenty feet or so between the back of the house and a patch of woods which served as playground, dog run, pig buffet, and home to a small flock of wild turkeys.

Alafair acknowledged Phoebe with a smile before she looked beyond the girl toward John Lee, who had stood aside to let Phoebe pass. He snatched the wool cap from his head when Alafair looked at him, releasing an untidy shag of black hair that fell across his forehead.

Alafair leaned against the support beam and placed the fist clutching the dishtowel on her hip. "John Lee Day," she greeted. "I haven't seen you since before there was dirt. What brings you around?"

John Lee drew himself up and looked her in the eye, shy but straightforward, and pressed his cap against the breast of his threadbare coat. Alafair caught her breath when the boy looked up at her. She hadn't realized what a looker he had become. For just an instant, she was bemused. The fist on her hip dropped to her side, and the dishtowel unfurled like a flag.

"Good evening, Miz Tucker," John Lee was saying, when Alafair came to. "I met Phoebe on the road yonder, and figured I'd walk her home and say hello to y'all, being as I ain't been by here in so long."

Phoebe came up to Alafair's side, quiet as a shadow. She slipped her hand into her mother's, but kept her gaze on John Lee.

Alafair said, "You've grown up since I saw you last, son."

"I don't get away from the farm, much," John Lee admitted.

"How is your mother?"

He hesitated. "Well enough, ma'am," he conceded. The words "given her husband" were unspoken but understood.

"And all them young'uns?"

"Growing right along, ma'am."

"What happened to your eye?" Alafair asked, in the same polite tone of inquiry, though more gently.

John Lee's hand flew to the gash next to his right eye before he could stop himself. It was a rather ugly gash of about three inches, not very old, since it was just beginning to swell and redden. It had been carefully cleaned, but still oozed a little. John Lee sighed a barely perceptible sigh and smiled a rueful smile. "Reckon I run into a door, Miz Tucker," he said.

Alafair nodded. She didn't look at Phoebe, but the girl's hand tightened around hers. Harley Day's reputation was well known in Muskogee county. It had long been rumored that he struck Mrs. Day, and Alafair expected that John Lee was plenty old enough to object. Her heart tightened. He probably ran into a lot of doors.

"Why don't you come in and let me doctor that?" Alafair offered. "It don't look too bad. Shouldn't take but a minute."

John Lee shook his head. "Thank you, ma'am. I expect my ma can put something on it."

"We're just about to sit down and eat a bite of supper. You're more than welcome to stay if you've a mind," Alafair urged.

The invitation seemed to alarm the boy. "No, no, thank you, Miz Tucker. Ma's expecting me. I got to get back or she'll be wondering what happened to me." He looked at Phoebe, and a transformation came over his face that gave Alafair pause. "I just seen Phoebe strolling down the road past our gate and I wanted to keep her company for a bit, if you don't mind. It's just a nice evening for a stroll."

Alafair couldn't help but laugh at that. It had been drizzling a freezing rain off and on all day. The wind was still, but if it were twenty-five degrees, she would have been surprised. The layered clouds warned of snow before morning. "I don't mind if y'all take a little stroll," she told him, "though you might have picked a better evening for it. I do wish you would take some supper with us."

John Lee tore his gaze from Phoebe and looked at Phoebe's mother. "Thank you, ma'am, but I got to get home. Maybe some other time." He looked back at Phoebe again, and that strange transformation again came over his face. "Good night, Phoebe," he said, backing out of the gate.

"Good night, John Lee," Phoebe replied in a voice like honey.

Alafair and Phoebe stood together in silence, hand in hand, and watched for a long time as he went back down the drive, until he turned out onto the road toward his own farm.

"So, you've started taking regular strolls on down by the Day place," Alafair finally observed. "Must be half a mile. That's quite an amble in this cold."

Phoebe did not normally have a high color, but the cold and her emotions had already reddened her face, so her mother's question caused her to flush alarmingly. "I get cabin fever staying in the house all the time, what with this weather, Ma. Sometimes I like to have a little walk. John Lee has spotted me a couple of times and come up to his gate to talk to me. There's nothing wrong with that, is there?"

"No, surely not," Alafair said. "I think you should invite him to supper, though. Let me and your daddy meet him. Especially if you're going to be doing any more 'strolling' in the future."

"He's a nice boy, Mama," Phoebe assured her.

"I'm sure he is, Phoebe. Especially if you like him. Now let's get inside before I freeze to death. I swear it'll snow before the night is out."

They turned and walked toward the deep porch that ran along the entire front of the long white house. Alafair paused and took Phoebe's arm before they went inside. "Honey, I know you'll use your sense now," she warned. "But I want you to be careful about going over there to the Day place. That father of John Lee's isn't the best of men. And I'd really like for your daddy to look this boy over before you get too fond of him."

Alafair feared that if Phoebe got any redder, the top of her head would blow off like an overheated thermometer. For an instant, Phoebe's mouth worked, but no words came out. "You're right about that old man Day, Ma," Phoebe finally managed, her voice rapid and low. "He's just an evil man. He strikes Miz Day sometimes, and John Lee, too. You could see that. And he drinks something awful, Ma. He makes his own corn liquor and sells it to the low types around. I think we ought to tell the sheriff about him. But John Lee ain't like that, Mama. He's so good. He feels real responsible for his mother and them kids, and he's so gentle and kind, even to animals. He's never been anything but a perfect gentleman, believe me, Ma. And he wants to improve himself, too, and learn...."

Alafair patted Phoebe's arm. "Calm down, now," she soothed. "I never said we were going to forbid you to see him. You just ask him over first chance you get."

Phoebe said, "Yes, ma'am," but she looked troubled, and Alafair thought that Phoebe was afraid that John Lee's father would be the real impediment to their relationship. It hurt Alafair to admit to herself that this was probably the case.

⌖

It was a relief to finally get into the dark warmth of the house. They walked together into the large parlor, which was brightened by tall windows that covered two walls. Two doors in the back of the room led to the bedrooms, and to the left was the entrance to the enormous kitchen. The parlor was furnished with a settee and two horsehair-stuffed armchairs, plus several slat-backed chairs, a rocker and a few side tables. A fine old upright piano graced one corner, and two narrow iron cots were discreetly tucked head to head into another. A large quilt frame was appended to the ceiling by a rope and pulley at each corner, to keep it out of the way when not in use. The pot-belly stove in the center of the parlor was fired up enough to take the chill out of the air, but the real heat came from the giant wood-burning cook stove in the kitchen, where all six of Alafair's other daughters were in a frenzy of meal preparation.

Dark-haired Martha, twenty and the eldest, was the general of this evening's repast, and directing her troop with a skill that was beginning to approach Alafair's own. Almost-nineteen-year-old Mary, the best if sloppiest cook in the house, was spooning fried potatoes into a ceramic dish. Alice was in charge of dessert, since she had a particular talent for pies, and tonight's offerings were already cooling on wire racks on the cabinet. The youngest girls, Ruth, Blanche, and Sophronia, ages twelve, seven, and six respectively, were setting the table with much rattling and clanking of dishes.

"You girls done with your lessons?" Alafair asked the young ones, as she hung Phoebe's coat on the rack next to the back door.

The two little girls shrieked and skipped and both spoke at once, somehow conveying the message that they had no homework tonight. Blanche dropped a serving spoon on the floor and gazed at it in befuddlement before Ruth scooped it up and handed it back to her. "Now you got to go wash it off," Ruth informed her disdainfully.

"Ma," Blanche implored, indignant, "I just swept the floor this afternoon."

"Go wash the spoon, Blanche," Alafair told her, ignoring the faces that the girls made at each other as Blanche flounced off toward the wash basin with the spoon.

"I see Phoebe has deigned to grace us with her presence," Mary interjected.

"Phoebe was occupied with her new beau," Alice explained.

Mary looked up from her spooning, interested. Mary was blond and blue-eyed, like Alice, but not so tall. She wore her light hair in a careless braid as thick as a rope down her back, and had a habit of flicking the tail of it against her cheek when she was contemplating devilment. Now, she fingered the blue-ribboned tail dangerously. "Phoebe has a beau?" she asked. "I thought she had made a vow to die a maiden because there's no man in the world good enough for her."

"No, you're thinking of Martha," Alice told her gleefully. "Phoebe's the one who would just dry up and blow away with embarrassment if a boy looked in her direction."

"Has Phoebe got a beau, Mama?" Sophronia asked. "What's a beau?"

"You all just mind your business and leave Phoebe alone," Alafair scolded. "Phoebe, go out to the porch and draw up a pitcher of buttermilk. And be quick about it. I hear Daddy and the boys coming up to the house already."

Phoebe gave her a grateful sidelong glance and left out the back door with a haste that was just short of unseemly.

"Now, you girls leave Phoebe alone," Alafair warned, giving Alice an especially stern glower. "She's just trying to be friendly to that poor Day boy, and I think he could use all the friends he could get."

"John Lee Day," Martha said, intrigued.

"Is Phoebe going to marry John Lee Day?" Blanche asked.

"No," Alafair assured her. "Go get some more big spoons for these dishes here."

The front door slammed open and Shaw Tucker and his sons and their dog, Charlie-dog, spilled into the parlor, ripping off coats and hats and scarves and piling them haphazardly on the coat tree. The two black, white and tan 'coon hounds, Buttercup and Crook, who followed Shaw almost everywhere, stayed outside. "We're home, Ma," Shaw boomed, like he did every evening of the world. "It's drizzling rain. We're froze!" The girls poured into the parlor to greet their father, and Alafair followed behind. She stood in the kitchen door and watched fondly as Shaw indulged in his favorite ritual of kissing his seven beloved daughters hello.

Alafair's dark brown eyes softened. After twenty-one years of marriage, the sight of Shaw Tucker still made Alafair's heart warm up. He was on the tall side, close to six feet, and slim as a rail still, hard from the physical work of a large farm upon which he raised horses and mules, a few cows, a few crops. Not one gray hair streaked his head full of dark brown hair, and his amber and green eyes shone with humor and intelligence. A toothy white smile flashed at his girls from beneath his big bush of a mustache. Alafair was always amused at how the girls clung to him like vines when he came in from work in the evening, as though he had been gone for weeks, and how he always gave each of them a showy smooch in order of age.

As Shaw and his daughters played out their evening ritual, the boys, finally skinned out of their winterwear, made their way over to their mother for their own quieter greeting. There were only two of them, sorely outnumbered in this house of females, but what they lacked in numbers, they made up for in presence. The elder, Gee Dub, was dark-eyed and curly-haired, but otherwise the image of his father, even down to his never-fail good nature. He was amazingly grown-up for a fifteen-year-old boy, and always had been old for his years. He had never given his parents any trouble to speak of, and Alafair could hardly credit her luck with him. Somehow, she just knew deep inside it couldn't last—no child was such an unmitigated joy. Charlie-boy, on the other hand, had kept his parents on their toes for all of his ten years. His big blue eyes were deceptively innocent. He wasn't a particularly noisy boy, or naughtier than most, but he was the hardest-headed child to ever draw breath. Once he made up his mind to do something, he did it in the face of punishment, or the wrath of God.

Gee Dub leaned over to give his mother a casual kiss. She was continually amazed at how easy he was about affection, for a boy. "Daddy's in rare form, tonight," he observed.

"Daddy always paints everything large," Alafair conceded. She grabbed Charlie and squeezed him to her with a noisy smack on the cheek, just to tease him.

"Oh, Ma, quit now," he managed, squirming, and Alafair laughed. The big yellow shepherd, who was Charlie's particular friend, nudged at her skirt, and she rubbed his head. "You've just got to have some loving, too, don't you, Charlie-dog?" She straightened. "You fellows are freezing! There's hot water for you on the stove. Go wash up."

The boys and the dog ran for the back porch as Shaw headed toward her with his arms full of daughters and Blanche and Sophronia dragging on his knees. "Y'all sit down, now," he ordered the girls, "while I kiss your mama and wash my hands."

"You couldn't wash your hands and then kiss their mama?" Alafair teased.

"First things first," he told her, giving her an authoritative kiss on the mouth. "Where's Phoebe?" he asked, when he drew back. "I'm missing a girl."

"Out on the back porch getting some buttermilk," Alafair told him. "She had a little adventure today and the girls were teasing her. I'm sure you'll hear all about it at the table."

⌐◦⌐◦⌐

When they were all seated properly in their places, including Phoebe, Shaw folded his hands on the table and silence fell. "Charlie, would you say the blessing tonight?"

Heads bowed and Charlie drew himself up. "Lord, bless this food to the nourishment of our bodies. In Jesus' name, amen," he intoned.

"Amen," all said, in chorus, and the clatter of self-service began.

Supper in the evening was a lighter meal than midday's dinner, and consisted mainly of leftovers from the main meal of the day, along with fresh cornbread and couple of newly opened home-canned vegetables from Alafair's store to round out the meal. Wednesdays' fare, according to custom, was a huge pot of soupy brown beans and fatback, and home fries with onions on the side. The butter, white at this time of year, and its resultant buttermilk, were fresh that morning. The sweetened carrots and cooked tomatoes had been canned in the summer. Shaw and Alafair both liked to float raw onion in their beans, so Martha had chopped a bowlful. Each member of the family had his or her opinion on the proper way to eat cornbread in conjunction with beans. Some liked to open a square of cornbread on the bottom of the bowl and spoon beans over it. Some considered cornbread wasted if it was not slathered with butter and eaten along with the beans. Others preferred to crumble their cornbread into their buttermilk. Some preferred a combination.

Shaw was a butter man himself, dolloping it into his beans and onto his carrots and potatoes as well as his cornbread. "Who has something interesting to tell me?" he asked in the midst of his buttering.

"I seen Mr. Leonard cutting across the back field over by the creek again today," Charlie told him. "He was riding a mule and toting some big old saddlebags."

"Which Mr. Leonard was that?" Shaw wondered.

Charlie shrugged. "I don't know. All them Leonards look alike to me."

"I swear, Shaw," Alafair interjected. "That path to the creek is getting to be a regular highway for the neighbors. Maybe you ought to post some signs."

"Oh, it ain't that big a problem, is it?" Shaw said. "The path only cuts across our property for about twenty yards, and it's a mighty long way from the house, more than a mile."

"Phoebe is going to marry John Lee Day," Blanche piped in, before Shaw could consider the path problem any more.

"Is that so?" he said offhandedly. A man with nubile daughters grew accustomed to unfounded rumors of marriage. "When did you decide this, Phoebe?"

"Oh, Daddy, you know that ain't true," she replied, dripping with scorn at her little sister. "I met John Lee on the road and he walked me up to the house and now nobody can talk of nothing else."

"It's true, Daddy," Alice admitted, her eyes bright with mischief. "We're just starved for entertainment."

Shaw laughed at that, for his children were masters of creating their own entertainment. "I see that boy out in the fields every once in a while," he said. "He sure is a worker, and always respectful when we've had occasion to speak. Truly, I think he's the only one who does a lick of work on that scraggly farm of theirs. I swear he's the only one over there I ever speak to, though."

"I barely know Miz Day to see her," Alafair confessed. "It's shameful not to know your neighbors any better, but it seems like they prefer to keep to themselves and shun company."

Shaw nodded. "It's strange," he agreed. "Do you remember Harley's old dad?" he asked Alafair. "He was a fine man. He had a share in the brick plant, I believe."

"I know Jeb Stuart Day," Charlie said in. "He's just my age, and we play sometimes. His daddy don't let him come over here, but I see him at school when he comes."

"Me and Fronie play with Mattie and Frances," Blanche contributed. "They're nice, but they don't come to school all the time, either."

"I talk at John Lee some," Gee Dub told them. "Sometimes our cattle get in together over by the pond, so every once in a while we meet when I go to bring in the stock. He's nice. He really admires the horses, Daddy. Said he wishes they could afford to raise horses. I used to be friends with that oldest girl, Maggie Ellen, but I haven't seen her in ages. I heard she got married and is living in Checotah now."

"They're poor, ain't they, Mama?" Ruth asked.

"There's no shame in being poor," Alafair told her.

"There's poor and then there's poor, Ma," Alice noted.

"That's hardly the kids' fault," Martha pointed out.

"No, it ain't," Shaw agreed, "and I'm pleased that you all have made friends with them sad ragamuffins. But the sadder truth is that Mr. Day is not a man I want you kids consorting with. So it's all right if they want to come over here and play or visit, as long as they come up to the house and say hello first. But I don't want you kids going over there onto the Day property." He looked at Phoebe. "Especially you girls," he said. "Y'all understand?" There was nothing stern about his tone, but all the children took serious note of what he was saying. There was a straggle of "yes, Daddy"s. Shaw's eyes crinkled over the cornbread he had raised to his mouth as he looked across the table at Alafair. A wordless parental agreement to discuss this topic later.

"Now, what have the rest of you been up to all day?" he wondered.

That night it snowed; fat, wet flakes that fell thick and drifted deep. In her dream, Alafair was running toward town, toward the doctor, as fast as she could go, her dying baby in her arms. Her lungs were bursting, but the faster she ran, the farther away the town became. Alafair awoke with a start, her heart pounding and her cheeks wet with tears. The snow sat deep and heavy wherever it fell, and as dawn approached, Alafair could hear cracks like pistol fire as tree limbs succumbed to the weight of the snow that blanketed them.

Chapter Three

The snow lay on the ground for three days, deep and white under a gray sky, ribbed with the black of bare tree limbs and half-covered buildings, a black and white world. On Saturday evening, the clouds began to break up and the wind shifted, and the thaw started. By nightfall, the roof edges had cleared and black ruts stood in the roads and footpaths. The thaw continued in earnest all day Sunday, and by Monday morning only patches remained under the trees and in the shady spots, and anomalous drifts on the north sides of buildings.

It was young Frances Day who spotted her father's ear protruding from the melting snow that drifted against the house. She sat for several hours next to the wall in the sun, playing with her corn cob doll and watching fascinated as the rest of the man emerged from the snow. He was lying on his right side with his hands pillowing his head, as though he had lain down against the house for a little nap. When he was pretty much uncovered, Frances notified her mother that she had found Daddy.

Not that they had been looking for him. Harley made a habit of going off on a drunk for a week at a time, which was always a nice respite for Mrs. Day and the children. He had been missing for five days this time, ever since the evening of the big snow. Now a general atmosphere of relief prevailed among the surviving Days once it had become clear they no longer had to anticipate his return.

Monday was washday in Alafair's scheme of things, as it had
been with the women in her family since time out of mind.
The clothes were gathered and the beds stripped while breakfast
was being made. After breakfast and before her help was called
away by the demands of work and school, Alafair and the girls
separated the clothes while Shaw and the boys toted her iron
cauldron and wash tubs and hand-cranked wringer into the yard
for her. Alafair started the fire as the girls formed a loose bucket
brigade between the pump and the kettle.

After Shaw and the kids had left, Alafair was joined by the
wife of one of their tenants, a Negro woman by the name of
Georgie Welch, whom Alafair paid to assist her in doing the
laundry for eleven people. Georgie was a pleasant, talkative,
competent young woman with an infant of her own. Alafair
enjoyed her company and loved playing with the baby, a boy
named Doll, whom Georgie kept in a large, willow-lath basket
while they worked.

While the water was coming to a boil, Alafair dumped a
measure of soap and the whites into the cauldron, which she
agitated with a broom handle for a while, then left to soak in
the soapy water while Georgie prepared the smaller tubs for
scrubbing, rinsing, starching, and bluing.

While the whites were being boiled and stirred to Alafair's
satisfaction, she and Georgie scrubbed and rinsed the clothing,
and starched selected Sunday pieces as stiff as wood. As she
finished each piece, she rolled it up and placed it into a wicker
basket. When the basket was full, the women stirred the sheets
for awhile before pouring the bluing water into the cauldron. It
took a lot of stirring and bluing and boiling before the whites
were eye-piercingly white enough to suit Alafair. When that
moment came, Alafair threw a bucket of soapy water on the fire,
and the women carried their baskets to the clothes line to hang
clothes while the sheets cooled enough to rinse and wring.

Alafair was thankful that the freeze was over and the wind was
moving, though the air was moist and it would take the clothes

longer to dry than usual. She rather enjoyed hanging clothes, since it gave her time to socialize, or when she was on her own, to think. As she hung the clothes, she took inventory of all the new holes and stains and rips that she had missed while sorting, planning her mending and deciding who needed a new shirt or skirt and what items were almost ready for the rag bag.

After the clothes were hung, Alafair and Georgie returned to the cooling kettle and lifted out the sodden whites with the broom handle. Wringing and rinsing and wringing and rinsing the unwieldy pieces of cotton big as sails was the most tiresome part of the job. When they finally got the things draped over the remaining clothesline and a couple of spare bare bushes, they were tired, and allowed themselves a couple of gusty sighs before they dumped the used water in bucketsful at the bases of the shrubs and trees around the yard. Alafair raked out the fire and Georgie rinsed and cleaned the smaller tubs, and returned them to their places on the work benches on the back porch, but they left the big iron kettle for Shaw to move back into the shed. Alafair paid Georgie a quarter and two quarts of canned apples, played with the baby in the kitchen for a few minutes while she caught up on Georgie's family, then both women retired to their respective domains to start dinner for their families.

Dinner on wash day always consisted of leftovers from Sunday dinner, since cooking from scratch was out of the question on such a busy day. Alafair had just built up the fire in the stove when Shaw got home. It had taken him almost half the day to deposit all the kids where they needed to go and to take care of some business at Mr. J.W. Brown's hardware store. The trip into Boynton only took twenty minutes in good weather, but a buckboard loaded with people took twice that long when it had to slog through the mud. His first stop had been to deposit the kids at Boynton Public School, including the twins, who along with two boys comprised the entire senior class. Mary had graduated high school in the spring, and now was helping Miss Trompler, the first-though-third grade teacher, while she decided if she wanted to be a teacher herself. Her parents had offered to send her to the teacher's seminary in Tahlequah, since she could get her education and live with Alafair's brother Robert's family there. And Alafair and Shaw were great proponents of education, for the girls as well as the boys.

It was the same when Martha had decided that she wanted to learn the rare and coveted skill of typewriting, because, she told her mother, she could always support herself and would never be totally dependent. Shaw had taken her to enroll in a six month business course in Tulsa, where she could, after all, get her education and live with Shaw's aunt Suley and her husband. Martha had come back armed with myriad sophisticated skills and immediately gotten a well-paying position as secretary to Mr. Lucas Bushyhead, president of the First National Bank of Boynton. The grandparents were scandalized.

After leaving Martha at the bank and doing his business with Mr. Brown, Shaw headed for home. He had already put in several hours' work with the animals before he had taken the kids to town, and Alafair knew that when he finally got into the house after unhitching the team, parking the wagon, and feeding the horses, he was going to be ravenous.

Alafair was standing at the kitchen window, tying her apron behind her back and watching Shaw drive toward the barn, when she caught sight of Sheriff Scott Tucker come riding up the drive on his tall roan mare.

She turned and walked through the parlor and out onto the front porch just as Scott reined at the gate. Alafair walked down the steps, clutching her sweater to her, and Scott removed his hat as she neared.

"Howdy, Alafair," he greeted cheerfully. "Finally warming up, ain't it?"

"I reckon," she responded. "I was glad it's warm enough to do a wash without the clothes freezing on the line. We'll be sitting down to dinner in half an hour or so. Come on in and join us. Have some coffee, gab with Shaw a spell."

Scott looked toward Shaw, who had almost reached the barn with the buckboard before he had seen the sheriff ride in. He had just begun to turn the wagon around and head back toward the house. "Sorry, Alafair," Scott said regretfully. "Can't do it. Just come to see if Shaw will help me in a bit of a chore. I'm on my way to the Day place." Scott Tucker was Shaw's cousin, owner of the Boynton Mercantile Company and the six room American Hotel above it, both of which were run by his wife. Scott was far too busy being sheriff to give much of his time to his businesses.

"What brings you hereabouts?"

"The oldest Day boy just rode in on that lop-eared mule of theirs to tell me that they found Harley Day froze to death out in the yard."

Alafair straightened. "Well, I'll be," she managed. "Froze, you say."

Scott, a shorter, rounder, and even jollier version of Shaw, laughed, seemingly unconcerned about the seriousness of the situation. "Yes, indeed," he assured her. "Apparently he wandered off from the house drunk on Wednesday night, and they thought he was just off on one of his benders. Turns out he lay down next to the house on the north side to take a little nap and promptly froze to death. Just this morning the drift melted enough for them to figure out where he'd gone."

Alafair contemplated this for a moment. "Where is John Lee?" she finally asked.

"He told me that he was going to tell his daddy's sister and brother-in-law, who live north of town, see if they'll take the kids for a spell."

Alafair nodded. "The ways of the Lord are strange," she observed.

Scott shrugged. "I don't imagine that the family will be overly broke up about the old reprobate's passing."

Unwilling to speak ill of the dead, Alafair didn't respond, but she thought Scott was probably right. More than likely it would be a great relief to Mrs. Day not to have that horrifying presence around herself or her children any more. But losing one's husband, even such a poor specimen as Harley Day, presented another whole set of problems. Especially if one were without resources, either financial or emotional.

Shaw pulled up in front, and Scott maneuvered his horse around to the side of the wagon. "What brings you out this way on such a sloppy day?" Shaw asked.

Alafair leaned up against the gate and rubbed her hands together to warm them. "Old Harley Day has died," she informed him.

Shaw looked at Scott for confirmation, his eyebrows rising. "Is that so?" he asked.

"It is so," Scott told him. "I'm going over there right now, and I figure I'm going to need some help moving the body after I see what's what."

"Did he get killed or what happened?"

"His boy says they think he died of the cold when he fell down drunk outside the house."

The corner of Shaw's mouth twisted up in his characteristic smirk. "Well, go along, then, and I'll follow you in the wagon directly."

"I'll come with you," Alafair interjected, and both men looked over at her. "Miz Day will be needing some help laying out the body," she explained, heading for the house to get her coat and wool scarf.

Scott plopped his hat back onto his balding head. "Y'all come along as soon as you can," he called, already cantering toward the road.

Shaw sat chaffing his hands and stomping his feet for ten minutes, calling to his hounds, who kept leaping in and out of the back of the wagon, before Alafair reappeared, bundled to the eyes and carrying a tin pail and a towel-wrapped tin jug that Shaw fervently hoped contained hot coffee.

He relieved her of the food and she climbed up onto the seat next to him. He snapped the reins and called to the team of mules, and they began to move as Alafair dug into her tin pail and brought out a couple of pieces of cold fried chicken. "There was a little chicken left over from yesterday, and I whipped up a couple of bean sandwiches with onion. It ain't much, but it'll tide us over."

"I'll sure have some," Shaw told her, "and pour me some of that coffee before my insides freeze solid."

Alafair pulled a mug out of the bucket and maneuvered the lid off of the jug with her mittened hands. "I'll swear, I haven't had one thought about the Days in a year, and all of a sudden they're all over the place."

"They're not the type of folks that one really gets friendly with," Shaw said, between bites, "though it is odd that we never saw them kids any more than we did."

"I think that father of theirs kept all of them on a pretty short leash."

There was a pause in the conversation when they reached the road. Alafair climbed down from her perch and swung the heavy wood and wire gate closed after Shaw drove out. He pulled up in the road and waited while she dropped a piece of looped wire over the end of the gate and the terminal fence post, then hauled herself back up next to him. "I'll tell you what I think is odd," Shaw said, as though they had never interrupted the conversation. "For somebody that's as much of a friend of the downtrodden as you are, I'm surprised you ain't Miz Day's best friend and protector."

Alafair knew he was twitting her a little bit, but she bristled just the same. "I tried to make friends with that woman dozens of times over the years, as you very well know, but she was having none of it."

"Yes, I very well know," Shaw admitted, amused. "Now that that skunk of a husband of hers has gone on to his reward, such as it may be, she might be more willing to be neighborly."

Alafair shrugged. "Truth is, I always got the feeling that she's more ashamed than unfriendly. No money, bunch of raggedy kids, an occasional black eye, if I read that situation right. I'd have helped her, if she'd have let me, but I couldn't very well force myself on her."

"No, that would have shamed her," Shaw agreed.

"You expect that they'll be able to stay on?" Alafair wondered anxiously. "I'm thinking the bank might foreclose on them."

"That's a possibility," Shaw admitted. "Though they won't if there's a brain to be had amongst them bank officers." He flicked a glance at his wife. "Which I wouldn't bet money on," he added. "But the truth is, it's John Lee that does all the work on that farm, along with help from all his little brothers and sisters, at least from what I've been able to see."

"Scott said the same thing."

"Problem is the boy is underage, and it wouldn't be him that holds the note on the farm. So my guess is that they'll be having to pack up and leave."

"That's a shame," Alafair decided. "I'm guessing that Phoebe will be broke up about it."

"So you think Phoebe is really sweet on that boy?" Shaw asked, sounding surprised.

Alafair laughed. "I hate to admit that I didn't know anything about it 'til this week, but from the way she turns all red and can't look me in the eye when his name is mentioned, I'd say yes."

Shaw sat up a little straighter in the seat. "What do we know about this boy?" he demanded.

"You know him better than I do," Alafair pointed out.

There was a short silence while Shaw pondered. "He talks a nice story," he said, "but I'm thinking he's going to have enough on his mind to keep him from going and courting for a long while. Perhaps it's just as well that they'll likely be moving on."

"Let's not be making any decisions that aren't ours to make," Alafair warned, "nor making assumptions before we know what's what."

Shaw made a harrumphing sound and fell silent, and Alafair busied herself with packing up the lunch leftovers. She knew Shaw well enough to know what was on his mind at that moment. He went through this every time one of the girls cast a sidelong glance at some boy.

❧❧❧

The gate at the Day place was standing open and they pulled through and started up the drive toward the house. Much of the snow had melted away, and the road was muddy and hard to navigate. It took them almost as long to drive from the road to the house as it had taken them to come from their front door to the Day front gate. They could see the house from the road, and a depressing house it was, weather-beaten and unpainted, standing in the mud.

"There's Scott," Shaw observed. Alafair could see Scott standing by the side of the house, looking down at something she couldn't see but had an uncomfortable feeling about. Mrs. Day stood a bit to the side, absently patting two urchins who clung to her skirts. Alafair studied the woman as they drove up to the house and Shaw jumped down to drape the reins over the porch rail. He whistled at the hounds, who had trailed them from home, and they obediently leaped into the bed of the wagon, out of the way. After her few unsuccessful attempts to befriend Mrs. Day here on the farm, Alafair only saw the woman rarely in town. Mrs. Day was a fairly young woman still, but looked older than her years, skinny and faded, with the demeanor of a whipped pup. When Alafair tried to speak to her, she had always murmured something and scuttled away with a look of mingled fear and longing. She always had at least two or three children with her, silent, big-eyed waifs who were ragged but clean.

Alafair got down and she and Shaw walked around the house. Shaw removed his hat as they neared, and Scott moved up to take charge of introductions.

"Miz Day, you know my cousin Shaw Tucker and his wife, don't you? I asked them to come on over and help us out."

The woman gazed at them for a second out of eyes that registered only blank surprise.

"Why, we know Miz Day, sure enough," Shaw replied, as though they were the best of friends. "We're real sorry to hear of your loss."

Mrs. Day's bewildered gaze moved from Shaw to Alafair, and they looked at one another in silence for the space of a breath. "Miz Tucker," the woman said, for a greeting.

"Miz Day," Alafair responded. "I come to help you lay out your dead." To be less forthright would have been disrespectful, to minimize what had happened.

Mrs. Day nodded. "I appreciate it," she said. She spoke matter-of-factly, polite, deferential as befitted the difference in their social status. But Alafair recognized the dreamlike look of shock in her eyes. Alafair looked down at the two little girls, one on either side of their mother. They both returned her gaze, wide-eyed and rosy-cheeked, infinitely more curious than upset by the untimely demise of their father. Alafair tried not to smile.

"Miz Day," Scott said to her, in his most solemn and official voice, "Doc Addison will be out before nightfall, but at this point it looks pretty straightforward to me. I don't see why we can't move him on into the house."

"Yes, sir, Sheriff," she said.

"Looks like he just lay down here and went to sleep."

"Yes, Sheriff."

"Me and Cousin Shaw here could probably use some help getting him inside. Where is John Lee?"

Mrs. Day's bemused expression didn't change. "He ain't got back from town yet, Sheriff."

Something sharpened in Scott's expression. "He ain't?"

Mrs. Day didn't seem to be aware of the subtle shift in Scott's attitude. "Reckon we got a load of relatives to notify, Sheriff."

"That so?" Scott responded, mollified. "Well, I expect we'll manage, though he's probably pretty stiff by now."

Alafair's eyes widened at Scott's casual tone.

"He's pretty dirty, too, ain't he?" Scott was saying. "Looks like he rolled around in the pig sty a mite before he decided to have a nap."

Mrs. Day dispassionately looked over at the earthly remains of her husband. "Yes," she said, as though she rather expected that was exactly what happened.

Scott looked toward Shaw and Alafair and gave an almost imperceptible shake of his head, acknowledging that questioning the woman right now was probably useless. Shaw moved forward, and Alafair stood aside with Mrs. Day and the girls as the two men hunkered down on either end of the body. They hefted what was left of Harley Day, Shaw at his head and Scott at his feet, and followed the widow up the porch steps and into the house.

Mrs. Day had already cleared the table, and the men deposited Day on the warped and well-scrubbed surface.

"You want me to send for the undertaker?" Scott asked, and Mrs. Day looked up at him.

"No, thank you, Sheriff. I reckon we'll just keep him in the shed 'til I can get a hole dug in the plot out back."

Scott nodded. He hadn't expected that she could afford the services of Mr. Lee, and the weather was still very cold, after all. "The county will provide you with a box, if you like," Scott told her.

"Me and some of my folks would be proud to help you with the grave digging," Shaw added.

She looked relieved. "I'm obliged, Mr. Tucker," she admitted. "It would have been hard for John Lee to do all by hisself."

"Now, you men just go out on the porch and wait for Dr. Addison," Alafair ordered, "while we do what we have to do. Girls," she said, looking down at the two little clinging bundles of curiosity, "y'all go outside with Mr. Tucker and Sheriff Tucker and let your ma and me get to work."

All tasks allocated, the men withdrew, each with a little girl by the hand, and left the two women to the grim and intimate task of preparing the body.

It took the women a few minutes to tug Harley's stiff limbs out and arrange him supine on the table.

Alafair rolled up her sleeves as Mrs. Day removed the big pot of water warming on the stove and brought it to the table. They worked in silence for several minutes, straightening the body and drawing off the wet, muddy clothing. Alafair turned her back as Mrs. Day tugged off the long johns and decently draped Harley's privates with an old dishtowel.

Alafair took a wet cloth and lathered it well with lye soap, then began washing the greasy black hair as Mrs. Day started at the feet. Alafair noted with distaste that this was probably the first bath that Harley had had in quite some time. The clothing they had removed from the body was amazingly filthy, as if he had indeed been rolling in some very black mud. The whole right side of his body was coated with a thick layer of it, from tip to toe. His clothes had been well-mended, though. Mrs. Day probably did the best she could under bad circumstances. Alafair glanced at the silent woman.

"Where's the rest of your children, Miz Day?" she wondered.

"Harley's sister from over north of Boynton come and got most of them just a little while ago," she replied. "Mattie and Frances wanted to stay. Naomi is around here, somewhere. I swear, that girl is always going off by herself, lately. The others will be back tomorrow, probably."

"How many kids you got?"

Mrs. Day looked up at her, perplexed, and Alafair thought that the woman was not used to someone being interested in anything she might have to say. "They's seven still alive and at home. Oldest girl run off last year. Got married, I believe. I ain't seen her since, but I hear she's still around here somewhere. Three other kids died when they was pretty little, back when the whooping cough was going around."

Alafair nodded while squeezing her already blackened rag into the bucket. "None of mine are married. Their daddy says they're way too particular, but really, we're both glad."

"I married up with Harley when I was thirteen," Mrs. Day commented dispassionately. "He weren't so bad when I first met him. Always was full of vinegar back then, and big ideas, looking for ways to make himself rich. Seems like all he could ever find was ways to get himself in trouble. John Lee come along directly."

Alafair looked up sharply. Eleven kids in nineteen years, and the woman couldn't be much over thirty. Alafair was filled with compassion and a nameless anger, quite unaware of any irony that might be inherent in the fact that she had borne eleven children herself, and was two years shy of forty. She, at least, could afford to feed and clothe her happy brood, and had been fully compliant in the conception of every one of them.

"I got nine living," Alafair told her. "I lost a couple of little fellows when they were babies. It's hard."

Mrs. Day shrugged without looking at her. "Sometimes it's God's mercy."

For an instant, Alafair was shocked at the comment. She hadn't felt the hand of mercy when her boy had choked to death in her arms, blue and staring, as she ran for the doctor. But the shock abated when she admitted to herself that she did not think life so horrible that she would have been grateful to see her children spared the experience.

"What do you plan on doing now?" Alafair wondered.

Mrs. Day didn't answer right away, just dipped her cloth and washed, dipped and washed, until Alafair wondered if the woman had heard her. But she had heard. She straightened suddenly. "I ain't thought," she managed. "I expect I have to plan, don't I?"

A sob escaped her, and tears spilled down her cheeks in a flood. "He's really gone, ain't he?" she choked out, her voice full of wonder.

Not for an instant did Alafair imagine that Mrs. Day was overcome with grief at the realization of her loss. It was not grief that had overcome the woman, but profound, unspeakable relief.

Alafair dropped her cloth and went to Mrs. Day's side. "You just cry, now," she soothed, gripping Mrs. Day by the shoulders. "He's truly gone. He can't bother you no more."

Mrs. Day's eyes widened at Alafair's perception, and she succumbed to more sobbing that took a few minutes to subside. Finally she wiped her face with the corner of her apron. "I expect you think I'm evil," she said shyly.

"I do not," Alafair assured her. "Folks have to earn the love of others. I expect you done your duty by him and more than your duty. It wasn't your fault that God decided to take him and free you and your kids."

"I could have gone looking for him."

"Phoo!" Alafair puffed her disdain. "He could have stood away from the corn liquor. Don't you go berating yourself for anything, any more."

Mrs. Day gazed at her warily for a long minute before a small, unaccustomed smile formed on her lips. For a moment, she looked as young as she was. She began bathing her husband's cold limbs again. "Maybe my Maggie Ellen, my gal that run off and got married, will come visit me now that Harley has gone. Me and the other kids miss her awful. Maybe I'll pack up and head back to Idabel. My folks can't take us in for long, but my ma's a Chickasaw, so I'm half. I expect the Nation will watch over us 'til I can get on my feet."

"You won't be trying to stay on here?"

She shrugged. "I miss my folks."

"So you'll be selling."

Mrs. Day looked surprised. It hadn't occurred to her that she now owned something. "Why, I reckon I could," she managed. "I'll have some money then, won't I?"

If you can find a buyer before the bank forecloses, Alafair thought. "My husband can help you," she offered, struck by sudden inspiration. Why not? The Day place adjoined theirs. It had buildings and woodland, one good plowed field, and Bird Creek ran right through it. If she knew Shaw, he had probably already considered buying, and would pay the widow a good price for it, too.

"Thank you," Mrs. Day was saying. "I don't know nothing about them things."

Mrs. Day had finished washing the entire front of the body while Alafair was still working on the filthy hair and grimy face. "How'd Harley get this black eye and bruised jaw, here?" Alafair wondered. It hadn't been apparent under all the dirt.

"Oh, he was always getting in some scrape," Mrs. Day told her dismissively. "Him and Jim Leonard from up the road a piece just had a set-to the other day."

Alafair pushed the head to the side so she could get to the back of the neck. She scrubbed a bit of black crud under the left ear, perplexed at its hardness. Her hand barely hesitated when she saw the dirt take on a rusty hue as it came off on the cloth. She stopped washing and straightened.

"Are your husband's good clothes ready, Miz Day?" she asked.

"Oh, yes. I'll get his clean shirt."

Alafair stood still until the woman had bustled out of the kitchen, then bent down close to examine the mysterious clot under Harley's ear. She soaked her cloth and scrubbed vigorously. She stood up quickly when Mrs. Day came back into the kitchen.

"He ain't got no regular pants," Mrs. Day said. "Overalls will have to do, though I don't expect Harley would care."

Alafair dropped the cloth back into the bucket and rolled down her sleeves. "I'll leave you to dress him. Do you need some help drawing them clothes on?"

"No, I'm plenty strong."

Alafair nodded. "I'll be right out on the porch with my husband when you're done."

Alafair left her and walked quickly through the house to the porch. Shaw was sitting in a cane-bottomed chair with one foot propped on the rail, playing cat's cradle with a piece of string, to the vast amusement of the two little Day girls. He looked over at his wife when he heard the screen door, and assessed her expression at a glance. He leaned forward and eased the cat's cradle over the pudgy fingers of the eldest girl. "You girls go on out in the yard and practice for a spell," he instructed, and they scampered away. Shaw stood up. "What is it?" he asked Alafair.

"Where's Scott?" she asked.

"He's around to the side of the house looking the place over. For some reason he's got his suspicions up. He can't tell me why. I figure he's been doing this depressing business too long."

"I'd say he's got the second sight."

Shaw's eyebrows went up. "Did the wife tell you something?"

"No. She's so glad to be shet of the old sot that she doesn't know if it's day or night. But I think I found something that shows that he was helped out of this world."

Shaw regarded her skeptically. "What?"

"There's a bullet hole behind his ear."

"A bullet hole!" Shaw echoed, loudly enough that Alafair shushed him. "I didn't see no bullet hole in his head when he was laying out in the yard," he added, more discreetly.

"It's behind his ear, I told you, and it was all caked with blood and dirt. I didn't see it either, at first."

"Why wasn't his head blowed off?" he insisted, unable to accept that a bullet hole in somebody's head could get past him.

Alafair's amusement at his attitude momentarily overcame her horror at her discovery. "Well, it would have to be a pretty small caliber bullet, wouldn't it? I didn't have time to check for powder burns around the wound. Go look for yourself if you don't believe me."

"Oh, I believe you know a gunshot wound when you see one," Shaw conceded. "What I can't believe is that me and Scott missed it."

"You weren't looking. The point is that Harley Day didn't just freeze to death."

"Which ear was this wound behind?"

"Left."

Shaw's gaze wandered into space as he visualized how the body had lain. "Well, he was on his right side. Could it be that somebody shot him while he was lying there drunk? He couldn't have bled much."

"It would have killed him instantly. And it was cold."

Shaw nodded. "What does she have to say about it?"

"I didn't say anything to her, though she may have seen the wound by now."

"You expect she done him in?"

"No," Alafair assured him firmly. "I don't think she's sorry he's dead, that's for sure. But she doesn't act like somebody who just did an act of murder."

"Well, now. If she was scared of him, and driven to desperation, I can see her doing it like this," Shaw speculated thoughtfully. "Little gun, a woman's gun. She gets him right in the head while he's passed out in the mud like the pig he was."

"Makes sense. I'd be tempted myself if I was in her situation. But it don't feel right. She just don't act like a woman with something to hide."

Mrs. Day came out onto the porch, and they fell silent. The woman was white. "Mr. Tucker," she began, "would you kindly come in here and have a look at something for me?"

Alafair and Shaw glanced at one another, then followed Mrs. Day into the house. She led them into the kitchen where Harley's remains lay neatly washed, combed, and dressed in his cleanest overalls and least mended shirt. Mrs. Day put her hand on her late husband's cheek, and with some effort, pushed his head over to the side. "What do you make of this?" she asked.

Shaw bent down for a close look. He examined the little wound carefully for a moment before he stood and looked down at Mrs. Day. "My wife was just telling me that she found a bullet wound, and that's what it is, all right. The sheriff will have to know of this, ma'am."

Mrs. Day, who for a few moments had looked as though she was going to bloom, now wilted before Alafair's eyes. "You mean he was murdered," she managed dully. Suddenly her unexpected gift of freedom had a price that would have to be paid.

"I'm sure Sheriff Tucker will get to the bottom of this right quick," Alafair soothed, "and you can get on with your life. Shaw, maybe you'd better get Scott in here."

⌁⌁⌁

Shaw left and Alafair and Mrs. Day went into the front room. The stove was out, and it was cold as a cave. One of the two narrow windows had been replaced by a raw-looking board. The glass in the other window was glazed with ice. The furniture in the room consisted of two homemade cane chairs, one bed and two pallets on the floor. Mrs. Day slumped down on the bed, and Alafair clutched her sweater around herself and sat down gingerly in one of the chairs. There was a moment of silence in which Alafair watched her breath mist in the air.

Scott came striding in purposefully from the kitchen with Shaw on his heels. He had obviously been enlightened, and he was all business as he approached Mrs. Day with his hat in his hand, polite and sympathetic, but firm. Shaw took up a post behind Alafair's chair.

"Now, Miz Day," Scott began, "I want you to tell me everything you can remember about the night your husband disappeared. It don't matter if it was important or not. You just tell me everything in your own words, and I'll decide what's important."

It took a few minutes for the poor woman to get up the energy to begin, but no one was inclined to rush her. "It wasn't no different than a hundred other times," she said. "He opened a jug late in the morning, and by noon he was blind drunk. I done something that riled him. I don't remember what. Looked at him funny, I don't know. He started clouting me. My oldest boy, John Lee, was home and took exception. He's started doing that in the last couple of years. He pulls his daddy off me and Harley flies into a rage. John Lee leads him a chase out in the yard. It was drizzling a cold rain, and beginning to freeze and they both were slipping and sliding around. There was no way Harley could catch John Lee, drunk as he was. After a spell, Harley staggered off to the barn and John Lee come inside. Harley never came in that night, and the next morning we found the mule and saddle gone, too. He has rode off for days at a time before, so we didn't think nothing of it."

"What day was it this happened?" Scott asked.

"Wednesday. Had to have been. That's when it rained and froze. Mr. Lang who owns the grain mill was supposed to come out and talk to John Lee about money Harley owed him, but he never made it. I remember me and John Lee talked about it. John Lee and Mr. Lang had worked out this plan to pay Mr. Lang back over time. John Lee figured something had come up in town and Mr. Lang got hung up. That was after John Lee and Harley got in to it. When I got up Thursday morning, there was a deep snow on the ground."

"What time was it that Harley went out to the barn?"

"I don't know. Before dinner. Must have been one or so."

"And when did you notice the mule was gone?"

"Next morning early. Milking time."

"So you saw the mule was gone when you went out to milk the cow?"

"My girl Naomi did. Naomi milks the cow. I was making breakfast when she come in and told me."

"Did you go out to see?"

"I did go, after breakfast, about sunup. It wasn't anything unusual, like I said."

"Were there mule tracks in the snow?"

Mrs. Day shook her head. "I didn't see any. But I wasn't really looking."

"So he must have rode off before the snow started. Did the mule ever come back?"

"No. Lord, I didn't think of that. We'll need that mule."

Scott leaned back against the wall, relaxed but sharp-eyed. "How do you reckon Harley got back here and got himself shot in the head up next to the house in time to get covered up in a snow drift?"

Mrs. Day began to cry. "I don't know. Lord Almighty."

"Did you hear any shots in the night?"

"Not a one."

"Such a small caliber pistol would be pretty hard to hear in the house, Scott," Alafair offered.

Scott's gaze shifted briefly to Alafair and back to Mrs. Day, but he didn't acknowledge her comment. "Where's your kids, now, Miz Day?"

"They're with my sister-in-law, all but the two outside there."

"John Lee, too?"

A look of terror passed over Mrs. Day's face and she burst into sobs.

Scott leaned forward again. "Miz Day, where is John Lee?"

"I don't know. I sent him into town to notify you, then he was supposed to go ask my sister-in-law to come get the kids. I know he did, 'cause she come, and said she talked to John Lee, too. I thought he was still at her place."

"How did he get into town without the mule?"

"He borrowed a horse from the Tuckers."

Scott glanced over his shoulder at Shaw, who was still leaning imperviously on the door sill. Neither Shaw nor Alafair changed expressions.

Mrs. Day stretched out both her hands toward the sheriff, imploring. "John Lee couldn't have done it, Sheriff Tucker," she wailed. "Not John Lee. I stood on the porch my own self and watched Harley chase him around 'til he forgot what he was doing and went to the barn. John Lee came back to the house, then. We all ate dinner, then did our chores, just like always. I never saw Harley again after that 'til we found him this morning. After we settled in, none of us went out again all night. I know it because we all slept in here that night to be close to the stove. It was cold. And that mule was sure gone the next morning. I saw with my own eyes."

Scott didn't argue with her, but the look in his eye was skeptical. He nodded. "Miz Day, if I was you, I'd be worried about John Lee. Somebody shot your husband and stole your mule and now John Lee is gone. If he shows up, or you hear word of him, you let me know right quick, you hear? Now, I got to go back into town, but I'll be back as soon as I can to hear what Dr. Addison has to say. I want you to stay at home until I tell you otherwise, ma'am. You understand?"

She nodded, snuffling.

Scott turned around. "Shaw, can you or Alafair stay out here with Miz Day and the girls 'til I get back in a couple of hours?"

Alafair stood up. "One or the other of us will stay here, don't you worry," she said firmly, addressing herself to Mrs. Day. "We won't abandon you."

Scott walked out onto the porch with Shaw, and Alafair patted Mrs. Day on the back. "I'll be right back," she soothed. "Just going to have a word with the sheriff before he gets away."

When she found the men at the end of the porch, she confronted Scott with her hands on her hips. "Scott Tucker!" she exclaimed in an angry whisper. "Did you have to be so rough with the poor woman? Ain't she been through enough?"

"Murder's been done, Alafair," Scott answered.

Alafair puffed and looked out into the yard at the two little girls playing in front of the house, both red-cheeked and runny-nosed, apparently unaware of how cold it had gotten. Leave it to the men to be so legalistic, to completely remove the heart from a situation that was practically unbearable as it was. But it was no use to argue. One couldn't explain light to the blind or sound to the deaf. Best to let them stomp around blind and deaf and take care of the seeing and hearing yourself.

"Did y'all loan John Lee a mount this morning?" Scott was asking.

"No," Shaw assured him. "And none of my stock is missing, so none of the kids did, either."

"He never even came by that I saw," Alafair added.

"You really think he might have done it?"

"Oh, I suspect he done it," Scott answered grimly.

For an instant, both Shaw and Alafair were stunned into silence by his pronouncement.

"Now, what makes you say that?" Shaw asked.

"Because he lied to me twice. His mama says he went to her sister-in-law's place before he come to tell me about his father's death, which he must have done, since she has already picked up the children. But when John Lee came to fetch me, he told me he hadn't been to his aunt's house yet. Said he'd be home directly after he talked to her, and he ain't here yet. And, as I mentioned this morning, when John Lee came by the sheriff's office this morning to tell me his daddy was dead, he was riding their mule."

Chapter Four

Shaw and Alafair sat together glumly on the front porch of the Day place while Dr. Addison was inside with Mrs. Day and what was left of Harley. The two girls were in there, too, which distressed Alafair, but their mother wanted them, and there was nothing Alafair could do about it. She consoled herself with the thought that the two children were apparently quite unconcerned about finding themselves fatherless. She expected that Dr. Addison made the family wait in the parlor while he conducted the preliminary examination.

"Do you think John Lee killed the old scalawag?" Alafair asked Shaw, after a long silence.

Shaw shrugged. "Looks bad," he admitted, "if he lied about the mule and then run off."

"If he did, do you think Miz Day knows about it?"

Shaw looked over at her. "It would seem likely," he admitted. "She said she stood on the porch and watched Harley and John Lee chase around in the yard. She could just as likely have stood there and watched the boy put a bullet in his daddy's head."

"I don't like the sound of that," Alafair said with a shudder. "It's awful cold to shoot a man as he lies drunk, even if he deserves it. Of course, there was no love lost between Harley and his wife. If she watched her boy kill her man, I don't doubt she'd do anything to protect him. I would."

Shaw chuckled. "I know you would. You'd defy the Lord himself to protect one of yours."

It was Alafair's turn to shrug. "He'd expect me to. That's what he put me here for."

"So you think John Lee did it, too?"

"I don't know, Shaw. I haven't seen much of John Lee for five years. He and Phoebe used to be particular friends where they were little, and it looks like they are still. He was a nice little kid, polite and well-behaved. Biggest old brown eyes. It just doesn't seem like he could have grown into somebody who would murder his own father."

"Maybe he grew into somebody who would do anything to protect his mother," Shaw pointed out.

"Oh, this is a terrible poser," Alafair said. "Did the boy do the worst thing in the world for the best reason? I have to say, though, I suspect that Miz Day doesn't know herself who killed her man. Why would she have called the sheriff if she was in on it? She seemed genuinely surprised to find a hole in the man's head, didn't she? If they conspired to help Harley keep his appointment with the Grim Reaper, then why didn't they just bury the body in the woods and say that he run out on them? Nobody would have thought twice." She leaned forward in her chair, her finger poking the air eagerly as she punctuated her argument. "And if John Lee did it, why did he go ahead on and tell Scott what had happened before he disappeared?"

There was a flash of white teeth under Shaw's mustache as he smiled at Alafair's enthusiasm for justice. "It's early days, yet, darlin'. Things may come clear all by themselves as time goes on. We don't even know what Doc Addison has to say about all this, yet."

"Scott sure has his teeth into it," Alafair observed.

"That's his job. You know how he is. Easy going as the day is long until an injustice needs to be righted."

Before Alafair could make another point, the screen creaked open and Dr. Addison came out onto the porch and walked over to them. Four doctors had set up practice in the booming town of Boynton in just the last five years, but Dr. Jasper Addison and his wife Dr. Ann had been practicing medicine around these parts since before most folks could remember. He was an imposing old fellow in his mid-seventies with flowing white hair and an equally flowing white beard. He had been doctoring since he was a surgeon's assistant with the Union's Fifteenth Arkansas Volunteers in the War Between the States, and he was by far the most educated man from Muskogee to Tulsa. Shaw stood when he came toward them.

Dr. Addison held up a tiny object between his thumb and forefinger for their inspection. "Twenty-two slug," he said. "My guess is it was fired from a derringer—some small lady's gun. Point blank into the mastoid."

"So you think it is as it appears," Alafair said. "Somebody put a gun to his head as he lay drunk and pulled the trigger."

Dr. Addison sat down in the chair that Shaw had vacated and leaned back, crossing one leg over his knee elegantly. He slipped the distorted bullet into the inside breast pocket of his coat. "Obviously someone did just that, Alafair," he replied. "The question is, is that what killed the man?"

A surprised sound escaped Shaw, and Alafair leaned toward the doctor, interested. "Do you mean that he was already dead when he was shot?" she asked.

The good doctor shrugged. "Who is to know, my dear? There are signs in the body that suggest that Mr. Harley Day froze to death, and was already speaking to his Maker when his would-be killer wasted his bullet."

"So it wasn't murder!" Alafair burst out, infinitely relieved.

"I didn't say that," Dr. Addison hastened to disabuse her. "All I can say for sure is that Mr. Day was already in the process of freezing when he was shot. I cannot tell which event ended his life. I can only tell that one occurrence followed hard upon the other."

"Well, well," Shaw mused. "I doubt if our gunman intended to make a simple empty gesture by purposely shooting a dead man in the head. Whether Harley was already dead or not, someone intended murder."

"And it could be that murder was indeed done," Dr. Addison admitted.

Alafair didn't comment. Her moment of hope had flown.

The rest of the day proceeded in spite of Alafair's disappointment. Scott returned from town and received Dr. Addison's report. As Shaw had predicted, Scott was little troubled by the question of when the bullet entered Harley's skull. Alafair desperately wanted to stay and watch as the investigation continued, but duty intervened. Shaw took her home, and together they did the afternoon milking before he drove off to pick up the children from their various pursuits and she brought in the laundry and began supper.

To supplement the leftovers from Sunday's dinner, Alafair prepared the brace of rabbits that Gee Dub had shot a couple of days before. She had taken them down earlier from the eaves off the back porch, where they had been hanging, and cleaned them over a tin washtub, and now she washed them and cut them into joints. She dipped them into beaten egg and flour, sprinkled them with a little salt and pepper, and fried them in a mixture of butter and lard in her cast iron skillet.

It didn't escape Alafair's notice that while the other children spent the entire evening in excited speculation about the intriguing end of their neighbor, Phoebe withdrew into a troubled silence. As far as Alafair could tell, only Alice seemed to notice her twin's mood, but uncharacteristically refrained from teasing her about it.

The girls were well drilled in their after-supper duties. Alice and Ruth drew the water from the pump by the back door while Mary brought up the fire in the stove to heat the dishwater. Martha hauled out the dishpan from the pantry, and Phoebe led the younger girls, Blanche and Sophronia, in clearing the table. Alafair seated herself in a chair by the kitchen door with her mending in her lap, presiding over the cleanup.

"You haven't had much to say this evening," Alafair observed to Phoebe. Phoebe shot her mother a surprised and wary glance.

How do they know, her expression said, these mothers, when something is on your mind? "I'm feeling a little draggy, Ma," Phoebe managed.

Alafair eyed her. "Are you feeling poorly? Come over here."

Obediently, Phoebe let her mother feel her forehead and cheeks. "No fever," Alafair pronounced.

Phoebe straightened. Her eyes wouldn't meet her mother's. "I'm not sick, Mama. It's just that time of the month. I'm a bit wan."

"You feel like you need to lie down? Fronie, stop that." Her eyes returned to Phoebe's face after her brief aside to Sophronia.

"No, Mama," Phoebe assured her. "I can finish clearing."

Alafair studied Phoebe in silence as the girl made several trips to hand dishes to Mary.

"You haven't said anything about Mr. Day," Alafair finally noted.

Phoebe gave her a furtive glance. "I don't know what to say, Ma. It's an awful thing."

Alafair considered this comment. It was very much in character for Phoebe, who was by far the tenderest of all of Alafair's brood. "It's beginning to look like John Lee may be in trouble," Alafair finally said, in her best conversational tone. "He shouldn't have run off. Should have stayed around and explained himself. It'd look a whole lot less suspicious."

Phoebe had finished clearing the table. Blanche and Sophronia had scampered off somewhere and the other girls were still involved in the kitchen. There was a lot of noise. Phoebe sat down. "Maybe he felt like he had to run off, Ma. He had fought with his daddy and all."

"I can see where he might want to hide in the first heat of things, but if he'd thought about it, he'd have seen it looks bad."

For an instant, Phoebe looked as if she might cry. "Things always are bad for him," she said. "I don't think he'd expect much different."

Phoebe's response took Alafair by surprise, and she swallowed hard, touched. "Well, honey," she finally said, "if it makes you feel any better, I've been thinking about it, and it seems unlikely to me that that poor boy did it. If he did shoot his father, it wouldn't be very smart of him to hang around home for three days waiting for a thaw."

Phoebe bit her lip and nodded, but didn't answer.

"You want me to make you some chamomile tea?" Alafair asked, falling back on a practical action she often took for her daughters' discomforts, physical and emotional.

Phoebe smiled. "Thank you, Mama." She hesitated, then continued, "You think it would be all right if I made up a pallet and slept here in the kitchen for a couple of nights?"

Alafair didn't think that a particularly odd request. The family's normal sleeping arrangements had the parents in the smaller north bedroom, the boys on cots in the parlor, and the girls in the larger south bedroom. Martha and Mary shared a bed, as did Alice and Phoebe. The younger girls shared cots that trundled under the big beds during the day. Often, when one of the kids was sick, Alafair allowed her the luxury of privacy by fixing up a makeshift bed by the stove in the kitchen.

"I think that would be all right," Alafair decided. Not that any of the sisters would mind. Ruth, Blanche, and Sophronia would immediately take advantage of the vacancy by jumping into the big bed with Alice, who would spend most of the night devising story and deed to scare them silly and irritate the older girls with muffled shrieks and scuffles. "In fact," Alafair continued, "I'll be going out to the Day place tomorrow to take some food out to them. I don't see anything wrong with your staying home and helping me, just for the day. Would you be willing to do that?"

A look a relief and gratitude passed over Phoebe's face and she leaned over to give her mother a hug. "Thank you, Mama," she said.

~~~

Later that evening, the family gathered in the parlor by the dim light of kerosene lamps to spend some time entertaining one another before bedtime.

Shaw melted a glob of butter in the bottom of one of Alafair's soup pots and popped an enormous batch of popcorn on the pot belly stove. He and Charlie-boy took turns shaking the pan and shaking the pan until every last kernel of corn was popped. The popcorn was meted out in bowls, and while the family snacked, Martha and Mary alternated reading from a favorite book of poems.

> *"Listen my children, and you shall hear*
> *Of the midnight ride of Paul Revere..."*

Alafair sat in her rocker by the window, listening with one ear as Martha regaled the family with her tales of working for Mr. Bushyhead at the bank and Ruth picked out a couple of tunes on the old upright piano. She tried to observe Phoebe without being too conspicuous about it. The girl seemed as engrossed in Martha's story as the rest of her siblings, and not overly nervous or upset. The idea that was niggling at Alafair, that Phoebe knew something she wasn't telling about this whole Harley Day affair, must just be her imagination. Phoebe was not good at being devious. Not like Mary or Alice or Charlie, the imps.

Of course, love makes one bold.

Alafair stopped rocking. She urgently tried to remember what she had heard in the last year or two about John Lee Day in conjunction with Phoebe. In fact, she had heard little enough about John Lee at all since his father had forced him to quit school and work the farm. She and Shaw and their friends and neighbors had all known of and deplored the situation at the Day place, but it was not unheard of for a man to drink to excess, or to determine that work was more important than education for his children, or to keep his wife at home. It was no one else's business, and none of the neighbors would have interfered. They would have helped any member of the family who asked, but no one had asked.

Shaw was playing his guitar now, and singing.

"The old gray mare, she ain't what she used to be,
Got stung by a bumblebee,
Climbed up the apple tree..."

Little Sophronia, scandalized, cried, "Oh, Daddy!"

Alafair got up and began collecting popcorn bowls to carry back into the kitchen. It seemed increasingly obvious, she thought, that Phoebe had not only kept in touch with John Lee, but had developed a relationship with him. She couldn't quite figure out how Phoebe had gone about it so thoroughly in secret. She wasn't surprised, though. If she had learned anything in all her years of motherhood, it was that children have lives, inward or outward, of which their parents know nothing.

Chapter Five

Alafair ran the hat pin through her good black felt bonnet with the bunch of carved cherries on the band, anchoring it to the thick knot of dark hair at her crown. It was an ongoing battle of hers to keep her hair neatly pulled back out of the way, but it seemed to have a mind of its own, and exasperated tendrils were always escaping any coif she attempted. She spent a moment trying to force a few tresses back into place.

As her mother arranged herself in the mirror by the door, Phoebe stood aside, clutching a covered dish before her in two hands. In the mirror, Phoebe could see the dart of Alafair's sharp brown eyes as she sized up Phoebe's reflection. Apparently, she passed muster, since her mother offered no criticism.

⌐⌐⌐

The Day farm was a sad, sorry place. The frame house had been white once, but no more. The yard was scattered with trash and rusty farm implements, rangy chickens, a cat or two and a yellow dog. The thought of lockjaw immediately entered Alafair's mind as they rode up the rutted drive. "Watch where you step, sugar," she said offhandedly to Phoebe.

A well-appointed buggy stood incongruously in front of the the house, the horse hitched to a porch railing. "Looks like Miz Day already has some visitors," Phoebe observed.

Several children stood on the porch and watched them as they halted the shay in front of the house and climbed out.

The eldest child, an ephemeral brown girl, stepped toward them. "Good morning, Miz Tucker," she greeted with an adult solemnity that startled Alafair enough to make her look at the girl more closely.

She was a small girl for her age, which Alafair judged to be early teens. She looked stringy and malnourished, even wrapped in a coat two sizes too big for her. Her Chickasaw ancestry showed in her high cheekbones and broad forehead, and her dark coloring. She bore a striking resemblance to John Lee. She had the body and face of a young fairy maiden, but the black eyes that scrutinized Alafair were the eyes of a forty year old woman who had not led a particularly pleasant life.

"You must be Naomi," Alafair acknowledged. "Will you please tell your mama that she has some callers?"

The girl smiled a weary smile. "Yes, ma'am. We've had a passel of callers today. Won't you ladies please come on in?"

"Why, thank you," Alafair responded, careful to accord this girl the respect that any civilized woman would show to another.

Naomi nodded, and her gaze shifted to Phoebe as they walked up the steps. "Hello, Phoebe," she said. "I'm glad you come."

"I didn't know you two were so well acquainted," Alafair said.

"We have spoke," Naomi informed her, as she led them inside. The knot of urchins followed silently.

Mrs. Day met them just inside the door, and Naomi took her place at her mother's side. "Y'all come into the parlor and look at how Harley turned out," Mrs. Day invited, "then have some tea with us in the kitchen. Naomi, take that there dish from Miss Phoebe and put it on the table with the others."

Alafair removed her coat and handed it to one of Mrs. Day's other minions, a boy of about ten, who appeared at her elbow. "You've been getting a bunch of callers, I hear," she observed.

"Yes, ma'am," Mrs. Day assured her. "I can't remember when we had so much food in the house." She led them into the parlor. The room had been cleaned and the beds removed, and Harley had been decently laid out in a plain pine box perched on two sawhorses in the middle of the floor. Alafair stepped up to the coffin and examined Harley's body, lying so inoffensively boxed. Well, Harley, she thought, look at you now. In all your pathetic life, somebody must have loved you sometime. "He looks right peaceful," she said.

"Don't he, though," Mrs. Day agreed. "Come on into the kitchen for some tea and cake, won't you? I'd like for you to meet some of our kin that's come to visit with us."

When they entered the kitchen, a tall, leathery man with graying hair stood up from a chair at the table. His companion, a pretty, black-haired woman, remained seated, but gave them a sweet smile. She had the most striking blue-green eyes Alafair had ever seen.

"Miz Tucker," Mrs. Day introduced, "this here is Harley's sister, Zorah Millar, and her husband, J.D. Zorah and J.D., meet Miz Tucker and her daughter Phoebe, my neighbors from over across the road."

J.D. muttered a greeting, and Zorah half stood and offered her hand to Alafair from across the table. "Yes, we've heard how your family has been so helpful since my brother met his end," she said. She looked at Phoebe with interest. "You must be John Lee's friend, Phoebe," she added.

Phoebe blushed charmingly, but responded with dignity. "Yes, ma'am. I hope I'm a friend to all John Lee's family."

Alafair studied the woman who was studying Phoebe. Zorah Millar may have been Harley's sister, but she resembled Mrs. Day in her size and features, except for the fact that she looked twenty years younger and thirty pounds plumper. It's a wonder, Alafair thought, what a useful husband and regular meals will do for a body.

Alafair knew of the Millars, but had never actually met any of them. The husband was a small cotton farmer who worked part-time at the brick factory. There were a few young children. They didn't go to her church, nor were any of their children particular friends of any of Alafair's. Alafair was not even sure that she had known that Zorah Millar was Harley Day's sister.

They settled themselves around the groaning kitchen table. Mrs. Day sat herself down with them to act as the official hostess, while the dignified Naomi took on the position of dogsbody, serving the guests.

"Y'all have a farm up north of town, I believe," Alafair said to the Millars. "I'm afraid I didn't realize you were Harley's sister, Miz Millar."

Zorah and her husband exchanged a glance before she replied. "I don't wonder that you didn't know, Miz Tucker. Me and Harley wasn't exactly close. Nobody in my family has been out here to Harley's farm in years."

"I fear Zorah and Harley didn't get along," Mrs. Day added.

"It's more like we had us a feud going," J.D. acknowledged.

Alafair shook her head. Was there no one in the world who could abide Harley Day? "Well, then, it's good of you to call on his folks in this time of loss," she said, at length.

"Oh, we never had no quarrel with the family here," Zorah hastened to assure her. She cast a sympathetic glance at Mrs. Day, who responded with a weak smile. "Why, we'd have done anything we could have to help these kids. They're all good kids, Miz Tucker, considering what they've had to put up with."

"That boy John Lee is the only reason this farm is making it at all," J.D. interjected. "Him and the older girls." He nodded toward Naomi, who was passing slices of cake on chipped saucers around the table.

"My sister-in-law has her hands full with all these young'un," Zorah said. "It's a wonder they've done as well as they have. How I wish we could have been more help!" She leaned forward, apparently anxious that Alafair understand their dilemma. "But it got so bad that we feared Harley would do us an injury if me or J.D. came out here."

"He threatened to," J.D. said.

Alafair looked over at Mrs. Day, who was listening to the conversation with an expression of polite interest. Nothing that anyone said about her husband seemed to cause her any consternation, Alafair observed to herself. Probably because she had been helpless to change anything for so long. Her gaze returned to Zorah and she smiled. Perhaps things would be different, now, she hoped.

"We'll be around more, now," Zorah said, answering Alafair's unspoken thought.

"Why, whatever could have happened to cause such a falling out between you and your brother, Miz Millar?" Alafair asked.

Zorah sighed. "Oh, it's a long story, Miz Tucker. I don't want to plague you with it."

"No, I'd like to hear it, if you don't mind," Alafair assured her, "and if it don't fret you to hear it, Miz Day. I'd be interested to try and understand something about Mr. Day. I don't believe I ever knew of anyone with so many enemies. What was it about him that would make somebody want to kill him in such a cold way?"

There was a moment of silence as the Millars and Mrs. Day stared at their laps and pondered Alafair's question. Alafair took a bite of her cake and cast a glance at Phoebe, who was watching the adults avidly. Naomi appeared at Alafair's side and refilled her coffee cup.

Zorah came to a decision and looked up. "Well," she said, "I kind of hate to talk ill of the dead, especially with Harley laid out in the next room and all. But the sheriff has already asked us about all this, so I suppose you'll hear the whole thing by and by." She looked at J.D. for support, and he nodded at her.

"Harley was always a rakehell," she began, "and irresponsible, but he didn't used to be as bad as he got. Nobody could be, I reckon. But he was a disappointment to our father. For years, Daddy kept trying to help him, don't you know. Kept giving him money, getting him jobs. Why, Daddy bought this piece of property here and let Harley live on it for just a little rent. Thought that maybe if he couldn't do nothing else, he could be a farmer. But Harley had big ideas. He didn't want to work on an oil rig, or at the brick plant, or raise crops. He was always looking for some way to make a lot of money fast."

"All he ever found was ways to lose his money fast," J.D. put in.

"That's the truth," Zorah agreed. "Before John Lee got old enough to take over, Harley pretty much squandered any money he made on a crop. Gambled most of it away, I think. He reached a point where he couldn't afford to buy seed, and had to go begging to Daddy for another loan. Well, Daddy give it to him. What could he do? Harley had a passel of kids to feed, and a new one every year. But he told Harley that that was the last money he was ever getting from him, and he better get to cracking."

"You can guess what happened, Miz Tucker," J.D. took up the story. "Harley lost every dime of that money on a Choctaw horse race over in Okmulgee. That was the last straw for old Mr. Day. I don't expect he wanted his grandkids to starve, but he figured that if he cut Harley off, he'd have to straighten up."

"Then Harley blamed Daddy for making him poor," Zorah added.

"Nothing was ever Harley's fault, as far as he was concerned," J.D. said. The silent Mrs. Day was solemnly nodding her agreement.

"Well, I blame Harley for busting Daddy's heart," Zorah said heatedly. Her gaze flicked guiltily toward the parlor, where the said Harley lay in state, unable to defend himself. Zorah sat up straight, stiffening her resolve. "Daddy died just a few weeks after that. His heart give out, Doc Addison said. Harley was his only son, and expected to inherit most of Daddy's estate. He actually gloated to me at Daddy's funeral. Can you imagine that, Miz Tucker?" Two spots of color rose in her cheeks. "I wanted to poke him in the face right then and there. But Daddy had the last word in the matter. He left everything to me, except for this pitiful farm. I don't think he would have left Harley that if it weren't for the kids."

"Well, Harley was fit to bust," J.D. went on. "He accused Zorah of turning their dad against him. He got him a lawyer and contested the will, but he lost, and then on top of everything, he was in debt to the lawyer. He threatened Zorah, said he'd hurt us somehow if she didn't give him some of that money, but I absolutely forbade her to do it."

"I didn't have no desire to, anyway," Zorah said. "But I did want to help my sister-in-law and these kids. I'd come out here for a while after that, bring food and clothes, but finally Harley said I'd stole everything from him but this farm, and if I set foot on it again, he'd be in his rights to shoot me."

"I declare!" Alafair breathed.

"Harley discovered moonshining after that," J.D. informed her. "Then there was just no hope for him at all."

"He grew to like his product too much," Zorah said bitterly. "Anyway, we saw John Lee every once in a while, and Maggie Ellen, when they come to town. Maggie Ellen had her a nice boy-friend in town, you remember that?" she asked Mrs. Day. "That Dan Lang who works over at Dasher's blacksmith shop."

"Is he any kin to the Mr. Lang the grain merchant?" Alafair asked.

"Yes, his second boy. I expected she'd marry up with him, but then I heard she'd found her somebody else. What ever happened to that Lang boy?"

For the first time, Mrs. Day looked uncomfortable. "Oh, he stopped coming around. Harley didn't approve."

Zorah snorted. "That figures, don't it? Harley couldn't stand anybody better than him. Which was just about everybody. Well, I'm glad Maggie Ellen up and took matters into her own hands."

"Why, that's quite a tale," Alafair acknowledged. "No wonder you've kept your distance."

"It's a sad tale," J.D. said.

"One that the sheriff knew all about," Zorah added. "I swear, after John Lee come to tell us Harley was dead, the sheriff was at our place with a thousand questions not more than an hour later."

"What kind of questions?" Alafair wondered.

Zorah shrugged. "He was real interested in what time John Lee showed up, what he said, when he left, which way he went. He asked where I was on Wednesday night. I told him I was home with the kids, and J.D. was out of town. He wanted to know all about where J.D. had gone and when he got back."

"I went to Tulsa earlier that week," J.D. explained, "on some business for Mr. Francis. I was supposed to be back Thursday morning, but the train was delayed by the snow. I had to spend the night on a bench at the station in Muskogee, and didn't get in 'til Friday afternoon."

"How is Sheriff Tucker's investigation progressing, have you heard?" Alafair asked Mrs. Day.

"I haven't heard nothing new from the sheriff," Mrs. Day told her. "I was kind of hoping maybe you know something, being kin and all."

Alafair smiled. "My husband's cousin Scott may be a funny old bear in private life, but when he's about an investigation, he's the most conscientious, single-minded creature that ever sat in a chair. He'll not go blabbing about, that's for sure. And you can rest easy that if Scott Tucker has anything to say about it, justice will be done."

Mrs. Day didn't reply, but the look on her face told Alafair that she thought justice had already been served, and she feared that any more justice would just lead to tragedy.

"Has John Lee showed up, yet?" Alafair wondered.

"No," Mrs. Day answered tersely. "But he will, and this foolishness will be cleared right up."

Naomi, who had just finished gathering up the dishes, shooed some stray children out the kitchen door and disappeared into the parlor behind them.

Unexpectedly, Phoebe stood up. "Mama, I'm going to help Naomi with the kids," she announced.

Alafair looked up at her, surprised, then nodded. She and the other adults took up their conversation after Phoebe had gone.

"Why do you think John Lee run off, Miz Day?" Alafair asked.

"I don't think he did," she assured Alafair. "I expect he went off on his own. Sometimes he does that. His timing is just bad this time, that's all."

"Well, who do you think put a bullet in your husband's head?"

Mrs. Day straightened, and her eyes showed an unaccustomed spirit as she prepared to defend her offspring. "I don't know, Miz Tucker," she said. "But it weren't John Lee, or anybody in this house. Doctor Addison said it was a .22 slug he dug out of Harley's head, probably from a derringer. Well, we ain't got a derringer, or any pistol of such small caliber on this farm. We just got Harley's daddy's old .45 Colt and a Winchester '86 and an aught-twelve shotgun. I don't think I ever even seen a lady's gun."

"Did you tell all this to Sheriff Tucker?" Zorah asked her.

"I did. He didn't seem much impressed."

"Well, I sure think John Lee is an unlikely killer," J.D. stated, "even though nobody had as much grievance against Harley as him. I don't think that boy has a mean bone in his body."

"Is there anybody you suspect?" Alafair asked Mrs. Day.

"Lord Almighty, Miz Tucker, it could have been anybody," the woman declared. "Harley had more enemies than you could shake a stick at. He was always getting into beefs with them lowlife scum he sold his home-brew to. Why, just a couple of weeks ago, Mr. Lang that we just mentioned was out here complaining that Harley hadn't paid him for that last fifty bushels of corn that he bought. I never seen him so mad. He said Harley wasn't getting another ear of corn from him if he didn't pay for the last batch that was delivered. John Lee made a deal to meet with him and arrange a way to pay."

"Harley bought the corn for his brew?"

A tiny smile, shy but defiant, appeared. "Didn't used to. Used to use the corn we growed ourselves. But three years ago John Lee wouldn't let him have none, and sold every bit of it before Harley could get his hands on it. He has done that ever since, and now Harley has to use the money from his moonshining to buy his corn."

"I expect he had plenty," J.D. commented. "I hear bootlegging is a going concern."

Mrs. Day shrugged. "I don't know," she admitted. "We always figured that Harley has a cache of money hid around here somewhere, but none of us ever could find it, if he does."

Alafair noticed that Mrs. Day was still using the present tense when referring to her husband, but didn't correct her. "So John Lee really ran things around here."

"He did and he does," Zorah assured her. "Harley never bothered with the farm. So you see there wasn't no reason for John Lee to kill him."

No reason but rage, Alafair thought.

When Alafair was ready to leave, she realized that Phoebe had been gone for quite a while. She stood on the porch with Mrs. Day and the Millars, saying her good-byes in a vague quandary, when Phoebe came around the house with Naomi. Naomi walked up the porch steps to stand beside her mother, and Phoebe climbed into the shay. The girls did not take their leave of one another. They didn't even look at one another. Naomi wished Alafair a solemn good day, and that was all.

Alafair didn't speak to Phoebe until they were out the gate and back on the road toward home. "Where did you and Naomi get yourselves off to?" she finally asked.

Phoebe skewed her a glance. "She was showing me around the farm," she said.

"That little old girl must be five years younger than you," Alafair observed. "I wouldn't think you'd have much to say to one another."

Phoebe shrugged. "I wanted to ask her what she thought about John Lee," she told Alafair. "Besides, Ma, you may have noticed that Naomi is older than her age."

"I did notice that," Alafair admitted. "Sometimes that happens, when the parents aren't very mature. The kids become older than their folks. Fortunately, you kids don't have to worry about that," she added dryly.

Phoebe's mouth twisted up in the corner with the little ironic quirk of a smile that all of Shaw Tucker's children had inherited. "I reckon not," she replied in a toneless voice that implied that maybe she reckoned so.

Alafair stifled a chuckle. "Have you ever met John Lee's aunt and uncle before?"

"No, I never met them, but John Lee did tell me not long ago that his uncle had come over and took his dad to task in an awful way for something Mr. Day did over at their farm. I guess Mr. Millar is the uncle he was talking about."

"Really? Do you know what Harley did to the Millars that called for such a dressing down?"

"John Lee didn't tell me. Maybe he didn't know himself."

"When did this happen?"

There was a pause while Phoebe figured. "Well, John Lee told me about it a couple of weeks ago."

"It's interesting that Mr. Millar didn't get home when he was supposed to," Alafair mused. She glanced at Phoebe, who was staring thoughtfully at the road. "So what did Naomi think about John Lee?"

"She thinks he didn't do it," Phoebe said, without looking at her.

"Does she have any thoughts on who did do it?"

"Not that she told me. And I certainly asked."

They were practically home already. Alafair pulled up in front of their outer gate and Phoebe jumped down to pull it open. Alafair drove through, then stopped while Phoebe closed the gate. She climbed back up beside Alafair and they drove to the barn. Not another word was exchanged between them on the subject of John Lee Day.

Something was up. Alafair's mother-sense was all aquiver. Phoebe was not acting strangely. She had not said anything suspicious or unusual under the circumstances. But something had changed in the ether that surrounded her daughter. Phoebe had found out something while they were at the Day place. Alafair considered how to proceed while she and Phoebe unhitched the horse from the shay. She was going to have to be careful. She decided to say nothing for the moment. Phoebe was preoccupied, and didn't notice the increased intensity of her mother's gaze.

The evening proceeded as usual; housework, animals, supper, cleanup, the ritual of going to bed. Phoebe made her pallet in the kitchen for another night.

"Aren't you getting tired of sleeping out here in the middle of everything?" her mother asked her.

"I kind of like it, Ma, having the bed all to myself."

"Suit yourself. But you're feeling better, now?"

"Not quite tiptop, but a lot better."

"Sleep well, then, honey."

Chapter Six

There was no possibility that Alafair was going to fall asleep. She lay on her back next to Shaw, listening to his even breathing, and staring at the ceiling for close to an hour. She was practically in a state of super consciousness, her ears as sharp as any cat's, hearing and classifying every sound in the house, and dismissing most as unimportant. The clock in the parlor ticked evenly. Charlie, full of little boy energy, even in his dreams, flopped on his cot in the parlor a few times before sinking into the catatonic sleep of the innocent. Blanche sighed in her sleep. One of the older girls in the next room shifted.

Alafair was drifting in that state between sleep and wake when she heard the brief click click click of Charlie-dog's toenails on the kitchen floor. Her eyes flew open. There was one tiny rustle, another half-dozen clicks, then silence. The brief, almost imperceptible creak of the back door screen.

Alafair didn't move, didn't breathe for a minute, giving the night-mover a brief head start. The instant she heard the back door latch settle into place, she rolled out of the bed and grabbed her shoes. She didn't worry about waking Shaw. She could have jumped on the bed without bothering him.

Alafair glided through the bedroom and the parlor into the kitchen. She was not surprised to see that Phoebe's pallet was empty. She had been half expecting just such a move since Phoebe's unusual behavior at the Days'. She snatched her coat off the coat tree by the door, and struggled into her shoes as she peered out the kitchen window into the yard. The moon was winter bright, illuminating the yard whiter than a torch. All was black shapes, except the few patches of unmelted snow, and the white quilt-wrapped shape of Phoebe floating quickly across the ground, past the outhouse, past the hen house, tool shed and barn, even past the stable at the top of the long rise behind the barn, accompanied by the yellow shepherd.

Alafair's brow wrinkled. Where was she going? She would have thought the barn the logical place to hide someone, especially in the winter, up in the loft, with the hay for warmth.

Alafair wrapped a scarf around her head and slipped out the back door, walking hurriedly after the receding figure. The thought of hay had given her the answer. Phoebe was heading for the soddie, or course—the original dwelling Shaw had thrown up when they had first bought the land fourteen years earlier and needed a place to stay while the house was being built. It was used for storing baled hay, now.

It was small, snug, well-insulated with hay and earth and safe enough as long as the foolish youngster didn't try to make a fire. Alafair puffed along in the cold and dark, keeping well back from Phoebe, who had the dog with her.

It was a twenty-minute walk to the soddie in the dark, long enough for Alafair to brood on every aspect of Phoebe's uncharacteristic behavior. Just how deep did this secret friendship with the Day boy go? Was it only a friendship, or something more? They were both just children, after all, not at an age known for levelheaded and thoughtful behavior. Oh, Lord, had sweet innocent Phoebe fallen for a murderer? Worse than a murderer, a parricide? Tears of anxiety stung Alafair's eyes. She'd wring that silly girl's neck. Look at her, so intent on meeting her sweetheart that she didn't even know she was being followed, traipsing around in the freezing cold wrapped in a quilt. She'd catch pneumonia. Alafair made a mental note to force hot rose hip tea down her and wrap her feet over a hot water bottle. To wet a strip of flannel with camphor and bind it around Phoebe's throat. She inventoried her fever medicines in her mind. Did she have enough onion and garlic in the house?

She shook herself back to the task at hand. She could see the soddie in the middle of the stubble-field, now, and Phoebe and the dog's ghostly forms making a beeline for it. Phoebe stopped in front of the doorless door and stooped to say something to the old yellow shepherd. Alafair quickly squatted down herself, to avoid being seen. Phoebe ducked into the soddie, leaving the dog sitting beside the door gazing after her. Alafair counted to sixty, then moved up to the shack as stealthily as she could.

The dog saw her, of course, but knew who she was long before she drew very near. He made no noise other than a few dull thumps as his tail hit the ground when he wagged his greeting. Alafair put her hand on the dog's head and urged him to accompany her around the side of the soddie, where one high window, unstuffed with hay, might enable her to hear what was happening inside.

She could hear them, all right, two young voices, one female, one male, speaking softly to one another in a murmur, just below Alafair's ability to comprehend. She anxiously pressed herself up to the wall near the window, her ears strained to the limit.

She listened, frustrated, as the young people talked for ten, maybe fifteen minutes, and then fell silent. Alafair sank down next to the house and draped her arm over the dog, feeling like she might explode. She desperately wanted to burst into the soddie, fling the two apart, and dash the boy's brains out against the wall.

If he cared for Phoebe, even if he only felt himself to be her friend, how dare he involve her in this nasty business? She indulged herself in her fury at John Lee for a minute, even as she was perfectly aware that there was enough guilt to go around.

She only had to restrain herself for a couple of minutes before she heard Phoebe step out the door again and whistle softly for the dog. Alafair pushed the dog away from her before Phoebe could come around the side of the shack to look for him. The dog shook himself and walked calmly around the corner to

Phoebe, with a single backward glance at Alafair, unsurprised by the inexplicable vagaries of human behavior. Alafair squeezed herself into the littlest package she could.

"There you are, you old Charlie-dog," Phoebe said, very plainly. "Let's get on back."

When Alafair heard Phoebe's footsteps recede, her breath escaped in one huge whoosh of relief, and not simply because she had not been discovered. Phoebe had not been alone with her fugitive friend long enough for anything untoward to have happened.

Alafair sat still for a minute, pondering. As she saw it, she had two long-range problems. First, she had to find out what there was between Phoebe and John Lee. Second, she had to know if this boy had killed his father, and if he had, were there mitigating circumstances? Her two long-range problems were momentarily precluded by two more immediate questions. Namely, was she going to rush into the soddie and demand that the boy tell her what he thought he was up to? And if she was not going to do that, how was she going to get back into the house without alerting Phoebe?

How long had she been away from the house? Forty-five minutes, probably. What if one of the kids had awakened and wanted her? Well, it would be a disaster, that's all. But it was unlikely.

Alafair rubbed her cold hands together and blew into them. She knew she wasn't going to confront John Lee, not right now. He wasn't going anywhere in the short run, and if she kept her counsel for a little while, she might learn something. She would have to be subtle as a summer breeze, she knew, since dealing with a wary teenager is more difficult than approaching a scared deer. And that included not just Phoebe, but all of Alafair's older kids, as well. They might not know everything about the situation, but as sure as the sun rises, they knew more about Phoebe and John Lee than she did.

She settled back against the grassy wall to wait a while, until Phoebe was settled back on her pallet and dozing, and Alafair could slip back through the front door.

A shuffle from the entrance froze Alafair as still as a rabbit. She held her breath as she listened to footsteps move away from the door of the soddie and the figure of John Lee appear just within her line of vision at the corner of the soddie. Alafair didn't panic. She knew if she stayed still, he probably wouldn't see her in the dark shadows. He walked out into the field about twenty paces and proceeded to relieve himself.

Alafair studied his compact figure with interest as he did his business. It didn't occur to her to be embarrassed. She had lived her life too close to nature to be bothered by a little pee.

The moon was bright and she could make out considerable detail about the boy, even if it was too dark to see his features. He was not a tall youngster, maybe five feet eight, but at nineteen, likely to add an inch before he was done. He was pretty broad in the back already, and narrow hipped, with lanky limbs and an untrimmed shag of hair. Years ago, he had been just one of the flocks of kids who had hung around when all the offspring were little. He hadn't been a brat, she remembered that. He said, "Yes, ma'am," and all. Usually barefoot, even when Alafair thought it too cold.

John Lee finished his task and put himself back together, then stood for a few minutes gazing up at the full moon before he visibly shuddered with the cold and turned with some reluctance and returned to his den in the hay bales.

Alafair felt a twinge of compassion for the fugitive. Maybe he was guilty and maybe not, but he was young, probably scared, and definitely cold, dressed as he was in nothing but a long-sleeved shirt and overalls. At least he was shod. She hoped Phoebe would have the sense to smuggle some old quilts or blankets to him.

She thought about Phoebe disappearing with Naomi earlier that day, and wondered if Phoebe was telling Naomi about John Lee's hiding place, or if it had been the other way around.

She could hear him scuffling around inside the soddie as he resettled into his lair. He emitted a sigh loud enough for Alafair to hear, and then silence. Alafair glanced at the moon. She stood up slowly, stiff and frozen-toed, and made her way home.

⌒⌒⌒

Alafair figured that the longer she waited to make her move, the more likelihood there was that John Lee would escape or be caught. She decided to do it early, while Shaw was taking the kids to their various pursuits and she was alone on the farm for an hour or so. The idea that she might be in danger from John Lee never occurred to her.

It was a miserable morning, still dark long after it should have been because of the heavy overcast. The wind was like a knife, freezing cold and full of little stinging bits of sleet. Alafair wrapped herself up like a mummy and filled a lard pail with some biscuits and bacon and hot coffee in a jar. She practically ran the quarter-mile to the soddie, partially because she was in a hurry and partly because it was so cold she feared that if she slowed down she would freeze solid in her tracks. She slowed a little as she neared the shack, and approached warily, not wanting to startle John Lee if he was watching. She stood before the door for a couple of seconds, took a deep breath, and ducked inside.

She saw nothing, except the u-shaped wall of hay bales that Shaw and the boys had piled floor to ceiling. Alafair stood still and studied the wall, her gaze sweeping slowly from side to side, top to bottom, trying to find the hay equivalent of a secret panel. She knew that in the fall, Shaw and his hired day-laborers had packed the soddie cram-full of baled hay, and as winter progressed, he had pulled out bales by the half-dozens, through windows and doors, until little packets of emptiness existed around the shack, like the anteroom she was standing in.

She was reasonably certain that the boy didn't have to remove a bale to reach his hiding place, since a bale of hay is heavy, and Phoebe certainly wouldn't be able to maneuver one with any ease. The bales were stacked in a flat, straight wall to within six inches of the ceiling. Climbing over would be so difficult that it was practically impossible.

Her eye followed the six-inch opening along the top. The bales were flush with the east wall, but stood out from the west wall about eight inches. Not enough to allow a human body to pass through. Not at first sight, anyway. Alafair stepped up and examined the opening, passing her hand around the hay wall. Only the front bales stood close to the wall. The bales behind were set back a good eighteen inches. She took a deep breath, blew it out, and making herself as skinny as she could, squeezed between the hard, scratchy hay and the soddie wall. For half an instant, she thought she wasn't going to make it, and an image of herself permanently wedged solid, waiting for rescue by some unsympathetic and highly amused offspring, popped into her mind. The very thought caused her to shrink another couple of inches and pop through into the corridor formed by the bales and the outside wall. She blew out a relieved breath, then paused a moment to pick hay out of her clothes and hair. The little hallway she found herself in was only about six feet long, and turned at an abrupt right angle at the back wall of the soddie. Alafair tiptoed forward and hesitated at the corner. For the first time she felt apprehension. She expected it might not be wise to startle a well-grown young fugitive in his hiding place. It was much warmer inside the soddie, with its tons of hay insulation, but she could still see her breath in the air. She held her breath and inched her eyes around the corner.

He was there, all right, sleeping like a baby, curled up in one of her better down comforters on a bed of loose hay and rough blankets. His nest was in an opening not six feet by six feet, as cozy and padded as a vixen's den. Alafair stood and looked at the sleeping boy for a long time. He was lying curled up on his side, swathed in blankets up to his eyes, so that all she could make out was a shock of black hair and two long fringes of black eyelashes. Light, such as it was, and air, were coming in from the high, narrow window just under the roof. The sun was fairly up by now, but it was still very dim, and chilly. A bucket of water sitting next to the wall was covered with a dark skin of ice.

Alafair looked at the sleeping boy and saw just that—a boy. Certainly no violent murderer. Any fear she may have felt vanished.

She took a step or two forward so that she was standing over him. "John Lee," she said in a normal voice. When he didn't stir, she tried again. "John Lee Day," she said, louder.

In the dimness, Alafair saw his eyes open and regard her dreamily for a second, then fly open in consternation. He sat up abruptly, and the comforter fell away from his shoulders.

There was a long silence as they gazed at one another. Alafair was pleased to see that John Lee's startle had faded quickly, and he sat looking at her matter-of-factly, plainly trying to decide if she were friend or foe.

And Alafair realized clearly that whether he had done it or not, she was his friend. Not that she would help him go unpunished if he were guilty. Rather that Alafair Tucker, mother of children, wasn't going to allow this child to suffer needlessly if she could help it.

John Lee, for all his rough condition, had the aura of innocence about him. And not just innocence of the death of his father, but soul innocence. How is it that some people can grow up in grinding poverty, in an atmosphere of violence and oppression, forced into literal slavery, and still maintain their innocence? Some are simply in a state of grace, and why God chooses whom he does, Alafair thought, is a mystery.

John Lee unfolded himself from his blanket and slowly stood up to face her.

"Miz Tucker," he greeted warily. "How did you find me?"

"Phoebe didn't tell me, if that's what you're wondering."

"Phoebe?" he echoed, with entirely convincing wonder. "Phoebe ain't got nothing to do with this."

An involuntary smile curled Alafair's lips. Good for you laddie-boy, she thought. But she said, "It's no use, John Lee. I followed her here last night."

He drew a breath, but said nothing.

"She's in big trouble, you know," Alafair observed.

"I made her help me," he replied evenly. "She didn't want to."

"Why did you run away, young'un?"

There was barely a pause before he answered. "Because I killed him."

Alafair's heart dropped. "Killed who?" she asked, giving him every chance.

"My daddy," he answered, throwing the chance away. "You don't need to pretend, Miz Tucker. I know he's dead. I seen him there, next to the house, all dead and froze."

"Doc Addison says your daddy froze to death," Alafair said.

"No, ma'am," John Lee said with conviction. "I shot him."

Alafair folded her arms across her chest. "Why did you do that, son?"

"Well, ma'am, he was trying to brain me with a rock. I had socked him, you see. I struck my own daddy, and he wasn't having none of it."

"Why'd you hit him, John Lee?"

John Lee bit his lip, then answered slowly. "He liked to hit my ma, Miz Tucker. He done that a lot when he was drinking, and sometimes when he wasn't. I finally had all I could stand, so I jumped on him. I guess I pummeled him a mite. He chased me around a while, but later that evening, when he come at me with the rock, I shot him. I didn't know I killed him, not 'til we found him that morning. He acted right shocked, when the bullet hit him, but then he just staggered off toward the barn. Didn't seem to bother him that much. He didn't even bleed that I saw. When I seen that the mule was gone the next morning, I figured that he just had rode off down to his still like he's done a hundred times before. I didn't know he was dead 'til my sister found him a few days later. Then I got to thinking about hanging, and after I fetched the sheriff, I run off. I know I shouldn't have done it."

Alafair was listening to John Lee's story with a growing sense of confusion. "What kind of gun did you shoot him with, John Lee?" she managed to ask.

"A little old two-shot derringer. I wouldn't have thought it would kill a flea."

"Them things aren't easy to come by," Alafair observed. "Kind of expensive, too. Where did you get hold of such a thing?"

John Lee hesitated for so long before answering that Alafair was fairly certain that the answer was a lie. "I saved up money for it," he told her. "I was going to give it to my ma for protection, but I had it in my bib pocket that evening."

"Was that before or after you met Phoebe on the road?"

"Well, it was before. I was trying to cool down, walking along the road, when I run across her. I didn't tell her nothing. She didn't know. She was just so calm and gentle, and made me feel better, so I asked if I could walk her home."

Alafair's hand went unconsciously to her forehead, which wrinkled with perplexity. "Sheriff Tucker says you were riding the mule when you came to tell him that your father was dead."

"Yes, ma'am. I came across him as I was walking over here, thinking to borrow a horse. He was just grazing by the side of the road as calm as you please, all saddled and everything. I caught him and rode him to my Aunt Zorah's and told her the situation. She didn't seem much surprised. She went to get the kids straight away, and I just rode off to think a spell."

"Where is the mule now?"

"I let him go out in the fallow field behind the pin oak stand, close by the creek. He'll have plenty to eat, but nobody goes out there much this time of year. I expected I'd throw the sheriff off a little."

"And how did you end up in our hay store?"

"I was just wandering around looking for someplace to hide where I wouldn't freeze. I thought my own farm was too easy to figure." He paused. His big dark eyes were shiny with tears, Alafair could tell, even in the dim light. "I done the worst thing in the world," he said. "I reckon they'll hang me." He sounded quite calm, but Alafair detected a catch in his voice. She resisted an urge to touch him, to comfort him. He sat down on a convenient bale of hay and perched his forearms on his knees. "Wish we had some light, don't you, Miz Tucker?" he said. "Course, I don't have no matches in here. But I wish you'd sit down a spell, ma'am, and let me talk a bit before we go to the sheriff."

Alafair was too curious to protest, and even if she had not been, she was in no hurry to make a decision about the boy. She folded her full skirt around her knees and sat down.

Her move encouraged John Lee, and he smiled, grateful for her—well, if not trust, then suspended judgment. "I'm sorry I run away," he began. "I don't mind paying for my sins. I ought to, I reckon. I just got afraid of going to hell. I don't see how God is going to forgive me for killing my own father. I guess I was looking to put off my eternal punishment as long as I could."

Alafair felt a physical pain in her chest as she listened to him talk. "If you face what you did, John Lee, if you're truly sorry, and you take your earthly punishment like a man, you can look to the Lord for mercy. I don't think God is so harsh."

He gazed at her. "You think so, Miz Tucker?" he asked, with tentative hope.

Alafair hesitated. This was the most important thing in the world John Lee was asking, and she wanted to be as honest as she knew how. "I don't know the mind of God, but I'll tell you this, son. I know how I feel about my own children. If one of them killed their daddy, now, I'd be practically killed myself. But I couldn't stop loving that child no matter how bad he was. And no matter what he did, I could never send any child of mine to burn forever in hell. And I'm only a mortal woman, John Lee. I figure God's love must be infinitely bigger than mine. So I don't think you ought to be scared of God."

John Lee's bottom lip, pushed out in youthful bravery, quivered a bit, and a couple of solitary tears escaped the corner of his eyes and slid down his cheeks. He let them go unheeded. "What shall I do, Miz Tucker?" he asked.

"You're going to have to turn yourself in."

"What do you expect will happen to me?"

"I don't know, John Lee," she said. "If what you say is true, it sounds like self-defense to me. They don't hang you for that."

"They don't? What then?"

"I'm not your judge and jury, son. I don't know what will happen. You'll probably have to go to jail for a while. But if you'll trust me for a day or so, and not stir a hair, I'll try to see which way the wind blows with Sheriff Tucker. Will you promise not to run away?"

"Yes, ma'am, I give my word." He paused. "What about Phoebe?"

"Don't you worry about Phoebe. I'll see to her."

"Please don't blame her for helping me," he pleaded. "She's a good, kind girl. It's my fault she got led astray."

"Now, John Lee," Alafair began.

"Can I see her before they send me away for good?" he interrupted anxiously.

"Oh, John Lee, you worry me like a dog with a bone! Let's see how things fall out. Now, I'm going to go make the best arrangements I can for you. Will you trust me, young'un?"

"Yes, ma'am, I will."

"You know that if you run again, they'll find you eventually, and it'll go worse for you," she warned, "and I'll see to it that you never see Phoebe again."

"Yes, ma'am, I know."

"Then you just sit tight here for a while. I brought you some breakfast here." She handed him the pail and eyed the quilts and blankets critically. "I reckon I can spare a pillow, too. Looks like you're set for bedclothes."

A ghost of a smile appeared on John Lee's face. "Phoebe allowed as how you might be peeved that I have your best comforter."

"Phoebe knows me pretty well," Alafair admitted. "You just stay stuck, now, 'til you hear word."

⌁⌁⌁

Alafair ran back across the field, through the scrub oaks, past the barn and outbuildings, and slammed into the house. It was getting colder by the minute, and blowing a gale. There would be an ice storm before the day was out. All the way back, she prayed that John Lee Day would get an attack of sense and stay where he was. She had already determined to delay telling Shaw where the fugitive was hiding until she had thought about this for awhile. Shaw may have been Alafair's partner in all things, and the finest man ever to set foot upon the ground, but he was a man, after all, and had a different way of seeing things. Shaw was more apt to stick to the letter of the law, and Alafair, in her own humble opinion, would cling more to the spirit.

And her spirit was telling her not to turn over an innocent boy for hanging. For Harley Day could not have staggered off to the barn after receiving the wound she saw. He would have dropped like a stone.

She had to have more information. Of course, it was entirely possible that John Lee was lying. An innocent face certainly didn't always mean an innocent man. If he was lying, he was not only a killer, he was so stupid it strained the bounds of credulity, and he did not strike her as such a dimwit. More likely, he could have thrown her that bit of disinformation just to give her pause. Which is exactly what it had done. If that were the case, he would be long gone before anyone could get back to the soddie. No, Alafair's intuition, in which she placed great and justified store, told her that John Lee sincerely had no idea that his father had been shot in the head. And in that case, someone else killed Harley Day.

Chapter Seven

There were innumerable people with a motive to kill Harley. In fact, to Alafair's way of thinking, Harley had invited killing. But who, besides Harley's immediate family, could have had the opportunity? Alafair had no doubt that everyone in town was speculating about the murder, and she felt a surge of frustration that she was isolated on the farm when she really wanted to be gathering information from anyone who ever knew Harley Day. Somebody had that piece of information, that one little illuminating fact that would cause the truth to dawn. It was clear enough to Alafair where to start asking questions. No one in town knew more about what was happening or what people were saying than Mrs. Fluke, the postmistress.

After feeding John Lee, Alafair figured she had a while before Shaw returned from town, so she dashed out to the barn and saddled the small mouse-grey filly that she usually rode. Missy, the horse, was as housebound as any of the people on the place, and was quite happy at the prospect of a trip to town. She stepped lively into the cutting wind, carrying Alafair to Boynton.

The town of Boynton hadn't even existed when the Tuckers had settled in the area. So many people moved into the region after the Creek Nation privatized the land that an enterprising fellow by the name of Finley laid out the town in 1902, and now, ten years later, Boynton boasted a population of close to a thousand people. There were two banks, five churches, and two schools, one for the white children and one for the colored children. The lively weekly newspaper was called the *Index*.

The Francis Vitric Brick Company, located just northeast of town, and the Boynton Refining Company employed one hundred and fifty people between them. Main Street was paved with Francis' brick. Homes in town were lighted by the Boynton Gas and Electric Company and supplied with running water by the city's own waterworks system. There was an automobile garage and machine shop to go along with the two livery stables, as well as four general merchandise stores, three hotels, two groceries, two drug stores, a furniture store, hardware stores, grain merchants, a farm implement store, a bakery, a cotton gin, an oil well supply, and representatives of any other business or profession for which any reasonable person might find a need. For the past few years, the town had even had its own telephone exchange. And right in the middle of Main Street, in pride of place, stood the Elliot and Ober Theatre, which showed moving pictures every Saturday night.

On the two mile trip into town, Alafair thought about John Lee huddled in the dim hay-store, wrapped in his quilts. She wished that she had taken a book out to him to relieve his boredom. But then, it was probably too dark out there to read. If indeed he could read very much. It had begun to snow again by the time Alafair got to town, another fat, wet, clinging snow like the one that had buried Harley. She rode Missy directly to the livery stable, loathe to leave the little mare hitched outside and exposed to the elements.

Mr. Turner, the owner of S.B. Turner and Sons Livery, popped up from his desk beside the door as Alafair dismounted and squeaked open the rough wooden door.

"Well, Alafair Tucker," he exclaimed. "I almost didn't recognize you under all them clothes. What are you doing out and about on a day like this?" The little grasshopper of a man had been old ever since Alafair had first known him in 1897, when they had moved to the area where Boynton would be. That had been the family's second move in three years. Before that, they had migrated to Cherokee County from Arkansas, in 1894, when she was twenty-one years old with two baby girls and pregnant with twins. They had come out in covered wagons, with Shaw's parents, siblings and their families, and three uncles and their extended families. They had been a wagon train unto themselves. The country had still been the Indian Territories then, and since the Tucker clan was part Cherokee, they were more welcome than most. Shaw's stepfather and uncles had seen the land runs in the west, in the Oklahoma Territory, but had preferred this greener country to the east. They had settled on tribal land near Tahlequah at first, and had even enrolled in the Cherokee Nation, but after a couple of years, many of the Tucker clan had traded up for several beautiful wooded parcels in the newly privatized Creek Nation.

The frisky Mr. Turner, who was a member of said Creek Nation, had a face both the color and texture of a walnut, covered over the top by a stiff gray buzz of hair that stuck up like a scrub brush. The lively gray eyes that examined Alafair with such human delight betrayed the fact that at least one of Mr. Turner's grandparents had been white.

"I was just stir crazy, Mr. Turner," she told him. "I came into town to see if we have any mail and to visit a while with my sister-in-law Josie Cecil. Do you mind if I leave Missy here for a spell? Too cold to leave her standing outside for long."

"Not a bit," Mr. Turner assured her. "Not like I'm doing much business today, and none at all if it wasn't for you Tuckers. Shaw's pair is right over there."

"Shaw? Did he say where he was going? Might ride home with him."

"Said he was going to drop into the sheriff's office and jaw with Scott a while."

She handed Mr. Turner the reins. "Well, if he comes back before I'm done visiting with Josie, would you tell him I'm here in town?" she asked.

"I'll do it," Mr. Turner called after her, as she ducked back out into the cold.

The town Post Office was directly across the street from the livery, at the corner of Second and Main. The tiny establishment consisted of one long wall of cubbyholes and a little counter, presided over by Mrs. N.C. Fluke, the postmistress. There was no one in the town of Boynton who knew as much about what was happening in the vicinity and what people were thinking about it. Every person who lived within a ten-mile radius of town had to pick up his or her mail from Mrs. Fluke, and if there was anything Nadine Fluke loved, it was gossip. At this hour, she was throwing mail, and Alafair could just see pieces of her through the jigsaw of postboxes.

"Morning, Nadine," Alafair called, and the entire Mrs. Fluke appeared from around the corner with a stack of letters in her hand. Nadine Fluke was a pretty, fair-haired widow of about Alafair's own age. She had been postmistress for three or four years, now, since the death of her husband. She lived in a little apartment behind the post office with her only child, a ten-year-old son.

"Alafair!" Nadine exclaimed. "I never expected to see anybody but townfolk today. If you're here to get your mail, you're too late. Shaw already picked it up. He had something from the Grange, and there was a letter for you from Enid. Your sister, I reckon."

"Oh! Well, I'll look forward to that. I haven't heard from Ruth Ann in a while. Since I can't get the mail, I'll just have to pass the time of day for a while. What are you hearing about this murder out to the Days' place?"

Nadine sat down on her stool behind the counter. "Nobody can talk of nothing else," she assured Alafair. "And just between you and me and this stool I'm sitting on, it's pretty shocking what people are saying. I mean, I know Harley Day wasn't no prize or nothing, but most everybody I've talked with seems to think it was about time somebody done him in. Can you imagine? And to just say it straight out like that! You know he must have had some good quality somewhere in him."

Alafair shook her head, but didn't comment. Nadine's charitable attitude toward Harley was rather nice for a change, and Alafair felt somewhat guilty that she didn't share it. "Anybody have any ideas on who might have done it?" she asked.

"That boy of his, John Lee, seems to be the leading candidate, since he disappeared and all. But if he did do it, nobody wants to blame him much."

"I sure don't want to blame him, either," Alafair told her. "He's such a nice boy. Have there been any other names bandied about?"

"Why, to hear tell of it, just about everybody in the county could have done it. Ara Kellerman thinks it's likely that it was the wife, since she had the most grievance. But since Harley sold that home brew, he was always consorting with murderous types. For my money, I'm picking one of them. You know, Bud Ellis that works over at the Mill and Elevator company was telling me just yesterday that his boss Mr. Lang was supposed to go out there to the Day place on the very evening that Harley disappeared. He said Mr. Lang was mighty unhappy when he came into work Thursday morning because he had made that long trip out there in the ice and snow and all for nothing."

"For nothing," Alafair repeated. "So he never saw Harley at all on Wednesday?"

"That's what Bud says."

"You know, Zorah Millar told me that Mr. Lang's son Dan used to be sweet on Maggie Ellen Day awhile ago, but he broke it off with her because Harley didn't approve."

"Oh, he more than didn't approve," Nadine assured her. "Them two planned on getting married, is what I hear, but Harley flat out forbade it. I don't know why he took against the boy. Dan Lang seems like a fine catch to me. You'd think he'd be glad to see his daughter settled. Anyway, the story I hear is that Dan went out to the Day place to confront Harley about it. Intended to tell him that he was taking Maggie Ellen off and that was all there was to it."

"Why didn't he, then?" Alafair wondered.

Nadine shrugged, then leaned forward over the counter, looking conspiritorial. "Somehow the two of them got into it, and Harley caught Dan one up the side of his head with a hoe handle. Knocked him silly. I gather Harley would have beat Dan near to death if John Lee and Maggie Ellen hadn't put a stop to it."

"I'll swan!" Alafair declared.

"Well, Harley got in a lucky blow. I'd think that healthy young fellow would have killed Harley, otherwise. Even so, I reckon Dan figured he'd had enough of the Days after that, because I never heard another word about him and Maggie Ellen."

"That's a shame," Alafair said. She was thinking that the situation sounded a little like Phoebe and John Lee's. Had Harley Day decided that if he couldn't be happy, none of the rest of his family could be, either?

"That gal must have been determined to clear out of there, though. Last I heard, she had married a bricklayer and was living in Shawnee. That Maggie Ellen is a feisty little gal, from what I know of her."

"Miz Millar has a high opinion of her, too."

"Speaking of Miz Millar," Nadine said, "she may have been Harley's sister, but there was no love lost between them, either."

"I got that impression, myself, when I met them during a visit to Miz Day," Alafair confessed.

"Yes, they must have called the sheriff out to their place ten times in the last few years with some complaint or another about Harley. Him and Zorah's husband had some bad blood about an inheritance, I believe. The Millars had all kinds of mischief going on at their farm—fences pulled down, garden ripped up, that sort of thing."

"Why didn't Scott arrest Harley, then?"

"I don't think they could ever prove it was him doing it, though J.D. was sure of it. In the last couple of years, though, Harley took to showing up at their front gate and hollering cuss words at them, until J.D. would threaten to fill him full of buckshot if he didn't get gone."

Alafair shook her head. "What a poor excuse for a human being that man was. Have you talked to Scott since this all began?"

Nadine chuckled. "Oh, he's been in here, but you know how he is. He just teases and jokes, and in the end you don't find out anything. Hattie was laughing and complaining that her husband never tells her anything interesting, either."

"Well, I'll be interested to see how it all falls out," Alafair said. "I just hope John Lee ain't involved. I'd hate to see him go to jail. So how is Freddie these days?"

Nadine smiled at the mention of her son. "He's just fine. Growing like a weed. I saw your girl Martha early this morning. She was picking up mail for the bank. I swear, Alafair, she looks more like you every day."

"Mercy, don't tell her that!" Alafair joked, though the comment pleased her. "Well, I'd love to stay and talk more, Nadine, but there's chores awaitin', and I mean to visit my sister-in-law before I head home."

⌁⌁⌁

The women said their farewells, and Alafair stepped outside. She caught her breath at the shock of the wind, but pressed on grimly. She took a left at the corner and ran the half-block to her sister-in-law's square white frame house, thinking about Russell Lang and wondering what the man knew. She was surprised to see Shaw's two hounds snuffling around Josie's yard. They trotted up to her with wags and whuffs of welcome, but she was too cold to pet them.

She rushed through the gate, picking up speed as the cold insinuated itself deeper into her bones. She didn't stop to knock but flung the front door open and ran inside at full tilt.

"Josie!" she called through the wool swathing her face. "You here?"

Josie Cecil keeled out of the kitchen with her sails at full. Josie was a large woman, generous in every way the word could be applied. She was five years older than Shaw, and like him, a typical Tucker, with the rosy-brown complexion, the honey-hazel eyes and black hair, and the wide toothy grin that dazzled all and sundry. The selfsame grin was now warming Alafair as she felt herself enfolded in a voluminous embrace.

"Girl, you're a block of ice!" Josie exclaimed. "Get in here and eat something this minute." She practically carried Alafair into her big, warm kitchen. "If you're looking for Shaw, you've come to the right place. Nothing's wrong, is there?"

"No," Alafair said, extricating herself with some regret from Josie's grasp. Shaw stood up from the table when he saw her, a look of momentary alarm on his face turning to curious delight. Alafair smiled when she saw him. She couldn't help herself. The sight of him always gave her a lift. "What are you doing here?" she asked him. "Mr. Turner told me you were at Scott's."

"I came here to get fed," Shaw told her. "How'd you get into town?"

"I rode Missy. It was fast, but I may lose some toes. I didn't know you were here 'til I saw the dogs."

"You're not going anywhere 'til you try this cobbler," Josie informed her. "I opened a quart of the peaches I canned last June. It's still hot." She was ladling sweet, runny peaches and crispy-gooey crust into a bowl as she spoke.

"Josie," Alafair attempted to protest, with a laugh.

"I'll put some cream on it," Josie interrupted her, snatching a pitcher off the windowsill. "Put some meat on you so the cold won't bother you so much."

Alafair sat down next to Shaw at the table without further protest. Josie's cooking was lore and legend, and the smell of the cobbler was making her mouth water.

"Want some more, Shaw?" Josie asked, as she set the bowl down in front of Alafair.

"Naw, I couldn't hold any more, Josie."

"I guess you won't be needing any dinner, then," Alafair teased him.

"It's three hours 'til dinner, Alafair," Shaw pointed out.

"Oh, well, then. Give him another bowl to tide him over, Josie," she said. "What's been going on with y'all?"

Josie lowered herself into a chair at the table after filling Shaw's coffee cup. "Not much," she admitted. "I haven't hardly been out of the house since the snow, except to go to church on Sunday. Jack says everybody at the bank is all agog over Harley Day being killed like that. Wonder what that poor woman is going to do with all them kids and no man? Does she intend to keep the farm, you think?"

"I doubt she can," Shaw opined. "It may be that John Lee has been working off the mortgage these last couple of years, but I imagine Harley owed the note. I'm guessing the bank will foreclose."

Josie's brow knit. "I think he owned the farm. Day's daddy left it to him, and I don't think he ever mortgaged it, according to Jack."

Alafair was so enthralled with the cobbler that for a moment the conversation didn't register. The heady aroma of peaches dripping with sweet heavy cream had just about knocked every sensible thought out of her. "There's cinnamon in this crust," she observed dreamily.

"I grated a stick over the top before I baked it," Josie told her.

"Y'all aren't going to start discussing recipes, are you?" Shaw exclaimed in mock horror.

"You don't mind eating what we discuss," Josie admonished.

Suddenly Alafair came back to earth with a wrench. "You say Day owned that ugly little farm himself?" she asked.

"I expect so," Josie said. "Jack told me that the bank doesn't own it."

"So who gets it now?"

"Probably his wife," Shaw told her. "John Lee is underage, even if he wasn't under suspicion of murder. I can bet you money Day didn't have a will, so it will have to go to probate court, but I don't know why she shouldn't get it. Even so, she'll more than likely have to sell it to pay the taxes."

"I hope you have things arranged so that Alafair doesn't have to sell the farm if you get kicked in the head by a mule," Josie interjected.

Shaw, who had been watching Alafair's pie ecstasy out of the corner of his eye, reached over and spooned a bit from her bowl. "Of course I do," he assured Josie, while chewing. "I even have insurance. I'm no John D. Rockefeller, but I ain't no Harley Day, either."

Alafair pushed her bowl over to the delighted Shaw, who finished the remains of her cobbler in two bites. "Shaw Tucker, I came into town to visit your sister. Are you going to hang around here and bother us for the next hour, or are you going to visit your cousin Scott like you said you were?"

Shaw's white grin flashed, and he stood up. "I can tell when I'm not wanted, yes, sir," he said. "You want to ride home with me?"

"I do. I expect I'll need to be home by eleven-thirty, if you want a proper dinner."

Shaw was already pulling on his coat beside the back door. He checked his pocket watch with one arm coated and one free. "I'll be back in an hour, then," he said.

"I'll be ready," she told the door as it swung shut behind him. She looked back at Josie with an ironic look in her eye. "I hope he thanked you for the cobbler."

"Many times. Mostly with his mouth full," Josie assured her. She leaned back in her chair and crossed her arms comfortably over her chest. "Now, what's up?

"You think you know me pretty well, don't you?" Alafair said, with a smile.

"I do," Josie stated.

Alafair sighed. "Yes, you do. Josie, you ever want something to be a certain way so badly that you can't even conceive of it being some other way?"

Josie shot her a piercing glance. "If I'm figuring that sentence right," she said, "I'd have to say yes. But of course, like everybody does, I've learned that wishing for things to be other than they are is folly."

"I know it," Alafair agreed unhappily. "Tell me, Josie, do you expect that there's still innocence in the world?"

"That's a strange question for somebody with as many kids as you have."

"I reckon I'm getting cynical in my dotage," Alafair admitted. "Of course, you know as well as I do that kids may be innocent, but they aren't necessarily honest, or compassionate, or good."

"Did one of your kids do something disappointing?"

"I don't know yet. Maybe."

Josie studied her a minute. "Here's the way I see it. You can proceed one of two ways, if you don't know the truth. Either you can decide the child is guilty, or that he's innocent, and base your actions on your decision. Now, the law of this land says that a person is innocent until proven guilty. I'd hope that my own ma would give me the benefit of the doubt until all the evidence was in."

Alafair shrugged. "All the evidence I have right now points in a direction I don't want to go. I know this child in my heart, and I cannot believe he would do wrong."

"You can't tell me what this is about?" Josie wondered, after a moment.

"No, I'm sorry. Not until I know for sure. I can't conscience slandering the innocent. I'm sorry to be so infuriating."

Josie shook her head. "Don't fret yourself. I'm a mother, too. I know how it is. It doesn't matter that you raise them all just the same way, they all just go off in their own directions and there isn't anything in God's world that you can do about it. You just love them, and there's nothing you can do about it."

If Alafair had been the type to cry, she might have done it. Instead, she gazed at Josie for a long minute with a steady solemn gaze, then asked for her cobbler crust recipe.

⌐⌐⌐

Alafair only had to run a matter of yards, across Second Street to Main and up two or three doors, to reach Boynton Mill and Elevator Company, owned by Mr. Russell Lang, the town's most prosperous grain merchant. At first glance, the place looked deserted, and Alafair puffed in disappointment. But she tried the door and found it open, and she stepped in to the pleasant warmth. Lang's office was a rather sumptuous affair, as grain merchant's offices go. Three large, cubbyhole-filled desks stood at right angles to the door, all messy with papers but unoccupied at the moment. Lang's imposing oak desk sat at the back of the establishment, separated from the ordinary workaday mortals by a gated wooden railing. The proprietor himself was ensconced in his place, and looked up with interest when Alafair walked in.

Alafair was acquainted with Russell Lang, of course, since Shaw patronized his business exclusively, both to buy and sell. She knew Mrs. Lang rather well, from church and all, and liked her. As for Lang himself, she didn't have much of an opinion. Shaw said he was honest and businesslike, but not given to socializing. Alafair thought him polite enough and not totally devoid of charm, if you held your mouth just right.

Lang smiled and stood up when he recognized Alafair. Apparently he was not adverse to an interruption on a cold, boring day.

"You seem to be left to your own devices, Mr. Lang," Alafair observed.

Lang stepped out from behind his desk to greet her. "I am indeed, Mrs. Tucker," he granted. "The clerks are at the warehouse today. What brings you here on such an unpleasant day?"

"I was in town to visit my sister-in-law," she extemporized, "and while I'm here, I wondered if I might have a word with you? I won't take up but a few minutes of your time."

He looked properly curious about what she might possibly have to say to him, and opened the gate in his little fence for her. "I'd be pleased," he said. "Do come in and have a seat."

She took the proffered chair in front of his desk, and they settled themselves comfortably. Lang was not a bad-looking man, Alafair noted. Smooth as silk, and apparently always in a good mood. A good way to be if you were in business. Alafair calculated in a split second how to broach her subject, and smiled.

"What can I do for you, Mrs. Tucker?" Lang opened.

"Mr. Lang, I expect you heard that Harley Day has gone to meet his maker," she said.

He folded his hands on his desk. "Yes, I heard that," he replied.

"I expect also that you have heard that a .22 bullet found its way into Mr. Day's brain on that night, and that the sheriff is proceeding on the assumption that the same bullet is the cause of Mr. Day's demise."

Lang's lip twitched. "Yes, Mrs. Tucker, I heard that as well," Lang told her. "It has also come to my attention that young John Lee Day rests under suspicion of having shot that selfsame bullet into his father's skull."

"That is true, Mr. Lang."

"Additionally, I have heard that young John Lee Day and one of your lovely daughters are friendly," Lang added. "Therefore, I might assume that being a loving mother, you wish that evidence existed proving that this young man is not the perpetrator of this ugly deed."

Alafair pursed her lips. Lang was astute. "You would be assuming correctly, Mr. Lang," Alafair admitted. "In fact, knowing the young man as I do, I'm convinced he didn't do it, and I am going to speak to everyone who could possibly have been in the vicinity of the Day farm that night, and might have seen something that could shed some light on this."

"I'm curious as to why you have come to see me, then, Mrs. Tucker."

Alafair paused, mildly surprised. Surely he knew that Mrs. Day would have told the sheriff that Lang was scheduled to meet with Harley the evening he disappeared. "I understand that you told John Lee that you intended to drive out to his farm that very evening to discuss the fact that his father owed you money."

There was a brief silence as they regarded one another. One of Alafair's eyebrows inched upward in curiosity. Mr. Lang's florid face grew more florid. But his expression remained as placid as ever. "Where did you hear that, may I ask?" he wondered.

"Miz Day mentioned it."

Lang nodded. "It is true that I intended to go out there that evening, Mrs. Tucker. But if you will remember, the weather was wretched. It rained a little, then froze. I didn't even get a quarter-mile out of town before the buggy slid off the road on a curve."

"Oh, my. Didn't hurt your horse, I hope," Alafair commiserated.

A smile passed over Lang's face. "Fortunately, no. Thanks for your concern. He kept his feet. Scared the wadding out of the poor creature, though. Took us close to an hour to haul the buggy out of the ditch."

"Us?"

"Me and the horse," Lang clarified. "By that time, I had lost my enthusiasm for a confrontation. I intended to go out there Monday afternoon, after the thaw, but by noon it was all over town that Day was dead."

Alafair nodded. She didn't need to pursue this line of questioning any further. Scott would check out every detail vigorously. From the look on his face, Lang knew it, too, and wasn't too happy about the prospect. He had been smart enough to answer her, she thought, with the truth. Or as close to it as he dare.

"Do you intend to sue the estate for your money, Mr. Lang?" she asked.

He answered her in the same civil tones he had been using since she walked in, but his face was so red now, that Alafair feared that his eyeballs might pop out and bounce around the room. "I'll try to make arrangements with the widow, first, but if that doesn't succeed, then I do, indeed, intend to sue, Mrs. Tucker." He paused, then added, "I am not insensitive to the fact that Mrs. Day and her children might be facing some financial difficulty now, but I am, after all, in business. I'm sure that there will be several claims on the estate."

"I'm sure there will be," Alafair agreed. She stood, unwilling to risk antagonizing Lang further. "I thank you for being so forthcoming," she said. "I'll leave you to your work now, and not bother you any more."

She moved toward the door, and Lang stood up to see her out. As she walked past him, Lang put his hand on her arm with such fleeting delicacy that she barely felt it. She looked up at him. He was smiling down on her with benign amusement.

"I'll tell you the truth, Mrs. Tucker," Lang said to her. "I wasn't exactly heartbroke when I heard that Day was dead. He was the scum of the earth, and what happened to him was only justice. That black-haired girl of his, the one who ran away, she was a friend of my son's. Told my boy that she hated her father like sin and corruption, and from the stories I heard, I can't say as I blame her. He was such a miserable creature that my son couldn't stand to go out to his place after a while."

Since Lang gave her an opening, Alafair took a deep breath and plunged ahead. "The gossip around town is that Mr. Day beat your son," she said.

Lang's eyes narrowed, but his expression didn't alter. He didn't exactly respond to her observation, either. "His wife and kids will be better off without him, and that's the truth," he said. "Whoever killed him probably had good reason. I can think of a dozen people who do. But it wasn't me."

Alafair studied his face for a second before she replied. She couldn't think of a way to ask him where his son was that night without making it sound like an accusation. "Well, I expect it wasn't you, Mr. Lang," she said to him, still hoping it might be him after all. "I hope you'll understand my concern, and I wish you'd tell Sheriff Tucker about some of those dozen people who might wish Harley Day was dead."

His face was not quite so red now. Apparently her comment had relieved him somewhat. "I'll do that," he assured her.

I'll bet you will, now, she thought, as she stepped back out into the cold. Lang had just proven himself pretty darn acute, and now that she had informed him that she knew he was abroad and in the vicinity that night, he would make haste to give Scott what information he had before Alafair did. His story about his buggy ending up in a ditch sounded suspicious to her. Why would he even admit to being anywhere near the Day farm that night? Any reasonable person would have canceled an unnecessary trip on such an unpleasant night.

Alafair and Shaw drove home together in the buckboard, with Alafair's mare tied to the back and Shaw's hounds trotting along side. Alafair was uncharacteristically quiet, Shaw noticed. After so many years together, he knew not to prod her. Her little troubled periods came and went, and sometimes he found out what they were about, and sometimes he didn't. Instead, he chatted about this and that, new gossip he had heard from the kids, the funny stories Scott had told him, the condition and personality of one or another of their animals. He told her he might be hiring a couple of wranglers on permanently. That elicited a grunt from her. The frigid weather was always a good topic. And it was in the midst of a complaint about the weather that Alafair turned on the seat of the buckboard and gazed at Shaw with that look in her eye that told him she might deign to answer him should he ask what was bothering her.

"Something on your mind, honey?" he asked easily.

"This business about the Day boy is driving me out of my mind, Shaw," she said. "I'm just so concerned that Phoebe might get a broken heart out of this. And I just have a feeling, a real strong feeling that no matter how it looks, John Lee didn't do it."

An unexpected feeling of alarm rose up in Shaw's chest at the look of determination on his wife's face. "Now, Alafair Gunn, you be careful about getting yourself involved in a murder investigation."

She forged ahead as though he hadn't spoken. "Did Scott mention to you whether or not he talked to Russell Lang, or to his son Dan? Nadine Fluke told me that Harley whipped Dan pretty bad last year."

"No, Scott never said anything to me about the Langs. Why would Harley want to whip Dan Lang?"

Alafair shrugged. "I understand Dan and Maggie Ellen Day were sweethearts, and Harley didn't care for the idea."

"Oh. Well, I'm sure Scott knows all about it," he reassured her.

"Did Scott say anything else to you about the murder just now? Anything new come to light?"

"I don't know if I ought to tell you," Shaw said perversely. "You're looking to me like you plan to rush to the rescue again."

Her bottom lip pushed out in a pout. "You ought to know by now that I'm not going to do anything foolish. But somebody's got to watch out for the youngsters."

"And that somebody's got to be you, I suppose."

Alafair laughed. "I don't expect it has to be, Shaw, but it probably will be. Now, don't torture me any more. Did Scott tell you anything new?"

Shaw sighed. "Let's see, now. Seems his deputy Trent Calder found John Lee's mule on the back forty behind that stand of oaks on their property, saddle off and let loose, he thought. So they're thinking the boy is still around here somewhere."

"Wouldn't be surprised if his mama's hiding him there on the farm," Alafair said, without looking at him.

Shaw didn't notice her evasion. "Wouldn't be surprised," he agreed. Distracted, he whistled at one of the hounds, who had taken off across a rime-covered field, nose to the ground.

Chapter Eight

Alafair awoke slowly. She was lying on her side, curled up into a tight knot under the quilts. Her body was warm enough in her wool flannel nightgown, but her nose was freezing, and she snuggled down under the covers. It was still dark, but she sensed that it would be time to get up before long. She turned her head enough to see that she was still alone in the bed.

When she and most of the children had gone to bed the night before, Shaw and Gee Dub were still out in the barn with a mare who was in the process of giving birth. Alafair flopped onto her back and sighed. A difficult foaling, then. She hoped drowsily that Shaw had sent Gee Dub to bed at some reasonable hour. She opened her eyes, suddenly wide awake. She hoped it was a hard foaling keeping Shaw out until all hours, and not the discovery of a fugitive on the property. She chided herself for borrowing trouble. Shaw wouldn't have left her to sleep if he had discovered John Lee hiding in the soddie.

She screwed up her resolve before throwing off the covers and standing up. The cold hit her like a slap in the face. She drew in a breath between her teeth and skittered into the parlor in her stocking feet, casting a glance toward the boys' beds in the corner as she made for the pot bellied stove in the center of the room. A lump under a heap of quilts testified to Charlie's presence. The yellow shepherd curled on the bed at the boy's feet lifted his head and gazed at Alafair benignly through the gloom. Gee Dub's bed, however, didn't appear to have been slept in.

Alafair peered at the pendulum clock on the shelf by the door, and could barely make out the time—four o'clock. She built up a coal fire in the stove, using as a starter a corn cob which had been soaking in a jar of kerosene, which she kept next to the clock on the high wall shelf. She lit a lamp, then took it and the quart jar of cobs with her into the kitchen to start the fire in her big wood burning oven. She was still scraping last night's ashes from the fire box into the ash bucket when she heard the sound of boots on the back porch. Shaw and Gee Dub.

She got up and walked across the kitchen to lean out the back door. By the weak yellow light of the lantern they had hung on a hook, she could see that Shaw was pouring a bucket of water into one of her washtubs on the bench in the corner.

"I just got the stove going in the parlor," she called to them. "Y'all get on in there and warm up. You must be ready to drop."

Shaw paused in his pouring and looked over at her. Even in the dim light she could see the dark circles under his eyes. "We washed off in a bucket before we came up to the house, but we're mighty filthy, darlin'," he informed her. His breath fogged in the air. "A little more soap wouldn't go amiss."

"I'm laying the fire in the kitchen right now. I'll have some hot water for you in a minute. Now, come on inside. I'm afraid you'll both die of the ague."

Shaw nodded at Gee Dub, and the two of them dragged their weary bodies into the house. They hovered over the stove in the parlor while Alafair kindled a roaring fire in the kitchen and heated a kettle of water that had been standing on the stove all night.

While her husband and son cleaned up on the back porch, Alafair went back into the still-frigid bedroom. She dressed as quickly as she could, taking her arms out of her nightgown and pulling on her clothes underneath. The two stoves had begun to warm the front part of the house enough that while she was measuring coffee into the pot, Alafair noticed that her teeth had stopped chattering. Shaw and Gee Dub, however, were still shuddering with cold when they finally came into the kitchen, their faces shiny from scrubbing with the water she had warmed, and their wet hair slicked back.

"Sit down," she ordered. "I've heated some milk with a little honey. Drink it up and get to bed. It's still early enough that y'all can get some sleep before the workday has to start."

Alafair drew more water from the pump outside the back door and poured it in a large pot to heat at the back of the stove. Then she added more water to the oats which had been soaking all night and put them on a front burner to slowly cook for breakfast.

"It must have been a hard foaling," she commented, as she worked at the stove. No one answered at first, and she looked back over her shoulder at the two sitting at the table. Shaw looked up at her dully from over the rim of his cup. He set the mug down on the table and absently wiped the milk foam from his mustache with the back of his index finger.

"It was," he affirmed. "Blackberry has produced a lot of fine mules in her time, and with no trouble at all, but this little fellow wanted to come out sideways. It took us a long time to get him turned around proper. He made it, though. He's a fine, strapping mule."

"How's Blackberry?"

Shaw shrugged. "She's wrung out, but I think she'll be all right. She took to the new foal just fine, and we left them looking pretty comfortable and interested in their grub." Shaw took another sip of his hot milk, and nodded across the table at his son. "Gee Dub was a big help. I don't know if I could have done it without him."

Gee Dub, who was slumped over the table with his half-empty mug in his hand, didn't acknowledge his father's praise.

Shaw chuckled. "Gee," he said sharply, and the boy jerked upright and blinked at Shaw blearily. "Go to bed, son," Shaw instructed. "You did a good job."

Gee Dub smiled and hoisted himself out of his chair. He detoured to give Alafair a brief squeeze around the shoulders, then disappeared into the parlor. He had not uttered one word.

"I'll send a note to school with Mary," Alafair said, after he had gone. "I reckon he won't be much for going to school today." She poured herself a cup of coffee and sat down in Gee Dub's vacated chair at the table.

"I'm sorry I kept him all night," Shaw said, "but I wasn't fooling when I said I'd have been hard pressed to do it without him. And there's two more mares ready to drop in the next few days. I've got eight mares in foal, and buyers for every one. There's so many people moving in here that I can hardly keep up with the call for mules. I need to buy more mares, and another good jackass or two."

"You need to hire some help, Shaw," Alafair chided. "You can't keep the kids out of school, and your brothers are all too busy with their own places to help you much any more. Why don't you hire Georgie's husband Edgar? You always said he was a good worker."

Shaw made a little gesture of agreement. "He is that. I reckon I will ask him if he'll hire on to help me with the foaling, but I doubt if he'll want to come on permanent. He's got enough of a job with that shareholding of his." He smiled as Alafair prepared to protest. "Don't worry," he preempted her. "I'll start looking around for somebody." He sat up in his chair and rolled his shoulders. "I'm mighty sore," he admitted. "I about got my arms jerked out of their sockets. I'm afraid I'm going to be stiff as a post later."

Alafair leaped to her feet. "Move over here by the fire and take your shirt off," she told him. "I've got some liniment in the cabinet. You'll put on your flannel nightshirt after I rub you down, and I'll warm a brick for the bed before you get in it. You'll be frisky as a pup when you get up later."

"Aw, honey, that stuff smells like a veterinarian's leather pouch," Shaw protested weakly, unbuttoning his shirt all the while.

"I can stand it if you can," Alafair said, as she rummaged around on one of the high shelves. "Or you can go around all stove up for the next few days."

Shaw pulled his chair over next to the stove and Alafair took up a position behind him. She poured some liniment into her hands and began to knead the strong-smelling stuff into Shaw's shoulders. He felt hard and knotted as old rope, but she could feel him melt under her hands, and his head dropped forward to afford her better access to the back of his neck. He sighed. "On top of everything," he droned, as though he was talking to himself, "I'll be having to break the clods in the cotton field in just a few weeks. I've been looking at the sod-busting machines, and I think I'm going to have to replace several of the discs on that old harrow of mine."

"Now, listen to yourself, Shaw," Alafair admonished. "There you go talking like we're still as poor as we were when we first moved out here. You could afford to buy a new harrow."

Shaw laughed wearily. "You're mighty free with our money," he chided. "There's nothing wrong with that harrow that some new cogs and a bucket of grease won't fix."

"Well, then, it wouldn't cost very much to pay somebody to fix it for you," she said. As the words left her mouth, a thought occurred that caused her hand to pause on Shaw's shoulder. "In fact," she said, suddenly animated, "I understand that Dan Lang is a very good mechanic. He works over at John Dasher's blacksmith shop, I think. You could probably get Dan to come out here and have a look at that harrow right quick. I'm guessing he could fix it right there in the barn, once he knows what he needs."

Alafair couldn't see Shaw's face, but he was quiet for a moment while he considered this. "I expect it would be easier on me to hire somebody to fix the harrow," he acknowledged. "I'll talk to Dasher about it. Maybe he'll do it himself, though. Don't know why I should settle for the student when I could have the master."

"But I hear that Lang boy is right handy," Alafair protested, dismayed. "He might be cheaper, too…." She paused when Shaw's shoulders began to shake with mirth under her hands.

"Alafair, I can see right through you, you schemer," he said.

She slapped his back, annoyed. "Oh, you plague me," she huffed. "Tell me, then, what's wrong with killing two birds with one stone? I can't just go in to town and start questioning the boy, you know that. If Dan Lang was to come out here for some honest work, I could have a little talk with him about that Day girl."

"And maybe that fight he got into with her murdered daddy?"

"If it comes up," she confessed.

"You just ain't going to let this go, are you?" he observed.

"How can I, Shaw, when Phoebe's happiness is involved?"

"Young people's affections blow with the wind, sugar. Besides, it ain't your job to be catching murderers. That's Scott's job, and he's pretty good at it."

"I know that Scott will find out who killed that awful man eventually," Alafair admitted. "But by that time it may be too late for Phoebe. And don't dismiss those young folks' feelings so lightly. A broken heart hurts like sin, no matter how old you are. Besides, I think this murder is hanging over everybody like a storm cloud. Nobody knows who to trust, who might be a killer. I'd sure like to have it done with."

"And what if the Lang boy is the killer, and you go to prodding him? Poking around in things like this can be dangerous, Alafair."

"Well, I hope I'm more careful than you seem to think," she said, slightly offended. "I don't intend to go accusing anybody to their face."

Instead of replying, Shaw nodded toward the kitchen door. "Look who's up."

Alafair turned to see a frowzy, nightgown-clad Sophronia padding toward her through the pre-dawn gloom. Alafair wiped her hands on a towel before she picked the child up and sat down at the table. Sophronia settled into Alafair's lap and laid her head on her mother's breast.

"What's that smell, Mama?" she mumbled.

"It's liniment to make Daddy feel better."

"It stinks, Daddy," Sophronia informed him.

"Why, I thought it smells like violets," Shaw teased, and Sophronia mustered a drowsy smile to acknowledge his witticism.

"Is it morning?" she mumbled.

Alafair enfolded the girl in her arms and pushed the curly auburn hair, fine as cobwebs, back from her forehead. "It's not time for you to get up for quite a spell, honey," Alafair told her. "Did we wake you up?"

"I'm cold," Sophronia complained. "I was dreaming about that man that got buried in the snow."

Alafair and Shaw looked at one another for a minute before Shaw said, "I'll see if I can't get Dan Lang out here later today. You can talk to him if you want, but I intend to be there when you do."

Alafair nodded, relieved. "He won't feel a thing."

Alafair pushed the door to the tool shed open with her foot and carried the old tin coffee pot and the bucket of cornbread and sliced fatback into the dim interior. The large shed, which was appended to the back of the barn, was lined at the back with stacks of good lumber and extra bricks, cabinets and shelves filled with nails, spikes, bales of wire, bolts and nuts. Tools of every description were hung neatly from pegs or leaning in their places along one wall. On top of and under workbenches which stretched along another wall lay items in need of repair, from pots with holes, to harness that needed mending, broken furniture, and a doll with one leg. In the center of the room, Shaw and Dan Lang sat on stools at a rough wooden table. Strewn across the tabletop were bolts, a long axle, and several platter-sized discs from a harrow.

The room was fairly warm, since Shaw had a small coal fire going in a makeshift oil drum brazier. A lantern on the table supplemented the pale winter light that filtered in between the boards of the uninsulated walls. Shaw looked up at Alafair when she entered, and his expression sharpened. She gave him a reassuring smile. Dan Lang twisted in his seat, then stood to greet her as she bumped the door shut with her hip.

Alafair knew Dan Lang to see him, but she couldn't remember ever having spoken to him. He looked very much like his father, Russell, the owner of the Boynton Mill and Elevator Company, tallish, with sharp eyes and a high color. Alafair noted with interest that a puckered white scar ran for a couple of inches across his cheekbone and temple before it disappeared into his hair.

"Oh, sit down, now, son," she told him. "I just brought you fellows some food to keep your strength up and some coffee to warm your innards."

Dan relieved her of the pails. "This is mighty welcome, Miz Tucker."

Alafair removed the two tin cups she had stuffed in her apron pockets and placed them on the table. "How's it going out here? Do you think you can fix the harrow, or is Mr. Tucker going to have to bust loose for a new one?"

Dan sat back down and accepted a piece of warm cornbread that Shaw had just unloaded from the bucket. "Oh, I don't think there's too much wrong with this one, ma'am," Dan assured her, as he pulled the cornbread apart and placed a piece of fatback between the layers. "I expect I'll have to take this axle back to the shop, but I can have it forged by tomorrow. These here discs don't need anything more than sharpening. I can do that right now."

Alafair crossed her arms over her chest. "How's business these days?"

Dan swallowed and nodded. "Not bad," he admitted. "There's not much a farmer can do during weather like this besides fix up his machinery and tools."

"How's your dad and mother?"

"They're doing well, ma'am, thanks for asking." He smiled at her, perfectly willing to eat cornbread and exchange pleasantries. It was the usual way of doing business with company-starved farm people.

"I visited with your dad at his office when I was in town a couple of days ago," Alafair said. "Talked to him about this ugly business with Harley Day."

A shadow passed over the young man's face. He hadn't expected this, Alafair thought. She felt a pang of guilt at ambushing him. He didn't appear to want to bolt, however. "Yes, ma'am, he told me about that," he responded.

Alafair glanced at Shaw. She couldn't tell if he was about to laugh, or choke, or leap up from his chair and hustle her out of the room. She plunged ahead, just in case. "He told me that you were friends with Maggie Ellen Day, a while back."

Dan lowered his cornbread to the table and studied it absently for a moment before he answered. "A mite more than friends, Miz Tucker," he confessed. "At least as far as I was concerned. I was mighty partial to Maggie Ellen."

Shaw shot Alafair a stern look. Apparently, he was having second thoughts about this scheme. "Dan," he said, "you don't have to talk about this if you don't like to."

Dan leaned forward on his elbows and quirked up an ironic little smile. "I don't mind," he said. He looked up at Alafair. "My pa told me that you're worried about your girl Phoebe, Miz Tucker, because she and John Lee are sweet on one another. I reckon that's why you want to ask me about this."

Alafair blinked at him, surprised. Either this young man was as astute as his father, or Alafair was going to have to admit to being a ham-handed interrogator.

"Well, yes," Alafair admitted, abashed. "I'm sorry to be bothering you with this, son. But I am worried about my daughter, and when I heard that my husband had hired you to come out, I just couldn't pass up the opportunity to ask you what you think." She didn't compound the matter by confessing that bringing him out to the farm for questioning had been her idea. "Do you have any thoughts about who might have shot Mr. Day?"

Dan shook his head. "I'd like to help you, Miz Tucker," he said. "I like John Lee, and I'd like it if he could be happy with a fine girl. But I don't have no idea who shot Mr. Day. He was such an awful old snake that anybody could have done it. He was a cheater and a thief. He tried to cheat my pa, and my pa was just about the only merchant in town who would do business with him when he did it. I'd have been happy to do the honors if I'd have thought of it before Maggie Ellen run off."

"I heard he came between you," Alafair said.

Dan looked up at her, then over at Shaw, as though he was trying to determine how much they knew before he answered. "He tried," he said at last. "But we just got sneakier about meeting. It was a lot harder to see one another, though. Sometimes I didn't see her for weeks as a time. I told her, though...." He paused and gazed into middle space for a few seconds, then resumed briskly. "I told her, though, that I'd be proud to marry her any time she wanted. We could get us a little house in Boynton. But she wanted to get completely away, out of the county, and take as many of her brothers and sisters as she could. I suppose she thought she couldn't wait any more, but I was surprised when she ran off like that. I expect that once she hears her old man is dead, she'll show up again."

"Do you think she keeps in touch with John Lee?" Alafair wondered.

Dan shrugged. His face was very red, now. "I don't know what John Lee knows. I wouldn't be surprised if she keeps in touch with Naomi, somehow, though. She was pretty protective of Naomi."

Shaw stood up. "All right, Alafair," he interjected firmly. "I think you've tormented this fellow enough for one day. We've got to get back to work, now, before the day gets completely gone." He seized Alafair by the arm and hustled her out the tool shed door into the cold.

"He seems like a good honest boy," Alafair observed, totally unaffected by the look of exasperation on Shaw's face. "But he never once mentioned that Harley beat him up, did you notice that?"

"I doubt if it was his proudest moment," Shaw said. "Now, if you're done with your questions, go on back up to the house and let us get on with it."

"Now, Shaw," Alafair chided. "If you're so set against my talking with Dan, why did you go ahead and invite him out here? I told you what I intended."

Shaw let go of her arm. "Well, maybe I did," he admitted reluctantly. "But I think that's enough. He's bound to get the idea you suspect him of something, otherwise. Did you even learn anything you didn't already know?"

"I learned that him and Maggie Ellen kept on seeing one another for a while after Harley drove him off."

Shaw made shooing motions. "Go home and think about that, then. I've got to get back inside before Dan thinks I've abandoned him."

Alafair trotted back toward the house, looking happy, and Shaw returned to the tool shed, feeling torn, and put out with himself for his own curiosity, and for indulging Alafair in her little plot.

"I'm sorry about that," he apologized to Dan, as he sat back down at the table. "She's got it into her head that maybe if she talks to everybody who ever knew Harley Day, she can figure out who did him in better than the sheriff can."

"And clear John Lee?"

"I expect that's the plan. Anyway, I hope you don't take offense."

Dan's complexion had cleared and he looked fairly sanguine about the whole situation as he took a bite of cornbread before responding. "I can't hardly fault a mother for wanting to help her daughter," he told Shaw. "I just hope she don't think I did it, or my pa, either." Another bite of cornbread, more chewing. His face underwent a subtle change as he pondered the death of Harley Day. "He was an awful man, though," he mused aloud. "It was like he took pleasure in making his own daughter unhappy. It was evil the way he did that."

Shaw sat back in his chair and studied the mechanic as he spoke, wondering if anyone was really as he first seemed.

When he left the tool shed an hour later, Shaw could see Alafair flitting around on the back porch, busying herself with washing out a few of the children's clothes. He smiled to himself as he trudged toward the house. Alafair had picked a chore that would enable her to keep an eye on the shed. He braced himself for the quizzing he was in for.

"Hello, sugar," he greeted, as he stepped onto the porch. Alafair was already wringing out the small shirt she had been washing. She hurriedly pinned it to her makeshift clothesline that was strung across one corner of the porch, and followed him into the kitchen.

"Y'all about finished with the harrow?" she opened.

"Dan is just packing up the axle right now. He's going to sharpen up another disc or two, and then I'm going to take him back into town, and pick up the kids, while I'm at it. I sure will be glad when it warms up some and the kids can get themselves back and forth by themselves."

Alafair knew that the kids could have managed by themselves very well if they had to, but Shaw was too tenderhearted to make them fend with the cold, so she didn't argue with him. "I expect you're here for some blankets and hot coffee for the trip, then," she said. "I've got a couple of hot bricks for you on the stove in the parlor, too. I've got a bit of dinner ready. Do you think Dan would like some?"

Shaw sat down while Alafair bustled around the kitchen retrieving dishes. "No, I asked him, but he said his mother is expecting him for dinner at her house. I'll eat, though. I'm peckish, and Dan won't be ready to go for a half-hour or so."

"Did he say anything else after I left?" Alafair asked casually, as she set a plate down in front of him.

"About what?" he wondered, feeling perverse.

"You know what," she said, annoyed. "About what we were discussing when I was out there."

"He said he hopes you don't think he did it."

Alafair poured him some coffee and began placing bowls of hot food on the table. "Well, I don't know, Shaw," she said. "He seems like a nice boy. I hope he didn't do it, too. But I hope more that somebody else other than John Lee did it. Where do you suppose Dan was the night Harley was killed? I couldn't think how to ask him. Well, I'm sure Scott did, but I might mention it to him, just the same."

"I wonder what Scott thinks about Dan's connection with the Day family," Shaw mused.

"Do you think Scott would tell you if you asked him?"

Shaw laughed. "No," he assured her.

"He sure keeps his thoughts to himself," Alafair said, exasperated.

"He's not going to say anybody is guilty 'til he thinks they are. That's a quality you want in your sheriff," Shaw noted wryly. "When I saw him this morning, though, he did tell me that they still haven't found a gun." He paused to mound mashed potatoes on his plate. "It would have to be a pretty small gun, he thinks, like a little muff pistol. Most derringers, the single-shots, take a .41 caliber bullet, but every once in a while you come across one of them two or four-shots that takes a .22 bullet. Useless little gun. I think of them as the kind of gun a St. Louis society lady carries when she has to walk down the alley."

Alafair's grip tightened on the spoon she was using to stir the squash on the the stove, and a sweat broke out on her forehead. Shaw obviously didn't remember, but Alafair was suddenly thinking of just the kind of pistol that he was describing. She owned one—a two-shot .22 ladies' derringer, silver-plated and ebony handled. Her father had given it to her when she was sixteen, just about the time she began to show an interest in boys, she remembered ironically. She kept it in its little velvet-lined box on the top shelf of her chiffarobe, along with a package of two bullets. She hadn't touched it in years. It couldn't be, she was thinking. She didn't recall that she had ever told any of the children about her little pistol. Of course, children snoop....

꜅꜀꜁꜂

It took every bit of the considerable fortitude Alafair possessed to get through dinner without alerting Shaw to her agitation. She made a typically huge meal just for him, sat down and ate her share, chatting pleasantly all the while, and was in the process of clearing the table when Shaw rebundled himself and went out to fetch Dan from the tool shed. The instant the door slammed behind him, Alafair was in her bedroom like a shot, pulling the little box down from behind a wall of folded quilts and hat boxes.

She had the box open as soon as both hands were on it, and so knew it was empty before she set it on her dresser, but she stood there for quite a while staring into it nonetheless. She couldn't think. Her heart was out of control. Suddenly this whole affair was infinitely more serious than it was even an hour ago. Could it be a coincidence that the gun was gone just at the time that someone was killed with something similar enough as to make no difference?

Oh, please, God. Phoebe wasn't just in danger of a broken heart. She was an accomplice. Maybe worse. No, mustn't even think that thought. Maybe it was one of the other children. No, why would it be? Besides, that wasn't any better. She had taken two steps toward the back door, intending to run back out to the soddie and confront John Lee, before she reconsidered and sat down on the bed. If she asked him where he had gotten the gun, and he had gotten it from Phoebe, he would lie. If she asked him where the gun was, he would lie. He would do anything to protect Phoebe, including run away. No, she couldn't alert him that she knew Phoebe was involved. She was going to have to wait and confront Phoebe herself. If she ran out right now and told Shaw what was happening, he would at the very least rush to the soddie and beat John Lee to a pulp and ask questions later.

And so, she was going to have to wait. Alafair, who seldom wept, began to weep softly with fear and frustration. How could Phoebe, of all people, get mixed up in such a thing? Sweet, gentle Phoebe, so quiet and obedient, so different from the rest of her sassy brood. Yes, she would have to say that, as much as she loved all her children, Phoebe might be her favorite. She stopped crying abruptly and sat up straight on the edge of the bed. Well, there was just no way, that was all. No matter what Phoebe had done, Alafair wasn't going to let anything bad happen to her while her heart still beat in her body. She stood up and smoothed her hair in the mirror, returned the box to its place in the chiffarobe, then got on with her housework.

Chapter Nine

Alafair was a lioness. She was in her hunting mode, her senses heightened to the point of clairvoyance, waiting and watching for the perfect time to pounce. Her prey, the little doe Phoebe, had no idea she was being stalked, and so when her mother finally went for the kill, she was doomed.

Alafair made her move after supper was cleared away, in that short happy period before bed when the family gathered in the parlor. She managed by some plausible ruse to get Phoebe alone with her out on the enclosed back porch. It was cold, and both women wrapped their shawls around themselves more tightly. But it was private.

"What did you want me for, Ma?" Phoebe asked, her breath fogging in the chilly air. She cast an innocent glance around the porch, looking for some likely task that needed doing.

"I wanted to talk to you," Alafair began. "Phoebe, you know that John Lee's dad was shot. What you may not know is that he was killed by a small caliber derringer."

Phoebe froze as still as a hunted rabbit. She paled so suddenly that it occurred to Alafair that she might faint, but she stood solid and gazed at her mother out of eyes huge with horror. She said nothing.

"Phoebe, where is my little silver pistol that I keep in my chiffarobe?"

Phoebe's lips parted and a little squeaky sound emerged, but she said nothing intelligible.

Oh, yes, you're caught now, my dear, Alafair thought. "Did you give my gun to John Lee?" she persisted.

"Mama," Phoebe managed with a gigantic effort.

"Girl, I'm not your enemy. I want to help you. I want to help John Lee if I can. I know John Lee is holed up in the soddie. I followed you out there the other night. Now, don't panic," she interjected quickly, grabbing Phoebe's arm when it looked as though she might bolt out of sheer inability to think of any other response. "I haven't told anybody, not even your daddy. Not yet. I talked to John Lee, and he told me his version of what happened. I want to believe him, honey, so I thought I'd see what was what before he turns himself in, and he has to turn himself in, Phoebe. You know it and he knows it, too. Of course, that was before I knew that my pistol is missing. Did you give it to him? And don't you lie to me, child. I'll know if you do, and it'll go worse for you."

Her horror at being caught out had subsided enough for Phoebe to think, and she was doing just that with manic speed. She knew very well that her mother had some sort of supernatural ability to tell when her children were lying, but she also knew that that ability wasn't 100 percent. What had John Lee told her? Knowing John Lee, he would have told Alafair as much of the truth as he could without involving Phoebe in it at all. But now her mother knew that Phoebe was involved, though not quite how. Phoebe's assessment of the situation was done in the twinkling of an eye. To deny knowledge would be stupid, dangerous, and an insult. "Yes, Mama, I took your pistol."

Alafair said nothing, but Phoebe could feel the heightening of the tension in the atmosphere. "I know it was wrong," Phoebe continued, "but I felt like I had to help John Lee. Things had got so bad that I was afraid his daddy was going to kill him, and I wanted him to have some protection."

"Don't they have their own guns over to the Day place?" Alafair asked. Her voice was crisp to the point of being brittle.

"Yes, but I figured that little gun would be easier to hide, and not make his daddy so mad if he saw it."

"When did you give him the gun?"

There was the briefest of hesitations before Phoebe answered. A look of fear came into her eyes that made Alafair's heart constrict. "I took it over there that evening that Mr. Day disappeared."

"What in heaven's name were you doing sneaking over there to the Day place?"

"Oh, Mama, I've been sneaking over there once a week to see John Lee for the last six months. I love him so much I couldn't help it. His pa was a monster, Ma. He wouldn't allow John Lee to court me proper, or come and speak to you and Daddy. He didn't want him to have a life or any happiness at all."

"Why didn't you tell us about this," Alafair asked, aghast, "instead of going behind our backs? Do you know what people will say? Do you know what your daddy will say?"

"I couldn't tell you," Phoebe protested, suddenly on the verge of tears. "John Lee couldn't come over here, and I knew you wouldn't let me see him on the sly, without his folks knowing."

"That's certain!"

"But, Ma, I have to see him! I love him. We never did anything wrong. Ma, please, don't you remember what it's like?"

For a second, Alafair was struck dumb. She gripped Phoebe's shoulders in an icy vice, trying to decide whether to comfort her or shake her within an inch of her life.

Did she remember what it was like? Did she remember Shaw Tucker with his honey-colored eyes and his lopsided grin? She was seventeen, just the same age as Phoebe was now. She had known of Shaw and all the Tuckers. She had disdained him, and all boys, until that strange day that was burned in her memory like a brand. She had gone with her mother to the drug store in Lone Elm, and while her mother had been replenishing her store of patent medicines, Alafair had noticed a rangy youth watching her from behind the counter.

Now, Alafair had seen boys before, and she had seen handsome boys before, and she had seen handsome boys ogling her before. But on that day, something about this handsome boy ogling her nearly caused her to stagger and catch at her breast as though a mule had kicked her. And Alafair Gunn, who until that moment had regarded all the male race except for her father with the contempt it so richly deserved, had instantly been reduced to an inner helplessness that she would rather have died than shown.

But in Shaw, she had been lucky, and she knew it. Little had he known, but she would have done anything for Shaw; gone against her better judgment, ruined herself, anything rather than lose him. If Phoebe felt like that about this boy....

Fear gripped her. Alafair had been lucky. Shaw was good. But what of sweet Phoebe, so vulnerable to hurt in a way the other children didn't seem to be?

Her hands dropped from Phoebe's shoulders in helpless resignation. "Well, you're in the soup, now, girl," Alafair said. "You might as well tell me about it."

"I went over there Wednesday afternoon. I can get away for an hour or so on Wednesday afternoons, because Martha doesn't work but half a day and everybody's home. You don't usually need me, and if I only do it once a week or so, nobody much notices I'm gone."

Alafair suddenly remembered an incident of two or three weeks earlier. Had it been on a Wednesday? "Where's Phoebe?" she had asked the milling crew of kids in the kitchen.

"Down to the root cellar," Alice had answered with timely ease, and Alafair had gone back to her cornbread unconcerned. When dinner was on the table, Phoebe had been at her place. Alafair made a mental note of Alice's complicity.

"We usually met way over behind their barn so John Lee's daddy wouldn't see. John Lee would always wait for me there on Wednesday evenings, even though I couldn't always make it."

"What did you do at these meetings?"

"John Lee never put a finger on me, Ma, I swear it on a stack of Bibles a mile high."

"I believe you," Alafair assured her. She did, too. She may have despaired of Phoebe's reputation, but she knew Phoebe too well to doubt her honor. "Now, go on."

Phoebe visibly relaxed. "Mostly we'd just talk. He likes to hear about my family. I think he likes to know that somewhere there's folks who are happy. Sometimes I'd bring him books to read. He can't read too fast, but he wants to know things. Sometimes I'll help him...." With no warning she burst into tears. "Oh, Mama," she sobbed. "He's so good. Why does God send him all this trouble?"

Touched almost to tears herself, Alafair enfolded her daughter in an embrace. "We can't understand the ways of God, sugar," she soothed, "but sometimes I think God tempers special people like steel. He makes them able to stand great sorrow and able to experience great joy."

"When is John Lee going to get some joy, Ma?" Phoebe asked, her voice muffled by her mother's shawl.

"Patience, child. The boy is only nineteen. Besides, you must be a great joy to him." She drew back and lifted Phoebe's chin, brushing the tears from the girl's cheeks with her fingers. "I know you are to me."

Phoebe mastered herself, calm again. "You may not think so when I tell you the rest of the story, Ma. You say you would have forbidden me to go over to the Day place, and you would have been right to do it. Mr. Day was a bad, dangerous man, and John Lee and I knew it. John Lee didn't want me coming over any more than you would have, and I'd never have done it, either, except that we couldn't figure out any other way to see one another without big trouble. We talked about running away. But John Lee felt he had to protect his ma and the kids. Besides, we'd have had to run far away so his daddy couldn't find him, and I don't want to be away from you. So we just met by his barn when we could. We never spent more than half an hour together, and we never got caught, until that night.

"There was more to it than just that Mr. Day wanted John Lee for a slave. John Lee told me that his pa hated us Tuckers.

Envy, I reckon. There's so many of us, and we aren't poor. And Cousin Scott is the sheriff, and Uncle Paul is the mayor, and Uncle Alfred is the president of the Grane. You can imagine."

Alafair was listening to this discourse in amazement. Phoebe, her little bunny rabbit of a girl. Well, still waters run deep indeed, and Phoebe had quite grown up while Alafair's attention was distracted by some of the more unruly members of the family.

"So we figured we'd just have to wait," Phoebe was saying. "We expected that things would change, somehow, someday."

"You might have had to sneak around for years!"

Phoebe's bottom lip pooched out in determination. "We knew that. But what else was there, unless we both just gave up on our families and our responsibilities? John Lee's sister Maggie Ellen did that, you know, ran away. He said it hurt his mother something awful. We just know that we are meant to be together, and that we'll get our opportunity someday." She took a breath. "I didn't want it to be this way. John Lee shouldn't have run away, I know it. But I saw what happened with my own eyes, and I offered to help him my own self, at least 'til we could figure out what to do. He was protecting me, Ma. If he hadn't shot at his daddy, Mr. Day might have done me an injury."

Alafair pushed Phoebe away from her and clutched her chest in shock. "Oh, my Lord, when your daddy hears this story, he'll have an apoplexy. I might have one myself right now. Let me sit down and tell me what happened, for pity's sake."

"Mr. Day come upon us. We were reading and didn't hear him in time to hide. He was drunk, of course. He called me a bad name, and him and John Lee got into it. They had already had one dust-up earlier that day. He caught John Lee one on the eye and knocked him silly for a minute, just long enough to reach over and grab me by the skirt. He'd dragged me over when John Lee came to himself and pulled out the little pistol I'd given him. He hollered at his pa to let me go, and when he didn't, John Lee shot. I thought by the way Mr. Day staggered that he was hit, but I never saw any blood. Mr. Day just let me go and wandered off toward the barn. Me and John Lee ran and ran. We stopped for a while by the creek and got our breath and brushed ourselves off. I cleaned his cut eye as best I could. Then he walked me all the way up to the house. It was the first time he'd ever walked me up to the door, and I was so proud of him."

"Did John Lee only fire once?"

"Yes, I think just once. Yes, just once."

"Now, think, honey. Are you absolutely sure beyond a shadow of a doubt that Mr. Day walked away toward the barn under his own steam?"

"Yes, ma'am, I know it for a fact."

"You said you thought at first that Mr. Day had been hit. Where did you think the bullet hit him?"

"Why, in the right side. He staggered a bit to the left. Sure not in the head, Ma. He would have dropped dead right then and there, wouldn't he?" Her cheeks flushed, and a look of excitement came into her eyes. "Ma, I can be his alibi, can't I? I mean, I saw the whole thing. I saw that John Lee didn't shoot Mr. Day in the head, that he was still alive when we ran away. That proves that John Lee didn't kill his father, doesn't it?"

"What did John Lee do with the gun?"

Phoebe drew up. "I don't know," she admitted. "I didn't pay no attention."

"That gun is a two-shot, Phoebe. Maybe John Lee came upon his dad passed out next to the house later that evening, after he left you, and finished him off. That fight Mrs. Day told us John Lee and his pa had, I don't know if that was before this business with you or after."

"Oh, no, Ma," Phoebe exclaimed. "It couldn't be. No, he threw the gun away, I remember now."

"Mercy!" Alafair clapped her hands against her cheeks in dismay. "Oh, my girl, God smite me for letting you get mixed up in this ugly thing."

Phoebe was surprised. "You didn't have anything to do with it, Mama. How can you know everything all the time?"

"Because I'm your mother. Oh, why didn't you tell me your problem? It's a hard one, I know, but maybe Daddy and I could have helped you some way. Maybe we could have got that man locked up for something."

"Are you going to tell Daddy?" Phoebe asked anxiously.

"Well, I've got to, darlin', can't you see?"

"Please don't, Mama," Phoebe pleaded with a vehemence that startled Alafair. "Not yet, anyway. Not until we find some way to prove that John Lee couldn't possibly have done this awful thing."

"Honey, you know your daddy and I don't keep things from one another." Not things of such monumental importance, anyway, she added to herself.

"I'm just asking you to hold off telling him for a little while. If Daddy finds out now, before we can clear John Lee, he'll turn him in. And once Cousin Scott has him, it'll just be too tempting to say that he's surely the one who did it, and leave off looking for the truth."

Alafair had not missed Phoebe's assertion that *we* could clear John Lee, and she smiled. The girl might have a grown-up life of her own, now, but she still depended on her mother with unconscious ease. I should encourage her to talk the boy into giving himself up right now, she thought. Then he'd be safe and warm and well fed while *they* went about the business of clearing him. If, in fact, he could be cleared. Alafair wasn't as sure of John Lee's innocence as Phoebe seemed to be. The way things now stood, Phoebe was implicated, perhaps as an accessory to murder. Right and proper behavior and legalities now all stood a distant second to Alafair's need to protect her daughter. There was no way in the world she was going to turn that boy in until she had unshakable proof that Phoebe was not involved in any way with the murder.

"All right," she said briskly. "But I think we need to find someplace to hide John Lee other than in that soddie. Your daddy goes out that way too often, and you can never tell when one of the other kids might get a notion to play there. Besides,

Scott and Trent will get to searching the vicinity pretty quick now, and that hay store is just too obvious. Let me ponder on it tonight."

Phoebe nearly swooned with relief. "Oh, Mama, thank you," she sighed.

"Don't thank me yet," Alafair warned her. "If I find out that John Lee did it, I have no intention of helping him escape punishment."

"No, no," Phoebe gushed. "You won't have to worry about that, Ma. Oh, thank you, thank you."

Phoebe's total belief in John Lee's innocence made Alafair feel a little better. "Get a hold of yourself, now. Tell you what. You make up a sandwich with that leftover roast pork and you and me can take it out there to him in a bit, while everybody's getting ready for bed." Phoebe's head was nodding wildly. "Right now we've got to get back in there before they come looking for us," Alafair continued. "But before we're done with this, you have to promise me that you will not go out there to see that boy without me along. Otherwise, I'm telling your daddy this minute."

Phoebe promised on her life.

Alafair had a side word with Shaw as the children were readying for bed. What she told him was the truth, though not the whole truth. She implied to the bewildered father that she was offering counsel and comfort to a girl teetering on the edge of heart-break, and that mother and daughter intended to step outside for a little walk and a heart to heart before sleeping. Shaw had no reason to find this suspicious, having lived through several girlish traumas in the twenty years he had had daughters. He did offer the opinion that it was too dang cold to go traipsing around outside in the dark, but after Alafair pointed out to him with some asperity that there was not a corner of the house that was beyond eight sets of prying ears, he admitted that she was correct. She comforted him by promising that they would go to the barn for a bit.

When Alafair and Phoebe finally left the house, bundled to the eyes and clutching food and drink under their coats, it was pitch dark and bitingly cold. They made their way to the soddie with a detour through the barn, because Alafair had said they were going to the barn, and she did what she said. When they reached the soddie, Alafair paused by the door and drew Phoebe over to her.

"I don't want you telling him anything about what Doctor Addison found, Phoebe," she warned the girl. "In fact, don't be talking to him about his father's murder at all, or about what's going to happen. You leave that to me."

"But I can talk to him?" Phoebe asked anxiously.

"Sure you can. I'll even let you two alone for a few minutes before we go back to the house, if you promise to do as I ask."

"You know I'll do whatever you say, Mama," Phoebe assured her.

John Lee was sitting on a bale of hay in his little cubicle, obviously waiting for them. He stood when Alafair squeezed herself through the opening in the bales. "Hello, son," she greeted. She reached back through to relieve Phoebe of the lantern, and was holding the light high when Phoebe popped into view, so she had a clear and unobstructed view of John Lee's face.

The greeting he was about to give Alafair died on his lips when Phoebe appeared, and the look of absolute adoration that came into his eyes when he saw her daughter startled Alafair. Oh, she had known beforehand that she had a problem on her hands with Phoebe's affection for John Lee. But in one moment of insight, she realized that these two children loved one another with the kind of love that would wither them if it were thwarted. She swallowed.

"Phoebe, I'm glad to see you," John Lee managed.

"Oh, John Lee, me too," Phoebe breathed.

Alafair cleared her throat ostentatiously, and both youngsters looked at her, abashed. "Well, John Lee, I'm glad to see you're still here," she said.

His eyes widened in mild surprise. "Well, I said I'd stay here 'til I heard from you, Miz Tucker," he noted.

She smiled. "So you did. And you've managed to keep from freezing, too."

"Yes, ma'am," he replied. He was trying to look at Alafair, but his eyes kept straying to Phoebe against his will. "I sleep mostly during the day. Got plenty of quilts and the hay is a good insulator. I jump around a lot at night. It ain't so bad. Worst thing is the boredom, that and not knowing what's going on with my ma and the kids. I'd have asked for some books, you know, to practice my reading, but it's too dim in here for that. I just been weaving things out of straw." He reached down behind his sleeping nest and proffered a couple of little straw dolls, deftly woven.

Alafair took one and examined it. "Pretty good," she admitted. "Best not to be idle."

"Do you have some news for me, Miz Tucker?" John Lee asked, managing with some effort to control the anxiety in his voice.

Alafair glanced at Phoebe, who had as yet made no attempt to say anything. "Well, first of all," Alafair began, "your ma and the kids are fine, though worried about you, of course. We heard that your daddy was definitely shot in the head with a small caliber bullet out of a small pistol, but they aren't sure whether that was what killed him or the cold."

John Lee's eyebrows rose. "The head," he repeated. A large puff of steamy breath escaped him, and he sat back down heavily on his bale of hay. "So I didn't kill my daddy after all," he murmured.

"It is not at all clear," Alafair pointed out firmly. But he looked back up at her with a face suffused with relief.

"No, ma'am," he said. "I don't mean I'm proved innocent. But now I know I'm innocent."

"You could be, son. But we've got to have proof. Now listen carefully, and tell me the truth. What did you do with that pistol after you shot at your father?"

The big black eyes, now suffused with the light of hope, widened at her question. "I threw it down, Miz Tucker, right there in the woods, by the hillock where we was sitting. It's lying there still, I imagine."

"You'd better hope so, boy, because if it is, and if it still has one bullet in it, then that means you didn't shoot your daddy while he lay beside the house. If it isn't there, then somebody came along and picked it up and probably used it to kill Harley, and that somebody could easily have been you."

"Or me," Phoebe interjected. "We're the only two who knew it was there."

"No," Alafair and John Lee said at once, and Phoebe almost laughed.

"I'm glad y'all have such faith in me," she admitted, "but the law could see it that way."

"Miz Tucker," John Lee said firmly, "I think we're agreed that we got to keep Phoebe out of this."

Phoebe started to protest, but Alafair cut her off. "Oh, we're agreed, John Lee. Question is, can we? We haven't got much time, is the problem. One more day, maybe two. I think me and Phoebe better go over to your place tomorrow and hunt for that pistol."

"I can show you right where," John Lee told her.

Alafair shook her head. "No, you don't stir a foot out of here 'til I tell you. It's too dangerous for you to go hotfooting it all over the county, and you being hunted. Phoebe can show me where you all were."

"What about school?" Phoebe wondered.

Alafair sighed. "I guess you'll be sick again tomorrow," she said.

━━━

That night, Alafair dreamed she was running toward town with the baby in her arms. She could feel the life going out of him, and she could hear a voice screaming in fear and desperation. She knew it was herself screaming, but she didn't have time to consider the fact because she had to run....

━━━

It was close to seven o'clock the next morning when Alafair and Phoebe finally were left alone and began their trek on foot through the fields and stands of pin oak to come up to the Day farm. Phoebe was a competent guide, having long ago figured the best way to get onto the neighboring homestead unseen. They crawled under the barbed wire fence, holding the bottom strand up for each other, and crossed over onto the Day place into a good sized grove of trees, their dried brown leaves like butcher paper shussing in the winter breeze, black boles standing out against a gray sky, and half melted streaks of white snow outlining the ground. They automatically fell silent when they entered the Day property, and picked their way warily through the trees. Alafair could see the back of the barn through the trees when Phoebe took her hand and halted her on top of a small mound just at the edge of the woods.

"This is where we were," Phoebe said in a voice just above a whisper. She bent down and picked up something off the ground. "See, here's the book I brought him, laying right here where I dropped it when Mr. Day surprised us." She handed the wet and ruined book to her mother, who looked down at it thoughtfully for a moment before eyeing her surroundings. It was a good place for a tryst. They could see out, but it would be difficult to see two lovers hunkered down in the trees with their heads together. She shook her head. How could a falling-down drunk have surprised two healthy young people? They had been reading, they said, engrossed in the book, or more likely, in each other. Oh, Alafair remembered how it was. An elephant could have charged them, ears all aflap, and they wouldn't have noticed it 'til they were trampled. Day had grabbed Phoebe by the arm, jerked her up. That's what they had said. Alafair could envision it. Phoebe would have screamed, the boy would have leaped up and shoved his father away. Then what? A blindly inebriated man, insane with drink, mad with rage, numb to pain, flails out at his son like he had a hundred times before. Beats him, blackens his eye. At first, the boy is inclined to take it, like he had a hundred times before, simply out of habit. But something new is added. Phoebe. Besides being shamed before his love, he knows that if he doesn't stop the man once and for all, his love may be in danger, too. His fair Phoebe, who has never known violence. She is a dream to him. Beauty and love and sanity to a boy who has known none of those things, when all the ugliness of his world suddenly bursts in and threatens it all.

He strikes back. Alafair could understand it. Faced with the loss of all that is dear to him, the boy pulls the derringer that Phoebe has given him for protection and fires.

She looked down at Phoebe, who was standing just below her on the hillock, looking up at her mother patiently. "Show me what happened," Alafair instructed.

Phoebe nodded. "Me and John Lee were sitting right here like this." She demonstrated by sitting down. Alafair moved down off the hillock and stood off to the side where she could take in all of Phoebe's reenactment.

And Phoebe was quite a little actor, Alafair noted to her amazement. She watched, skeptically, to be sure, as Phoebe hopped around the clearing, playing the parts of innocent maid, evil accoster, and heroic rescuer with desperate verve. Alafair interrupted the performance periodically with questions.

"Now, did Mr. Day fall down like that right on top of you?" she asked.

"Yes, ma'am, he did," Phoebe assured her. "Knocked the wind right out of me."

"And that was right about here?"

"Yes, near as I can remember, it was right here."

"When you and John Lee came to the house afterwards, you didn't look much like you had been rolling around in this leaf litter, here," Alafair noted.

Phoebe reddened. "John Lee and I hid out for a bit, like I told you, to get our breath back. Brushed each other off as best we could. John Lee picked a mess of twigs out of my hair."

"Couldn't disguise that black eye John Lee had, though," Alafair observed.

"No," Phoebe agreed with some heat. "It wasn't the first one his daddy had given him, either."

"Well, go on, then," Alafair urged. "John Lee fell down right over there when Mr. Day clobbered him, and then you two struggled and fell down here. Why didn't you run away when you had the chance?"

"I couldn't leave John Lee," Phoebe told her, surprised that she would suggest such a thing.

Alafair's eyebrows shot up. "No, of course not," she conceded. "So, anyway, you hollered, and John Lee sat up and pulled out the pistol. Is that when he shot at his dad?"

"He yelled at him to leave me alone," Phoebe told her. "But Mr. Day kind of staggered up to his feet and lunged at John Lee on the ground there. He looked like he meant to kill John Lee, with his fists all balled up and his face screwed up real mean. I think John Lee was still kind of woozy. It was my fault that he fired, Ma. I thought his dad would murder him, so I yelled at him to fire."

"*You* yelled at him to fire?"

"Yes, Ma. I thought it was kill or be killed. I was scared witless."

"And John Lee fired."

"He did. Mr. Day stopped in his tracks, I guarantee. He reeled a bit, and I thought he was hit. But he just stood there for a second, surprised, I guess. I reckon he suddenly thought better of whacking on John Lee. After a half a minute, he just sort of reeled off toward the barn."

"And then what did you kids do?"

"I helped John Lee up and we ran off back that way, further into the woods and down to the creek bank, until we figured it was safe. Then we made our way to the road and John Lee walked me home. He told me that when his pa was so drunk, he didn't even remember what he had done, so after I got my wits back and calmed down, I wasn't too worried that Mr. Day would still be after him."

"But you didn't see John Lee throw down the pistol?"

"No, I didn't even think about it. But now that I look back, I know he didn't have it in his hands when he helped me get up."

"Let's start looking for it here, then," Alafair suggested. "And look sharp. That little thing has been lying out there for a week and is surely covered up with ground stuff by now."

And the two women looked. They looked for an hour, covering every scrap of ground between the hillock and the property line, and then they covered it again. No leaf lay unturned.

"But he said he dropped it right after he fired it," Phoebe protested to no one, close to tears. "It has to be right here!" They had made their way back to the hillock for the second time.

"It isn't here," Alafair stated. "It isn't here, honey. If John Lee is telling the truth, then somebody has been here and picked it up."

The tears that had been welling in Phoebe's eyes trickled down her cheeks, and she scrubbed at them with the back of her mitten. "That's what happened, then, Mama," she assured Alafair. "'Cause John Lee wouldn't lie."

Alafair caught her bottom lip between her teeth thoughtfully. She stepped purposefully into the spot where John Lee was sitting when he shot at his father. "John Lee was right about here when the pistol went off," she said. She sat down on the ground. "He would have been, what? About like this?" She held her two hands straight out in front of her, aiming a phantom gun.

Phoebe sniffed and gazed at her mother, interest replacing frustration. She walked to a place behind the hillock. "I was lying on the ground right here," she said, pointing to her left. "Mr. Day was standing over there. Everything happened pretty fast, but it didn't look to me like John Lee aimed very carefully. Or maybe he was aiming at his daddy's knees, because I don't think he lifted the gun very high before he shot, just shot straight ahead."

"Did you hear the bullet hit anything?"

"Oh, heavens, Mama. I can't remember. I don't remember any ricochet or anything like that. What are you getting at?"

Alafair glanced at Phoebe before peering off into the woods again. "I'm thinking, my girl," she said, "that if we can't find the gun, maybe we can find the bullet. At least that would prove that your part of the story is true."

Phoebe's eyes widened. "You ever heard of the needle in the haystack story?" she asked.

"Don't be sassy, now," Alafair replied offhandedly. "Try and remember. You think he aimed right about this way?"

A thoughtful look passed over Phoebe's face as she gazed at her mother, trying to superimpose her memory of that evening over what she was seeing at the moment. She moved to where she remembered Mr. Day standing when John Lee fired. "This way, Mama," she said, and Alafair aimed her imaginary gun at Phoebe's knees. One hand clutching the phantom pistol dropped down, and the other pointed into the woods. "That tree, there," she stated. Phoebe turned to look at a scrubby oak about twenty yards from her that looked identical to all the other scrubby oaks in the grove.

"What if I was wrong about the angle?" Phoebe wondered.

Alafair scrambled to her feet. "We won't know until we look, now, will we?"

Phoebe reached the tree before her mother, and bent down to look at where Alafair had pointed. She nearly fainted when she saw it—a little pale bore in the black bark of the slender oak, right at waist height. It was too round to be natural, and it was new. Limp with amazement, she stuck her finger into the hole and felt metal at about half an inch. She laid her forehead against the tree trunk and prayed her thanks. It never occurred to her that divine guidance might not be involved. Only God could have led her to find a single bullet hole in a forest.

She heard her mother come up behind her. "Is it there?" Alafair asked.

"Yes, Ma, it's here," Phoebe said. "It's a miracle."

Alafair moved her aside and knelt down to look at the hole in a businesslike manner, more sanguine about God's intervention than Phoebe was. She nodded. "Well, girl, that's one piece of evidence down," she said. She picked up a rock and scored a white scar on the trunk, so that they would be able to find the tree again with ease. She looked up at Phoebe, her brown eyes full of determination. "Now we have to find that bothersome gun."

⌇⌇⌇

Alafair and Phoebe were approaching home, trudging hand in hand in grim consort against the cold. Alafair had her eyes on the ground before her feet and didn't see Scott's big horse tied up in front of the house until Phoebe squeezed her hand in alarm. Alafair's steps faltered. "Now, what is he doing here this time of day?" she wondered aloud.

They walked up the porch steps together, moving more quickly now, from anxiety. "You keep quiet, girl," Alafair instructed in a low voice, as they approached the front door. "No use to assume anything. Just let me do any talking that needs to be done."

Phoebe didn't have time to assent before they entered the house. From the front door they could see into the kitchen. They could see Scott and Shaw sitting at the kitchen table, both holding steamy mugs of coffee clutched in two hands. The men both turned and looked at the women when they came in. Alafair squeezed Phoebe's hand as a reminder, then calmly began to unwind the wool scarf around her head and face.

"What are you two up to, lolling around and this time of day?" she called to them.

Shaw picked up her bantering tone. "Just not in the mood to mend harnesses," he called back.

Alafair and Phoebe finished peeling themselves out of their outerwear, and walked into the kitchen. Alafair sat herself down opposite her husband and his cousin. Phoebe leaned uncertainly against the cabinet.

"Now, I might ask," Shaw continued, "what you two were doing strolling around out in the frigid for so long?"

"How long have you two been here?" Alafair asked.

"Oh, just about fifteen minutes," Scott told her. "Don't let him give you a hard time. Shaw and me met in town and I rode back out with him. Got a little news for you." He glanced up at Phoebe. "Seems John Lee Day marched into town a couple of hours ago, right into my office, and gave himself up."

Phoebe gasped, and Alafair shot her a stern glance.

The glance that Shaw gave Scott was even sterner. "Come sit down here by your daddy, sweetheart," he said to Phoebe, patting the chair next to him. She did as she was told in stunned silence. Shaw draped his arm over his daughter's shoulders and looked at Alafair. "We were thinking to tell you about it," he said to her, "so you could break the news to Phoebe, but it looks like the cat is out of the bag, now."

"Oh, come on, Shaw. Phoebe is hardly a baby, are you, honey?" Scott defended himself.

"No, she's not," Alafair answered for her, unaware that all three of the adults were treating the poor girl exactly like the baby they were professing she was not. "Where has the boy been hiding himself?"

"He says he's been in the corn crib out behind the Day house. Which he ain't," Scott assured them. "I searched that crib, that whole farm, in fact, and I'd have seen sign if he had been sleeping there. But it don't matter now, I expect." He leaned back in the chair, his blue eyes widening. "He apologized to me for hiding out, don't you know. Said he thought at first that he really had shot his dad, but now he knows it wasn't him, so there is no need to be afraid." The look he gave Shaw spoke volumes about what he thought of the naivety of youth. He looked back at Phoebe. "You try not to worry about your friend, darlin'," he soothed. "I already talked to Judge Sutton about getting him a lawyer. If he's innocent, like he says, we'll find out."

Innocent and naive herself, Phoebe was comforted by the sheriff's assurances. "Thank you, Cousin Scott," she said. "Will I be allowed to see him, you think?"

Scott glanced at Shaw again, whose eyebrows disappeared up under the dark hair that had fallen onto his forehead. "Maybe in a few days, Phoebe," Scott told her, "if your mama and daddy don't object."

Before Shaw could tell them whether or not he objected, Alafair leaned over the table and put her hand on Scott's forearm. "Have you told Miz Day that you got her boy?"

"Not yet. I was just on my way out there. In fact, I'd better get."

"Would you let me tell her, Scott?" Alafair asked, her voice betraying some anxiety for the first time.

It was Shaw who responded first. "What in heaven's name is on your mind, Alafair?" he wondered.

"I'm the one to tell her, Alafair," Scott interjected. "I want to tell her what her rights and obligations are, here, and answer any questions she might have about what to do now."

Alafair nodded. "Yes, I guess you do need to do that. But still. That poor woman never had anything but a hard time. It would be a kindness to let me break it to her first, woman to woman, rather than have the scary sheriff do it. You can come along in a half hour or so. I'll make you out to be just a big old angel in a badge."

Out of the corner of her eye, Alafair could see Phoebe gazing at her, perplexed. What *is* on your mind, Mama, Alafair could practically hear her say. Once again, Scott looked at Shaw, and they gazed at one another in silence for a moment, wordlessly commiserating about the unfathomable female mind. At long last, he looked back at Alafair. "I guess I could do that, if you think it's important," he conceded, as graciously as he could. "As long as you don't go to questioning her or giving her legal advice."

Alafair jumped up out of her chair with such alacrity that her feet left the floor. "Thank you. It'll be better this way, you'll see." She was halfway into the parlor by now, talking to them over her shoulder. "I'll just run over there on Missy right now. You give me, oh, forty-five minutes, then come on over." She was shrugging into her coat.

"You want me to come with you?" Shaw asked, standing up.

"No, no," she called, impatient. "This is woman stuff."

"Mama?" Phoebe wondered.

"You walk me out, Phoebe," Alafair instructed. "You might as well start supper while I'm gone."

Phoebe flew to her mother's side. Only one arm was in her coat when she and Alafair walked out onto the porch.

"Now, listen, girl," Alafair said to her, talking fast. "Something just occurred to me and I want to ask Miz Day about it before Scott gets to her. You offer Cousin Scott and your daddy some pie. Try to stall them a bit, give me some time. Just try not to act suspicious. When they start champing at the bit, let them go."

"What is it, Ma?" Phoebe huffed, straining to keep up with the longer-legged Alafair as they strode toward the barn. "What are you going to ask Miz Day?"

"I'd rather not say until I know more."

"Ma, why did John Lee turn himself in? He was safe where he was. He could have let us find out who done it."

Alafair swung the barn door open. "He was trying to protect you, silly girl," Alafair informed her sharply. "And he was probably smart to do it. If he'd been found out in that soddie with all our blankets and food, there's no way he could say somebody in our family didn't help him. And turning himself in makes him look less guilty, is another thing." She slid the halter over Missy's head, which was hanging serenely over the stall door, and led the mare out into the barn.

"As soon as Daddy and Scott get completely gone, you rush on out to the soddie and get rid of every trace of John Lee." The saddle made a hollow whump as it hit the saddle blanket on Missy's back. Alafair's voice was momentarily muffled by the horse's belly as she reached under for the cinch. "Don't put that comforter back on the bed," she warned. "Somebody's bound to smell hay. Shake it out good and fold it up with some cedar chips in it, and put it in the chest at the end of my bed." She took the reins and the saddle horn in her left hand and the crupper in her right and hoisted herself up into the saddle. She adjusted her full skirt with a flick of her hand. "If ever you had any stealthiness in you, Phoebe, you'd better use it now. Try to be invisible around Scott and your daddy, and if they ask you anything, try to answer with one word or less."

"I don't like to lie, Mama," Phoebe told her, anxious. "I'm not real good at it."

Alafair chuckled humorlessly. "You've been doing pretty well at it for the last few months, to my thinking. But don't worry, I doubt if you'll have to. Daddy thinks you have hurt feelings and he won't be bringing up anything he thinks might cause you pain. Just try not to raise Scott's suspicions, or he'll be all over you like a duck on a junebug." She kicked Missy and was out the barn door, leaving Phoebe watching after her.

Chapter Ten

Mrs. Day came out on the porch to meet Alafair long before Alafair reached the house. Alafair reined at the porch and dismounted in silence, and she and Mrs. Day eyed one another as she tied her horse to the porch rail and walked up the steps. Alafair couldn't see the woman's face, since she was wrapped up in a quilt, top to toe, and only her black eyes were visible. Those black eyes gazed at Alafair with a combination of curiosity and dread, and at first Alafair wondered if Mrs. Day already knew about her son. By the time she reached the top of the steps, Alafair had realized that Mrs. Day was simply not a woman who expected anything good to happen to her. It made Alafair feel bad that she was not going to do anything that would change Mrs. Day's mind about that.

"What can I do for you, Miz Tucker?" Mrs. Day wondered.

Alafair took a breath and came out with it. "Miz Day, I came to tell you that Sheriff Tucker has just arrested John Lee for the murder of your husband."

Mrs. Day's eyes widened, and the quilt fell back from her head. "Oh, no, it can't be," she said. "I can't believe he done it." Her voice was curiously detached at first, then without warning, a wail escaped her that literally made Alafair jump. "Not John Lee," she moaned. "Oh, mercy. Oh, Lord Jesus. Harley was a bad man. Harley deserved to die. But not John Lee. I can't believe he done it."

"I don't think he did it, either," Alafair interjected firmly.

Mrs. Day abruptly stopped wailing and stared at Alafair stupidly. "You don't?" she asked, at length.

Alafair glanced toward the screen door where several little Days were bunched around watching their mother's hysterics without much alarm. Alafair grabbed the woman's arm and drew her away, toward the end of the porch. "No," she assured her. "I've thought on it this past week until my head is sore. It just don't seem possible that John Lee could have so cold-bloodedly walked up to his dad and shot him in his sleep, but I didn't have any other good explanation. The sheriff is going to come out here in just a few minutes to tell you that John Lee has turned himself in. I think John Lee has told the sheriff that he and his dad got into a fight in the woods on Wednesday evening and that John Lee shot at him, then dropped the gun and ran, while Harley staggered off the other direction. Phoebe and I went to the place in the woods where this thing is supposed to have happened, and we did find a fresh bullet scar in a blackjack. But we didn't find no gun...."

"Wait now," Mrs. Day said, halting Alafair's narrative, "John Lee and Harley did go at each other that morning, but it was here in the front yard. And there weren't no gun involved. I saw it with my own eyes. Are you saying there was another fight later that day?"

"So John Lee says."

Mrs. Day blinked. "Miz Tucker, how do you know this? Have you spoken to John Lee? Where has he been?"

Reflexively, Alafair put her hand on Mrs. Day's arm. "I'd rather not say, right now. Let's just say that since my girl Phoebe likes John Lee, and I've found him to be a fine thoughtful boy, I'd like to help him if I can. What I've come to tell you is that I'm thinking that someone found that gun that John Lee threw down in the woods on Saturday night and used it to kill Harley. And I'm wondering if you can think of anybody who was around that night that might have done it."

A perplexed look crossed Mrs. Day's features, then relief and—Alafair didn't know what else to call it—enlightenment flooded into her eyes, and Alafair faltered, startled.

"Something come to you?" she asked.

"The answer, I think," Mrs. Day acknowledged. "Thank you so much for coming out, Miz Tucker. I think my family is saved, now."

Alafair's heart skipped. "What is it?" she wondered excitedly. "Who do you think done it?"

Mrs. Day smiled and shook her head. "I'll wait and tell the sheriff, Miz Tucker, if you don't mind. And don't worry. I won't tell him you told me anything. Now, where's my manners, making you stand out here in the cold? Please come in, and Naomi will heat up some coffee."

❦

Alafair went with Mrs. Day into the house, surrounded by a knot of small children, to wait for Scott. Try as she might, she couldn't get the woman to tell her what she knew, and she was filled with both fear and hope. Well, she had taken a gamble in telling Mrs. Day her suspicions, and now she just had to accept the consequences and pray everything worked out for the best.

Naomi was feeding wood into the Franklin stove when they came in, and she looked back over her shoulder at them with an expression of curiosity on her face.

"Naomi," Mrs. Day said, after she had installed Alafair at the table, "pour us some hot tea, girl, and see if there's any of that pie left that Miz Bellows brung over. The sheriff will be here directly. You make yourself to home, Miz Tucker." She draped her blanket over the back of a chair and sat down on it. Kids stationed themselves around her, and a toddler hoisted himself into her lap.

Naomi stood and wiped her hands on a cloth, then took two cups from the shelf and placed them on the table. "What's happening, Ma?" she asked, as she poured tea leaves into a tin coffee pot full of water and put it on the stove. "Did the sheriff figure out who killed Daddy?"

"He thinks he did. He thinks it's John Lee."

"John Lee," Naomi repeated.

"I mean to tell him different," Mrs. Day stated.

"What are you going to tell the sheriff?" Alafair urged.

"Who are you going to say done it, Ma?" Naomi asked, at the same time.

Mrs. Day shook her head. "I figure the sheriff should know first."

Naomi and Alafair exchanged a puzzled glance.

"Well, I'm mighty curious," Alafair admitted.

"I think it was one of them men that used to buy Daddy's home brew," Naomi offered, and Alafair looked over at her, taken aback. She couldn't recall ever hearing Naomi speak so many words all strung together at one time. It hadn't occurred to her that this shadow of a girl might have an opinion.

But Mrs. Day dismissed the speculation out of hand. "Wasn't them. Sure wasn't John Lee. Hurry up with that pie, Naomi. The sheriff will be here in a few minutes." Naomi retreated back into herself and moved toward the pie keep.

⤐⤐⤐

The two women met Scott in front of the house, and Alafair stood back as he explained to Mrs. Day what had happened, much as she had expected.

"Do you have anything to tell me, now, Mrs. Day?" Scott asked, after he had finished his story.

Mrs. Day drew herself up. "Yes, Sheriff," she said, soberly. "I must tell you that it wasn't John Lee shot his daddy at all. It was me. I found this little gun out in the woods behind the barn and I picked it up. I came back up to the house and I found Harley lying there all drunk and disgusting. I had the little gun in my hand and I put it up against his head and I shot him." She sat down in a wooden chair propped against the rail. "I ain't sorry he's dead. He was a evil man. But I done shot him and I'll take my punishment. It was worth it to me, for now my body may go to prison, or may hang, but my soul is free. The only thing I'm sorry for is that I let folks think it was John Lee did it. Believe me, though, when I tell you that I'd have confessed before I'd have let you jail him."

Alafair was dumbstruck for a moment. "Miz Day…" she managed, at length.

Scott raised a hand, silencing her. Alafair noticed that he didn't look surprised. They were still standing in front of the house when Naomi came out onto the porch, just in time to hear her mother condemn herself. Naomi stood next to Alafair with a dish rag in her hand and listened without expression. Was she moved? Alafair couldn't tell. The big solemn eyes regarded her mother with a blank resignation that made them look a thousand years old. Alafair's heart ached with pity.

"What did you do with the gun, Miz Day?" Scott was asking.

"I throwed it in Bird Creek," she told him without hesitation.

Scott glanced at Alafair, let his gaze slide over Naomi, then back to Mrs. Day. "I'm sorry things turned out this way, Miz Day," he said. "What arrangements do you want me to make for the kids?"

"Are you going to let John Lee out right now?"

"I reckon I've got no more reason to hold him," Scott told her.

Mrs. Day nodded. "Him and Naomi here can take care of the kids for a few days. I'll have him parcel them out to my kin soon as he can."

Scott nodded. "I'll be taking you into town, now," he explained, as though to a child. "You'll have to spend the night in jail, Miz Day, 'til we can get you on over to Muskogee in the morning. The judge will explain the charges to you there, and then you can enter a plea."

"What does that mean?"

"That means that after he tells you what crime you're charged with, you tell him whether you are guilty or not guilty."

"I'm guilty."

"No, Miz Day," Scott said patiently. "Don't tell me. Tell the judge. In fact, I think you'd better not do any more talking right now. I talked to Lawyer Meriwether about representing John

Lee. I expect he can represent you, now. We'll get him over to the jail as soon as we get back."

"What ever you say, Sheriff," Mrs. Day acquiesced placidly. She turned to Alafair. "Miz Tucker, can we hitch your horse to our buggy? I don't have no transportation since the mule disappeared."

"The mule is found as of this morning," Scott informed her. "John Lee can ride it back this afternoon."

Mrs. Day looked relieved, even smiled a little. "Oh, good," she said. "He'll be needing it."

"I'll be glad to let you borrow my horse right now," Alafair interjected. "But wouldn't you rather ride her in and let me stay with the kids?"

Mrs. Day shook her head. "If you don't mind, I'd rather take the buggy and ask if you'd come along with me, you've been so kind and all, and I ain't sure what will be happening. Naomi can get the kids some supper. They'll be all right 'til John Lee comes home." She didn't even glance at Naomi, still standing in silence at Alafair's elbow.

"Can Missy draw a buggy?" Scott asked Alafair.

"She's drawn light rigs in her day," Alafair assured him.

Scott nodded. "All right then, we'll do as you want, Miz Day. Alafair, if you'll help Miz Day get some things together, I'll hitch your horse to the buggy and we'll get to moving."

Alafair and Mrs. Day walked up the porch steps with Naomi trailing behind, as Scott disappeared with the horse toward the barn. "Miz Day," Alafair said to her urgently, "what is this? I didn't tell you about the little gun so you could condemn yourself. You don't have to do this. We can find whoever really did it. Your kids need you."

Mrs. Day paused with her hand on the screen door handle. "No, Miz Tucker, you don't understand. I really did do it. When you told me what you knew, about somebody finding the gun in the woods, I knew it was just a matter of time 'til the sheriff figured it out. Besides, I thought for a while John Lee had got clean away, which I'd miss him, but then I could have stayed with my children. But when I heard he was caught, well, I couldn't let him take the blame any more."

Alafair blinked. Was it true? It made sense, but nothing the woman had done or said until the moment she confessed had led Alafair to suspect her. Though a great barrier to her daughter's happiness had just crumbled, she took no joy in the woman's confession. "This is a sad thing, Miz Day," she finally observed.

Mrs. Day looked up at her, not at all sad. "Yes, ma'am, but as far as I'm concerned, I'm only sorry because I have to be leaving my babies, now. John Lee will be all right, being nigh grown as he is, and I expect my folks will divide the others among them. They'll probably have better lives now than they would have, so I'm glad of that."

She went into the house, leaving Alafair and Naomi on the porch, gazing at one another. Alafair didn't know what to think. Naomi had nothing to say.

"Do you need anything, sugar?" Alafair asked, finally.

"No, thank you," Naomi said, and followed her mother inside.

***

John Lee had been lounging on his cot in the little jail cell when Scott walked in with Mrs. Day. He stood up when he saw her. "Ma, what are you doing here?" he asked.

Scott unlocked the cell. "Come on out now, son. You're free to go."

For a moment, John Lee stood frozen. "What's going on, Sheriff?" he asked, wary.

"You come on out, John Lee," Scott urged. "I'll explain it to you."

John Lee hesitantly crossed the cell and passed in front of his mother, giving her a wondering glance as he passed by. Alafair took his arm, drawing him out into the outer office before he could see his mother jailed.

By the time the door shut behind him, he had well comprehended the situation. He turned his big dark eyes to Alafair and stood patiently, steeled for the story she would tell him while Scott was locking his mother in a jail cell.

"Son," Alafair began, "your ma has said that it was her who killed your pa."

John Lee's expression did not change. He nodded. "Miz Tucker, you know she's saying that just to protect me," he said calmly. "I told you that it was me who shot Daddy, and it was."

"I'm afraid not, John Lee. That original story you told us don't fit the facts. You have Phoebe as a witness, so you can't change your story now, or she'll come forward and we'll all be in the soup. Your ma had the opportunity, and the reason, and most important, she says she did it. I know what's in your mind, but you can't sacrifice yourself to save your mama."

John Lee never moved, but the determined lower lip quivered briefly, and he paled. Alafair reached out, but didn't touch him, lest she compromise the dignity he was struggling to maintain. "Remember the talk we had in the soddie?"

He nodded. "Yes, ma'am, right well, nor will I ever forget. I told the sheriff the story of how Pa came upon me in the woods and we got to fightin'. How he struck me and I shot at him and throwed the gun down. All the truth, except I left Phoebe out of it entirely, just so you know."

"I expected you would," Alafair admitted.

"Good. So we won't need to involve her, looks like. But right now, I can't help but think that old man reaches out from beyond the grave to do evil."

Scott came back into the room and carefully closed the door behind him. He glanced at Alafair, but addressed himself to John Lee. "Has Miz Tucker told you what's happening?"

"Yes, Sheriff," John Lee said.

"Do you have anything to say to me?" Scott asked. His sharp gaze held John Lee's ingenuous one.

"I think she confessed to protect me," John Lee said without hesitation. "I told you the truth about what happened, Sheriff. I shot at my father in the woods and he went back toward the barn."

"Your father only had one bullet wound, John Lee," Scott told him, "right behind his ear. He didn't stagger off nowhere after that. Your mama knew that. You didn't mention it."

John Lee blinked and shook his head. "Even so, she ain't the type. She never lifted a finger to help herself in her life, far as I know."

"That is as may be," Scott replied. "But it's now up to a judge to sort things out. Your mother is comfortable now for the night. She's got her a warm soft bed and a good supper and breakfast coming, so y'all don't need to worry about her right now. She wants you to go on home and carry on with the young'uns just as normal until you hear different. You reckon you'll be all right for a day or two on your own?"

"Yes, Sheriff," John Lee assured him.

Scott nodded. He had not expected it to be otherwise. "Miz Tucker will take you on home. You can pick up your mule at the livery. I'll give you a release."

"Will you be taking my ma into Muskogee in the morning?"

"Not 'til Monday. But you can't come along."

John Lee pondered for a second. "Can I be there when you get there?" he asked.

Scott tried not to smile. "Sure. It's a free country. But if I was you, I'd wait until your mother is arraigned. That means charged and a trial date set. A couple of days, maybe."

"I don't like to think of her being alone. She ain't never been alone, to my knowledge."

Scott finally allowed the smile to emerge. "Well, then, you don't know, son. She might enjoy it for a change."

"Can I bring her some things tonight?"

"You can come visit if you want, but my wife will provide her with everything she needs, otherwise."

Alafair watched John Lee ponder this for a moment. It was likely that whatever Hattie Tucker provided would be much nicer than anything Mrs. Day owned, Alafair thought.

"Can I see her in Muskogee?" John Lee persisted.

"Yes, you can," Scott said patiently.

"It'll be hard for me to be getting back and forth. Can't you hold her here until the trial?"

"That isn't up to me, son. We can ask the judge, but I expect not, especially on a charge of capital murder."

"What is capital murder?"

Scott shot Alafair a chagrined look. "Serious murder," he said. "Planned and thought of beforehand."

Alafair, who had stood silent through this exchange, jumped in hurriedly. "Scott, if it's all right with them, the Day kids can come home and eat with us tonight, then Shaw can bring John Lee back here for a visit with his ma and I can take the kids home." Her gaze switched to John Lee. "Or, you all can stay the night with us, if you don't mind pallets."

"Thank you, Miz Tucker. It's up to Naomi if we should take supper with you, though I think she'll be grateful. As for spending the night, I think the kids might feel better at home in their own beds. We won't be afraid."

Nothing to be afraid of, now, Alafair thought. "I'll ask Naomi, then," she said. John Lee and Naomi were just kids, but after what they had been through, Alafair was very careful of their feelings.

"You go on along, then," Scott ordered. "I'll see you this evening. I'll tell your mother what's happening with you, so don't worry about her."

⸺⸺⸺

John Lee and Alafair didn't speak to one another as they left the livery stable, or as they climbed up into the buggy after hitching John Lee's mule behind. She picked up the reins and they rode out of town together in silence. They had turned south onto the road that led to their farms before John Lee finally had something to say.

"How's Phoebe, Miz Tucker?" he asked.

Alafair smiled without looking at him. "She's fine. She's at home. She's put out with you for turning yourself in."

"Well, I had to do that," he said, matter-of-factly. "You see that, don't you?"

"Yes, I see it," Alafair admitted.

"Don't look like it was necessary," John Lee commented. He looked over at Alafair. "Miz Tucker, it don't seem possible that my ma plugged my pa. She just ain't got it in her. He beat out every bit of spirit she ever had."

"Maybe she just had enough, John Lee," Alafair said gently.

He shook his head. "I don't believe it. She never once lifted her hand to defend herself, nor us, either."

"Did he abuse you kids, John Lee?" Alafair asked.

John Lee shrugged. "Not like he did her. He mostly never paid us any mind at all, just to kick us out of the way. He's whacked me some in the last couple of years, since I got old enough to bother him. Only one of us he ever seemed know was alive was Maggie Ellen, and that's because she was the only one brave enough to sass him."

"Your sister that married?"

He glanced at Alafair out of the corner of his eye. His ears reddened. "Ma tell you that? Well, she would. We don't really know where Maggie Ellen went. She run off a couple of years ago, when she was sixteen. It was cotton time. Lots of itinerant pickers around, don't you know." He blushed furiously. "I blame Daddy. She was walking out with a fine boy, Dan Lang from Dasher's machine shop, but Daddy was such a misery that he run Dan off for good. Maggie Ellen was heartbroke."

"Yes, I heard that story. I heard your dad beat him with a hoe handle."

John Lee glanced at her. "Well, then, you can see why Dan thought courting my sister wasn't such a good idea. Can't blame him. But Maggie Ellen had these big plans to marry and set up a home, and rescue the kids from Daddy. Losing Dan was a disappointment to her. She hated Daddy for it, I'm thinking. Took the first chance she had to get away for good."

"Don't worry, son," Alafair soothed. "I don't judge her at all."

Alafair heard him swallow. "Poor Maggie Ellen. I hope she's happy," he murmured. "I think about her some. I'm always thinking that I see her here and there, in town sometimes, or even across the field when the sun's going down. My aunt told me once that she heard Maggie Ellen was living with a brick-layer in Sand Springs. I was surprised she'd run off and not say anything. At least to Naomi. Her and Naomi was always close. Daddy didn't seem to notice when she ran away. Ma cried a bit. She told me a while ago that she was hoping Maggie Ellen would come home now that Daddy wasn't here to torment her."

He blinked, then looked at Alafair again, coming back into the present. "But, Miz Tucker, I still can't see how it could be Ma. When could she have done it? By the time I got back from your place, Daddy and the mule were gone. We all went about our business the rest of that evening, and I guarantee Daddy wasn't curled up next to the house having no nap, not before we all went in for the night. We all slept in the parlor by the stove that night. Nobody went out that I saw. When we got up at cockcrow, there was six inches of snow, and still snowing. Daddy must have been laying there dead for hours."

"The ground under the body was wet, according to my husband," Alafair remembered. "Harley must have lain down there some little while after it started snowing. Now here's the question, John Lee, that hasn't been answered. Where did your daddy go when he got on that mule, drunk as a skunk, on Wednesday afternoon?"

"I figured he was making a run to the still. When I went out to the barn that night I noticed that his stash was low."

Alafair's eyebrows peaked with interest. "And where is this still?"

"He moves it around to fool the sheriff. It's usually right near the creek, though. It's pretty overgrowed down there."

"Suppose we could find it later?"

"I expect. I never had no trouble finding it before. What do you think we might find, Miz Tucker? Something that could help us?"

"I don't know, son. But we can't account for the last eight or so hours of your father's life, and I'm thinking that if there's a chance of clearing your mother, and you, too, by the way, we'd better figure out what happened from the time you noticed him gone 'til the time your sister found him dead."

They fell silent again, pondering the possibilities. Alafair clucked to the horse to hurry her up, excited about having a new tack to pursue.

Chapter Eleven

Naomi thought long and hard when Alafair invited her and her charges to take supper with them, but finally acquiesced. Not that she didn't feel herself perfectly capable of handling the task, but she knew that the family would doubtlessly eat better at the Tuckers'.

Shaw didn't bat an eye when Alafair showed up with seven extra mouths to feed. Martha, efficient as always, had already begun firing up the stove before Alafair had unloaded all the kids and gotten them inside. Mary and Alice jumped into the fray and helped part strange children from their winter wear. Alafair was pleased to see the ever-charming Gee Dub try to engage Naomi in the bantering excuse for conversation used by fifteen-year-old boys with thirteen-year-old girls. Naomi's response was desultory at best, but such a thing had never been known to deter Gee Dub. Ruth did her gentle best to help her brother entertain the shy guests, showing them the upright piano in the corner and how to pick out some simple tunes. Blanche and Sophronia flitted around like excited birds, sharing dolls and toys, beside themselves with the new playmate potential.

"Where's Phoebe?" Alafair asked Shaw.

"Charlie and her are milking tonight," Shaw told her. "They'll be in directly. Now, you want to tell me what's going on, here?"

She drew him into the relative privacy of their bedroom and explained the situation to him as quickly as she could.

"I'm glad it wasn't him," Shaw confessed, "but the boy's still got a pretty rough row to hoe, sounds to me."

"He does, and he's proud and slow to take help. So is Naomi. But I'm hoping we can be there if they need us."

"I'll offer to take him back into town this evening," Shaw assured her, "see if I can get him to tell me if he's made any plans yet, tell him we'll do what we can to help."

Shaw's concern for the boy touched Alafair, and affection for him welled up in her. "I imagine he hasn't had time to think of much, yet, since this has all come as such a surprise," she said. "Maybe if he'll talk to you on the trip to town it will get him to thinking. Now I've got to take our kids aside somehow and caution them before somebody asks John Lee why he isn't in jail."

"I already warned them not to ask questions when I saw you coming," Shaw told her.

"That showed some foresight on your part, Shaw Tucker," Alafair teased.

"I have been known to practice foresight in my time," he replied.

As Shaw and Alafair stepped back into the parlor, Charlie and Phoebe were just coming in from the back porch, after pouring their new milk through cheesecloth to strain it into the big milk can. When Phoebe caught sight of John Lee, Alafair thought the girl might swoon. The look that passed between them was so fraught with emotion that Shaw tugged Alafair back into the bedroom.

"What is this?" he asked.

"Why, Shaw, you are showing rare insight today. I told you that Phoebe and John Lee are sweet on one another."

"So I now see," he blustered, half amused and half alarmed. "I did not realize how sweet." He shot the young couple an appraising glance from the door. They were both involved with children and ignoring one another desperately. "Well, I don't know about this," he pronounced. "The boy has a shadow on him. Besides, she's just seventeen."

"I'll point out to you that I was seventeen and you nineteen, when we fell for one another, same as those two yonder."

Shaw looked startled. "I didn't feel as young as they look," he observed wistfully, then firmed. "Still, times are different, Alafair. Besides, I don't really know this boy. And you'll remember, that isn't the best family, what with the pa a drunken, bootlegging wife-beater and the ma a murderer."

Alafair put her hand on Shaw's arm to calm him. "He's a real nice boy," she said. "I've talked to him, and I think Phoebe could do a lot worse. You spend some time with him and you'll see."

"He couldn't possibly marry anybody while this mess is going on, and he ain't got a nickel, nor is he like to. Taxes will take that farm as sure as I'm standing here, and they'll end up with their kin. That's not for Phoebe."

"Now, now, I don't expect he'd ask her to marry until he thought he could support her well. But I'll tell you, I wouldn't be surprised if he pulls it off in a few years, because he reminds me of you."

Shaw looked over at her. "Me?" he managed.

"Well, he's not as happy and light-hearted as you were, but I don't expect his life has been as easy. But he's a thoughtful boy, honorable, and strives to do well. Best of all, he's very tender to Phoebe, and protects her as best he can. I remember all those things about you being dear to me, and if they're dear to Phoebe, I'm not surprised."

Shaw had been studying John Lee critically while Alafair was talking, and now he looked back down at her. "How do you know all this about the boy?"

Alafair hesitated before answering. "I spoke to him at length as we drove home from town. He was respectful and straightforward, and looked me in the eye. He has fine eyes, Shaw."

Two spots of color rose on Shaw's already ruddy cheeks. "Well, I'll reserve judgment until I've seen for myself," he said, as sternly as he could manage. "But I'm not happy that it's gone this far without that youngster declaring his intentions to me."

"I don't reckon they know themselves how far it's gone. These things sneak up on you, sometimes."

"Who'd have thought it would be Phoebe?" he asked with wonder. "Martha and Mary are grown women already and don't seem to be in any haste."

"Martha and Mary are formidable and proud, and it will take formidable men to woo them. Martha has already spurned a suitor and Mary just laughs that big old laugh of hers when a boy comes around. Alice is so pretty and gay that she'll have her pick. But Phoebe is like a little violet, all shy and hidden, to whom sweet things just come."

"Only a knight of old will be wooing Alice, or somebody else with a suit of armor on him," Shaw joked. But though he was laughing, a sadness had settled in his eyes. The little girls weren't little any more.

Alafair squeezed his arm, full of pity for him. Men never saw these things coming, and were liable to be blindsided. "I'd best be getting supper on the table now," she said, and thus Shaw and Alafair departed into their own realms.

❧❧❧

Martha had the stove properly banked and she and Mary were hauling down plates when Alafair came into the kitchen. Alafair dropped her apron over her head and tied the strings behind her back.

"What's it to be, Ma?" Mary asked her.

"I doubt if those kids eat very good, so let's do it up," Alafair said. "Got no time to kill a hen, so let's fry up some ham with gravy. Mary, I see you've already peeled some potatoes and chopped onions. Are you thinking of home fries? That's good, then. Martha, warm up all the leftovers from dinner, and make two or three pans of cornbread. Remember, there's seven extra of us tonight. I'll open some more jars from the pantry."

Sophronia and Frances Day came skidding into the kitchen, and Sophronia grabbed her mother's skirt. "Mama, can you get me and Frances a glass of milk?"

"Are your arms broke?" Alafair asked, while hauling out her frying pans.

"No, ma'am," Sophronia assured her.

"Well, then, you gals can go out on the back porch your-selves and draw off some milk in a couple of big pitchers for the table. Mary, get these girls some pitchers. Draw some but-termilk, too."

"I don't like buttermilk," Frances informed her, as she and Sophronia skipped off toward Mary.

"It'll make your hair curly," Alafair said.

"I only made two apple pies, Ma. Shall I make a cobbler, or another pie?" Mary wondered.

Alafair pondered, then shook her head. "I'm near to out of canned fruit. I suppose we could whip up a couple of molasses pies. Alice is good at molasses pies. Where is Alice?"

"In the parlor torturing Phoebe, Ma," Martha informed her cheerfully.

Alafair sniffed and headed toward the pantry. "Put out a jug of karo syrup and one of sorghum. Some may prefer to doctor their cornbread." She swerved enough to stick her head into the parlor. "Phoebe and Alice, we need you in here." She looked down at Naomi, who was sitting in an armchair with a toddler in her lap, and hesitated.

"I'm sorry about your mama, honey. This is a lot of respon-sibility to put on your young shoulders."

Naomi blinked at her. "It's all right," she said at length. "I'm used to it."

"I heard that you and your sister were close. I wish Maggie Ellen was still here to help you. You must miss her."

"Yes, ma'am," she acknowledged. "But she ain't. Maggie Ellen told me that if she ever did get away, she'd come back and take the rest of us off with her. Never did, though."

"Well, maybe now you can find her."

Naomi shrugged. "I don't reckon she'll come back. I won't come back, when I get me a place of my own." She stood up. "I can help you with supper, Miz Tucker," she said.

"You're the guest, Naomi," Alafair told her. "You take your ease. When we come over to your house, you can wait on us."

Naomi's mouth quirked slightly in an expression of irony, since the likelihood of the Tuckers coming to dinner at her house was nil, then sat back down.

"Shaw," Alafair continued, "we'll be needing some boards and sawhorses to extend the table, and something to sit on."

Shaw was half out the door before she finished speaking. "Boys, come on," he called. "You Day boys, too. I'm not so delicate a host as Miz Tucker."

All the males tumbled out into the cold except for toddling, thumb-sucking Alfred Day and three-year-old Otis Day, and all the females were pressed into mess service except Naomi, Ruth and Blanche, whom Alafair set to keeping Alfred and Otis out from underfoot.

After supper, Alafair made use of all the extra hands to help with the cleanup and the evening chores, while Shaw went with John Lee into town to visit Mrs. Day in jail. Alafair packed a basket of comforts for them to take to Mrs. Day, though she was certain that Scott's wife, Hattie, had already done the same. Alafair thought that the woman could use all the comfort she could get.

Alafair expected that Naomi would go into town with her brother, but when the time came, the girl demurred and set about scraping leftovers into the slop bucket. Alafair sat in a chair near the parlor door, as she usually did, and supervised the cleanup. She was interested to observe Naomi discreetly wrapping scraps of food in a napkin and slipping it into the pockets of her voluminous skirt. She quietly took Martha aside and had her pack up all the uneaten food for the Days to take home with them.

⌒⌒⌒

When the two men returned two hours later, Shaw drew Alafair out onto the porch. They sat down together on the porch swing while John Lee and Naomi roused their dozing siblings for the short trip home.

"You were sure right about the boy, Alafair," Shaw said to her. "He seems like a good upright young fellow to me, though knowing his situation, I can't see how that can be. Of course, you know as well as I that some people are ruined by trouble and others made strong and good by the same troubles."

"I'm glad you think so," Alafair told him. "When it looked like he killed his own daddy, I thought he was either the unluckiest good boy or the most cold-blooded bad boy I had ever met, and either way, I rued the day that Phoebe got mixed up with him."

"Speaking of which," Shaw said, "I'm still not thrilled with that situation. He's got character, all right, and spine, but I'd be happier if he had a pot to pee in. And not so many responsibilities."

Alafair shrugged. "You said you'd not let them marry right away. Now we'll see how they endure and if they can plan for the future. Did you ask him about his intentions toward her?"

"I did, and I let him know I wasn't happy with their sneaking around behind my back."

"What did he say to that?"

"Like you thought. He said the situation was such that he couldn't come calling plain, so it was snatch a moment as they could, or not see one another. I told him that if he regarded her he should have just not seen her rather than put her in peril. He said he knew it was wrong, but might as well say not to breathe, for he loves her."

"Oh, Shaw!"

Shaw looked at her askance. "Oh, Shaw?" he repeated. "Why do you sound surprised? You're the one told me, after all."

She had surprised herself with her exclamation. "I don't know," she admitted. "It just shocked me to hear that he said it straight out like that. I was hoping that the kids didn't know so plainly that they love one another, I guess."

"Well, I think you'd better have a talk with Phoebe. We both know that if the fire is on them that there isn't much we can do but ride herd on them as best we can. If he really loves her, he won't do anything to dishonor her."

Alafair nodded. "That sounds like the wise course to me. If we treat them like a proper betrothed couple, then they'll be less inclined to do anything rash. I can't see how he could be able to marry for years, and they may cool off by themselves if we don't pressure them."

"And if they don't?"

"Then they'll marry when they're ready. They may never be rich, but I think he'll work hard. She could do worse."

Shaw puffed out a laugh that hung for a fraction of a second like a white cloud in the frigid air. "You suppose our folks felt like this when we fell in love?"

"Surely. And I think John Lee and Phoebe will, too, in their turn. In fact, your ma will probably cackle when she hears about this, the evil old thing."

Shaw laughed, unoffended. He knew that Alafair loved his feisty mother.

"So you told the boy he could call on Phoebe?" Alafair asked.

"I told him I'd think about it. I expect I'll give him permission after you've spoken to Phoebe, and I think he's sweated enough."

They were chuckling together when John Lee came out on the porch and approached them diffidently.

"What is it, son?" Shaw asked.

"It's pretty late, nearly eight o'clock. I reckon we'll be going home now, Mr. Tucker, Miz Tucker."

"You're sure you don't want to spend the night, now?" Alafair wondered.

"Thank you, ma'am, but no. You all have been most kind. And we're indebted. But we'll be all right now."

Shaw casually lay his arm across Alafair's shoulder as he studied John Lee. "You know we'll be right here for you all the way through your trouble, John Lee," he said.

John Lee colored. "Yes, sir, I know it. And I want you to know that I won't speak no more on that other matter we discussed until this whole affair is honorably settled."

Only Alafair would have noticed the twitch that disturbed the corner of Shaw's mobile mouth. "I appreciate that," he said to John Lee.

John Lee drew himself up. "But then I'll be approaching you. I do promise it."

Alafair's eyebrows shot up at this boldness and she glanced sidelong at Shaw. His face had become the picture of inscrutability. "I expect," he replied coolly.

Naomi came out onto the porch, shepherding the younger children before her. They all spilled down the porch steps toward the buckboard, followed by a pack of Tucker children, closely followed by John Lee, Alafair and Shaw. As older people lifted younger people into the wagon, Alafair managed to maneuver herself through the throng to stand next to John Lee. She leaned in to murmur into his ear.

"Tomorrow is the weekend, and everybody will be home. But when you come back from visiting your ma on Monday, come on over here late in the morning while everyone's at their tasks and let's see if we can find your daddy's still."

John Lee skewed a sharp look at her, then nodded once before he climbed up into the driver's seat and unwound the reins from the brake. Alafair picked up Alfred and handed him to Naomi, who settled him on her lap. "You all have been right kind," Naomi acknowledged.

"Call on us if you need anything," Alafair told her.

"Yes, ma'am," the girl stated in a tone of voice that was not particularly enthusiastic.

Shaw and Alafair, Martha and Mary, Phoebe and Alice and Gee Dub shooed little hands and feet away from wagon wheel and mule hooves as John Lee released the brake and clucked at the mule, and they moved slowly off into the darkness. Most of the Tucker family headed back up the porch steps toward the warmth and their beds, but two or three little ones escaped into the yard, skipping and shrieking.

"You kids get inside before you freeze," Alafair called.

"Mama, Charlie tied a knot in my hair," Sophronia's voice yelped out of the darkness.

"You children get yourselves inside," Shaw interjected, "before the panthers get you. It's a cold night and the panthers need to eat little children to keep warm."

The quality of the shrieking changed as Charlie, Blanche and Sophronia charged around the corner of the house and up the steps in a rush to elude the panthers.

~~~~

Alafair dreamed that night. "Bobby!" she screamed, and the baby gasped and dropped the glass jar he had just drunk from. She scooped up the little boy in her arms. The parlor floor was covered with coal oil and glass shards and her bare feet were cut and bleeding. The baby was choking and turning blue. She crashed out the front door, leaving a trail of bloody footprints down the porch steps and across the yard. She started awake, and got up to check on her sleeping children.

~~~~

Alafair was too busy on Sunday morning to worry much about her upcoming foray into the woods with John Lee to find Harley's still. Shaw and Alafair rousted everyone out of bed long before dawn, so that cows could be milked and all the animals fed before breakfast, and Alafair and the older girls could prepare the dishes they would take to Grandma's house for Sunday dinner. Before eight a.m., everyone was fed and washed and dressed, and packed into the wagon for the trip to town. They stopped by Shaw's parents' house on the outskirts of Boynton to drop off the food, then proceeded to the Masonic Hall, where the First Christian Church met.

After the service, Alafair lagged behind in the cloakroom with the younger children, so that she could supervise and assist as they put on their coats and hats.

"Fronie has a loose tooth, Mama," Blanche informed Alafair.

"Is that so?" Alafair asked as she wrapped Blanche's scarf around her neck.

Sophronia gaped wide and wiggled a front tooth for her mother's inspection. Charlie, who was sitting on the floor adjusting his boots, looked up, intrigued. "I think she should show it to Grandma," he said.

Alafair shot Charlie a stern look. Grandma was notorious for asking permission to inspect a loose tooth, then jerking it out of the unsuspecting child's mouth amid howls of outrage from the victim and laughter from the siblings. Unabashed, Charlie returned an impish grin.

"Oh, I will!" Sophronia exclaimed, while skipping about and manipulating the tooth with her index finger. In spite of feeling guilty, Alafair smiled and kept quiet. Sophronia would undergo her rite of passage and join the sorority of the untoothed.

Alafair inspected buttons and knots, and dismissed the children one at a time. Blanche was suffering from a bunched-up sock, so Alafair knelt down to make the necessary adjustments, drawing off Blanche's shoe and straightening out the stocking.

"Hurry, Mama," Blanche urged, as her siblings disappeared out the door.

Alafair glanced up, but before she could say anything to Blanche, her attention was captured by a group of women standing in the foyer, visiting. She paused, and Blanche, whose foot was in Alafair's hand, grasped her mother's shoulder to steady herself.

Alafair recognized the plump woman standing nearest the door. It was Mrs. Lang, Russell's wife and Dan's mother. She released Blanche's foot and stood up with the shoe still in her hand, and took a few steps toward the women. Blanche hopped after her. "Ma!" she exclaimed, affronted.

Alafair handed the girl her shoe. "Here," she said, distracted. "Sit here and put your shoe on. I'll be right back."

Blanche obeyed, grumbling. Alafair insinuated herself into the group of women and sidled up to Mrs. Lang. For a few seconds, she stood silently at the woman's elbow, pretending to listen to the conversation, but as soon as a lull arose, Alafair touched Mrs. Lang's arm to gain her attention.

Mrs. Lang looked at Alafair blankly, then her eyes widened with alarm when recognition dawned. She mastered her expression quickly, and stepped back from the group, drawing Alafair with her.

"Hello, Miz Tucker," she said. "What can I do for you?"

"I was just wondering," she began gingerly, "if you had heard that Harley Day's wife confessed to the murder of her husband?"

"Yes, I heard," Mrs. Lang said. "I'm sorry for Miz Day, but I'm glad the killer is caught. I didn't like all the suspicions between folks."

Alafair felt her cheeks grow warm. Obviously, Mrs. Lang had been apprised of Alafair's interactions with Russell and Dan. By this time, it was likely that everyone in town knew. Did Mrs. Lang think that Alafair suspected her menfolk of murder? Did she bear Alafair ill will for casting aspersions on her loved ones? Alafair would, if the situation was reversed. Nevertheless, she forged ahead. "John Lee thinks his mother confessed to pro-tect…someone. He's thinking the killer is still out there, and I'm wondering if he's right." Was that statement innocuous enough? Maybe not, since Mrs. Lang's face reddened.

"I mean," she added hurriedly, "I know your son cared about Maggie Ellen Day and her family, at one time. I was thinking that he might be keeping his ear to the ground."

Mrs. Lang thawed a bit, and nodded. "Well, it's true that Dan liked that Day girl for a while, but that situation was just too big a mess to turn out well. Mr. Day gave Dan a hard time from the minute he got involved with his daughter. Russell and me tried to warn him, but you know how young folks are. I don't know what it was that made Dan and Mr. Day get into such a nasty fight in the end, but after that happened, Dan never went out to that place any more. Russell wanted to bring charges against Day after the scrap, but Dan wouldn't hear of it. Said he could take care of himself. He don't want to be treated like a child, I reckon."

"Did Dan and Maggie Ellen ever see each other again?" Ala-fair asked. Dan had told her that they did, but she wondered if his mother knew about it.

"I think they did, now and then, though Dan never discussed it with me. I'm just his ma, after all. I was surprised as all get-out when I heard she married somebody else all of a sudden. I liked that girl, too, until she up and broke Dan's heart. Dan blamed her father for the whole business, though. He still won't hear a word against her."

"Your husband told me that he was on his way out to see John Lee the night Harley got killed. Did he see anything suspicious?"

"Well, he said there wasn't hardly anybody on the road. Just one of those Leonard boys is all he could call to mind. Russell never got to Day's place, you know. His buggy slid off the road. It was a miserable night. He told me he'd just be gone a couple of hours, but after it got close to nine o'clock, I sent Dan out to look for him."

Surprised, Alafair opened her mouth to speak, but Mrs. Lang went on. "Russell had already got his buggy out of the ditch, though, and finally came back home not long after. Dan just missed him. Said he spent a cold and miserable hour searching, before Mr. Ross out there by the crossroads told him he had seen Russell riding back toward town a few minutes earlier."

"Dan went out to look for his dad? Did he tell that to the sheriff?"

Mrs. Lang bristled, and Alafair wanted to bite her tongue. "I didn't mean…" she attempted, but Mrs. Lang interrupted her.

"Isn't the sheriff your husband's cousin?"

"You must think me uncommon nosy, Miz Lang, but I'm concerned about my girl. I imagine you know she and John Lee Day like one another. Your son got mixed up with that family and got hurt. I'd not like to see that happen to Phoebe."

Mrs. Lang took her explanation as an apology, and nodded, though her manner had cooled. "If Miz Day says she done it, that's good enough for me. She had cause. I don't know what else I can tell you that you don't already know, Miz Tucker. Seems you already run Dan through the mill, and Russell, too. Yes, the sheriff talked to both of them, and I'll say to you what they said to him. Neither of them know a thing about that murder. In fact, Dan told the sheriff he ought to look to J.D. Millar for some answers."

Alafair blinked at her. "You mean Mr. Day's brother-in-law?"

"That's the one. Him and Mr. Day had quite a feud going. Maggie Ellen told Dan that her daddy and her uncle hated one another like poison, and that J.D. threatened to shoot Day more than once. Ask the sheriff about that, while you're asking."

Alafair put her hand to her forehead. "Hating Harley Day seems to be a popular way to pass the time."

"And keep this in mind, too, Miz Tucker," Mrs Lang added, "John Lee must have seen how his father came between his sister and my Dan. I'm sure he didn't want the same thing to happen to him and Phoebe. His mother confessed, and I'm sure she did it, but nobody had more reason to get rid of Harley than John Lee himself."

Alafair didn't respond, but she suddenly felt a little nauseated. Mrs. Lang had voiced a thought that she had no wish to ponder.

"Mama," Blanche called from her seat on the aisle, "help me tie my shoe. I can't get it right."

"Just a minute, punkin. Thank you for talking to me, Miz Lang. I will ask Sheriff Tucker what he found out about the bad blood between J.D. Millar and Harley Day. If I find out anything that might interest you, I'll let you know."

"I'd appreciate that."

"Mama," Blanche wailed, and Alafair reluctantly returned to her duties.

⌒⌒⌒

As Shaw pulled the wagon around the side of the Masonic Hall and out into the road, Alafair caught sight of the Langs, father and son, standing in the yard, engaged in intense conversation. Mrs. Lang was walking away from them, back toward the building. As the wagon passed, both the men turned and looked at her sitting next to Shaw on the bench. She was struck again by their resemblance to one another, even in the way they both stood, ramrod straight, in their matching black suits with tan vests, black boots and Stetsons. Dan's hand came up to finger the scar on his cheek, and Alafair's heart thudded. The three people eyed each other as the wagon moved away. Russell Lang gave her an ironic smile and tipped his hat.

Alafair looked away quickly, just in time to see J.D. and Zorah Millar's buggy coming down the road toward them from the Methodist church on the hill. Zorah Millar's piercing blue-green gaze followed her until they were out of sight. Alafair felt a thrill of fear in her stomach, and she swallowed. Lord help me, I'm seeing murderers everywhere, she thought.

"Is Scott going to be at your ma's for dinner?" she asked Shaw.

"I think his folks are going to Ma's house, so I expect Scott will be there with Hattie and the boys. Why? Are you expecting to pick his brain again?"

"I'm planning to try," she confessed.

Chapter Twelve

By late Monday morning, Shaw was long gone from the house, out in the fields with the livestock, hauling feed to them, making sure their ponds and water tanks weren't frozen over, checking the herds for signs of illness, injury or stress. Alafair and her helper Georgie had left the wash flapping on the line, and Alafair was on her own until dinnertime. She took an empty flour sack and a scoop to the root cellar and scooped a couple of cups of pecans from the big bag in the corner next to the bottom of the steps. The nuts had been curing in the cellar at the side of the house since the family had gathered them from the ground under the trees in Shaw's mother's pecan grove the previous November. She took the nuts back into the house and sat by the window in her rocking chair. She sat rocking nervously, stopping occasionally to chafe her hands, as she stared down the drive toward the gate and cracked and picked out pecans into a bowl in her lap, while her mind was otherwise engaged.

While she was at her mother-in-law's for Sunday dinner, she had tried to talk to Scott about her conversation with Mrs. Lang, but she had been unable to make any headway with him. She was never sure if he was taking her seriously or simply humoring her when she told him of her suspicions. He did tell her that he had investigated both the Langs and the Millars, but he didn't tell her what he had found out. She had expected him to tell her to mind her own business, but he had seemed more amused at her questions than annoyed.

In spite of a banked fire burning in the kitchen stove, and a good coal fire going in the pot belly stove in the parlor, the house was chilly. It was February, now, and spring couldn't come fast enough for Alafair. Winters in Oklahoma weren't as relentless as the winters she had experienced growing up in the Arkansas mountains, but even so, the weather alternated almost day to day from false spring to arctic blast, and a body never had time to get used to one or the other. It was a wonder, she thought, that they all hadn't died of pneumonia long ago.

She was worried that if John Lee showed up too late, they wouldn't have time to search the creek bank for Harley's still, and still get back home in time for her to fix dinner without alerting Shaw that she had been out. Therefore, she was most relieved to see John Lee trudging up the drive toward the house just before eleven o'clock. She carried the bowl of cracked pecans back into the kitchen and pulled on her winter wear in time to meet him by the front gate.

"Good morning, son," she greeted. "You made it in good time. Have you already managed to get into town to see your mother?"

John Lee snatched the stocking cap off of his head before he spoke to her. "Good morning, Miz Tucker. Yes, ma'am, I've been and gone already. Her and the sheriff's deputy are on their way to Muskogee right now. Ma is in fairly good spirits. As long as she thinks we're all going to be taken care of, she don't seem very concerned with what happens to her." They began to walk around the house and into the woods at the back of the yard, toward Phoebe's secret access to the Day property. "I have a pretty good idea where Daddy was set up before he died," John Lee interjected. "It shouldn't take us more than fifteen, twenty minutes to get there. Anyway," he continued, "I told Mama that I didn't think she really did the deed, and that she was just helping the real culprit get away. She told me that she did do it, too, and besides she'd just as soon that this all be over and us kids can start our new lives."

"But you still think it wasn't her," Alafair said.

He shook his head. "No, I don't think it was. I think she just saw the opportunity to confess and make this all be over with, and she done it. I'll tell you, ma'am, I think she's got it in her head that this way she can make up for not standing up to him all these years and putting us kids through it."

"Well, that's just crazy," Alafair opined.

John Lee shrugged. "That ain't all, I'm thinkin'. I expect she really believes that I did it, and she thinks she's protecting me, and making it up to me, as well." He looked over at Alafair, his black eyes hard with determination. "That's why we've got to find out who really done it, and quick, because I don't want my own mother thinking I'm a killer, even if it's of such a low critter as my father."

Alafair stared at him, taken aback. John Lee moved ahead of her to lead her through the trees as they neared the creek bank. The crunch of their feet on the carpet of brittle leaves was magnified by the papery rustle of the wind through the pin oak leaves that still hung on the trees. "Do you have some notion of who the culprit is, John Lee?" she asked his back, at length.

"I have two or three notions, Miz Tucker," he said, as he held a blackjack branch aside for her, "though they're just guesses. Pa was such a nasty piece of work that I'm sure there are a dozen folks who would welcome the opportunity to do him in. When we got to talking about the still, it reminded me that Daddy had got in some kind of a scrape with Jim Leonard over the last batch of 'shine he sold him. Seems Mr. Leonard didn't think highly of the quality of the batch and didn't want to pay. I heard them going at it down here a couple of weeks ago, while I was at the pond, them a'yelling and all. They took a couple of swings at one another. Daddy had a scrape on his cheek that evening, anyway. Daddy always met his customers down here on the creek, at the place where that willow hangs over the water and the bank is undercut. Lots of roots there for stashing quart jars."

"You said you thought your daddy was headed for the still on that last night you saw him alive," Alafair remembered.

"Yes, ma'am, the still or the willow root stash, though I don't know it for sure. It's just that his stash in the barn was low, and that's his usual way of doing things."

They were walking along the creek bank, now, their feet squishing and sliding along the wet, half-decomposed brown leaves that lay thick next to the water. A coating of very black mud was clinging to the bottoms of Alafair's shoes, which didn't help her footing any. The creek was running, but a thin skin of ice had formed up next to the bank. Alafair reached out and grabbed the back of John Lee's coat in her fist to steady herself as they picked their way along.

"So you're considering old Jim Leonard," Alafair observed. "Take a look at how black this mud is. You father's body was covered in black mud just like this. Maybe him and Leonard met that night and got into it again, and maybe old Jim followed him back to the house, all stealthy, and saw him lay down drunk beside the house."

"Then finished him where he lay with the gun he ran across in the woods. Yes, ma'am. It's worth finding out."

Alafair cocked her head as she thought about it. Stranger things had happened. Jim Leonard was a nondescript enough person when he was sober, but he was a pretty unpleasant drunk. "You said you had two or three prospects," Alafair reminded John Lee.

She saw his head nod. "Yes, ma'am. I was also thinking about Mr. Lang, the grain merchant. He was supposed to come out to the farm Wednesday afternoon and give Daddy what for, but he never made it. I expect he got busy that day. It was a real sloppy, dreary day, I remember. Daddy didn't have no love for Mr. Lang, I'll tell you. He sort of had it in for anybody with money, anybody respectable, don't you know. He always went out of his way to provoke Mr. Lang, and as nice as Mr. Lang has always been to me, I think he has something of a temper. Once or twice I thought he'd have a hissy fit while trying to deal with Daddy. There was that business with Dan, too. Mr. Lang was mighty put out with Daddy for the way he treated Dan."

"You know, I considered Mr. Lang myself," Alafair admitted. "Your mama mentioned that he was supposed to come by and never made it. I even went by the office and spoke to him. He says he started out to see you, but his buggy skidded into a ditch at the crossroads."

"Really?" John Lee exclaimed, interested. "It could be he went ahead and walked on out here, since he was nearer here than to town. It would be right on his way to cut across the back there where I dropped that gun. He'd have been a lot later than he expected to be, and probably in a pretty bad mood. And then after all that to find the no-good crook passed out all stinking drunk and revolting...."

"That's the story I concocted, more or less," Alafair told him. "And it's one story would be easy enough to check, when he left town to come out here on Wednesday, whether he came back late and disheveled. Somebody would have seen."

"Mr. Turner would know the when and wherefores of the horse and buggy," John Lee noted.

"I'll ask him when next I have the chance."

John Lee turned and took Alafair's mittened hand in his own in order to help her over a slim fallen tree. "I'll be in town this evening," he said. "I'll ask him."

Alafair gathered her skirt in her free hand to keep it from snagging on stray branches and stepped over the log. "Perhaps that's best," she acknowledged. "I'd just as soon my husband didn't know how deep I am involved in this."

"Not to mention Phoebe," John Lee agreed.

"Not to mention."

John Lee turned to take the lead down the path, and Alafair fell into step behind him. "You know," she said to his back, "speaking of Dan Lang, did you ever wonder whether Dan might have done Harley in?"

John Lee kept walking, but Alafair saw his spine stiffen before he answered. "No, I can't imagine that he'd have shot Daddy. He'd never done anything to cause Maggie Ellen to think less of him."

"Maybe he thought just the opposite," she speculated, "that she'd get wind of what happened and admire him for it."

John Lee shook his head. "No. I'd hate to think Dan was a killer."

"Do you know where Dan was that night?" she persisted. She was going to tell him that Dan had been riding around in the dark, ostensibly looking for his father, but John Lee responded before she got the chance.

"Not anywhere around here," he said, firmly dismissing this line of thinking.

They had reached the old willow, hanging precariously over the creek. The bank had been undercut by the current, washing the soil away from the tree's roots, which dangled in the water. Some day in the not too distant future, the creek would completely undermine the willow, and it would fall. But until that day, the bare, washed-out roots created a perfect little complex of hidden storage compartments, practically invisible to the casual passerby. John Lee squatted down and ran his hand under the overhung bank. After a couple of minutes of feeling around, he sat back on his heels and stared thoughtfully across the water.

"Empty," he pronounced. "Last time I was down here, just a day or two before he died, there was a couple of gallon jugs and maybe a dozen quart jars."

"You think somebody cleaned him out?"

John Lee looked up at her. "I reckon. I've got Jim Leonard on my mind, but Daddy did business with several of the less respectable types around here, and I imagine there's any number of folks would have thought of his cache when they heard that he was dead."

"So where is this still?" Alafair wondered.

John Lee stood and brushed himself off absently. "He moved it around, like I said. But he usually used one of about three or four places here on the property that was suitable. I kind of liked to know where it was, so I'd come down here once a week or so to see if I could spot it. He was a pretty good hider, and you could practically trip over it when he had it hid. He'd cover it up with brush and such when he wasn't cooking with it."

Alafair grunted appreciatively. A good working still was a fair sized operation, and had to be run at night, if you didn't want to be betrayed by the steam. Hiding one was not the easiest proposition.

John Lee pointed through the brush. "Last I saw the thing, it was over this way." He started walking east along the bank with Alafair right behind him. He left the path that had been beaten down by many feet following along the creek, and ducked into the tangle of dormant limbs. Once again, Alafair had to grab the back of his coat, this time to keep from getting lost in the dense undergrowth. Alafair lost her sense of direction in about ten seconds flat, but John Lee seemed to know where he was going. He crashed through the woods purposefully while Alafair covered her face with her arm to protect her eyes from slashing branches and hung on for dear life. In less than five minutes they broke through into a small overhung clearing, where John Lee stopped abruptly and Alafair crashed into his back. He looked back at her over his shoulder. "This here is the place, Miz Tucker," he told her.

Alafair blinked and looked around. She saw a small, room-like clearing that had been created when a large pin oak had fallen. Dead branches and leaf litter were at least ankle deep, and the surrounding trees had filled in with their limbs overhead, effectively creating a leafy roof ten feet up. It was a neat little hidey-hole. But there was no still to be seen.

Before she could question him, John Lee had begun tossing aside man-sized dead limbs from one end of the clearing, exposing bricks, a cauldron, copper tubing....

"Well, I'll be!" Alafair exclaimed. "I could have stood right on it and not found it! I can't even figure out how you found it again yourself."

John Lee, who was studying the still with his hands on his hips and his feet planted apart, shrugged. "Like I said, Daddy tended to use the same two or three spots. I've been here plenty of times." He squatted down, eyed the apparatus for a minute, then dug his hand into the ash pile under the makeshift brick fireplace. "These ashes are warm," he said.

Alafair thought about this briefly. "You mean somebody's made a fire within the last few hours," she observed.

He looked up at her. "Had to have. Looks like somebody's got himself a still." He looked back down. "I wouldn't care if one of Daddy's ne'er-do-well friends dismantled this thing and hauled it off, but I don't like the idea of somebody doing this on our property."

"If I was a thief and a bootlegger," Alafair told him, "I might think there was advantages to doing my business where somebody else besides me could get blamed if it was found out."

John Lee made a "humph" sound, then fell silent for a time, pondering the implications of this discovery.

"What do you think?" Alafair asked him, at length.

"I think I'd better come out here a few nights with the shotgun and catch this fellow," John Lee stated.

Alafair put her hand on his shoulder. "John Lee, don't you think you'd do better to turn this information over to the sheriff and let him pursue it?"

John Lee stood up. "No, ma'am, with all due respect, I don't. The sheriff has got his killer, or so he thinks. If I don't present him with the answer writ in stone, I don't see why he'd think it worth his time to mess with it."

Alafair glanced up at the light spot in the clouds that indicated the position of the sun. "I've got to get home and start dinner for Shaw," she said nervously, "but I really want to talk about this some more before you do something rash. What if this person is the killer? What does he have to lose by shooting you? Or maybe worse, what if you end up having to shoot him and then end up being the killer you're trying to prove you're not? Please don't do anything until we can get together again and plan this out. Maybe tomorrow...."

"Miz Tucker," John Lee interrupted. "I've got to move fast. The sheriff is taking my ma into Muskogee today to charge her with murder."

"Please, son," she pleaded. "We'll get it figured out. Please promise me you won't try to take this all on yourself."

John Lee eyed her doubtfully. "I'll think on it, Miz Tucker," he finally said. "Now let me take you out of here and get you headed for home."

Alafair opened her mouth to argue with him, but suddenly realized that this was the best she was going to get. She nodded, and followed him as he led her back through the brush to the path by the creek, all the while anxiously wondering what she was going to do next.

⌐⌐⌐

Alafair had set a stew on slow heat early that morning, and it had cooked to soupy perfection by the time Shaw got back to the house at about 12:30. Alafair baked a short batch of biscuits and fried a few slabs of bacon, creamed a quart of corn from her pantry, fried some potatoes in drippings with onion and a bit of her dried sage, sliced some onions into thick chunks, and poured a couple of glasses of buttermilk. They discussed the homely business of the day as they ate, sitting companionably at the table for a little longer than necessary when they finished, lingering over mugs of strong bitter coffee, a bit of warm apple cake with butter, and a slice or two of homemade cheese. It was close to two when Shaw went back to work, leaving Alafair to clear the table and store the leftovers for supper. She took her time over the dishes, staring out the window over the dish pan, pondering the mysteries she found herself involved with.

Things had become too complicated. She was desperately trying to protect her daughter from—well, from anything that might hurt her. In the process, she was afraid that she was keeping things from Shaw and Scott that perhaps she shouldn't. Alafair was beginning to fear that there was no way that she could continue to keep the law from finding out that Phoebe was involved in the events that may have led to the murder of Harley Day. That little gun. Somebody was going to find out where that little gun had come from. She really hoped that Mrs. Day or whoever had used the derringer had indeed flung it into the creek, never to be seen again, because if it were found, and Shaw saw it, he would recognize it immediately. Alafair felt some dread of what Shaw would think of her if he found out she had been keeping things from him, but that was only of peripheral importance to her compared to sparing Phoebe. Also, Alafair was not fool enough to believe beyond a shadow of a doubt that John Lee himself was not the culprit here, howsoever much she may have wished it weren't so. She had to prove to herself most of all that he was innocent, for if he was not, then Phoebe was in for a broken heart. And that prospect horrified Alafair almost as much as the idea of the girl being in trouble with the law.

———

After dinner was cleaned up and put away, Alafair took the slop buckets out to the sties next to the barn to slop the hogs. The two yearling boars were waiting for her by the troughs as she trudged across the yard lugging the heavy pails of scraps from last night's supper and today's breakfast and dinner. She made soothing noises to them, under her breath, "pigpigpig," as she tipped the buckets over the fence into the troughs, practically over the hogs' heads as they inhaled the tasty leftovers. She added a couple of buckets of Shaw's blend of corn and sorghum pig food from the barrel just inside the barn door, then went inside to feed the sow and piglets in their warm nursery sty. Two barn cats insinuated themselves around her ankles while she fed the sow. Her usual companion for this chore, Charlie-dog, was absent, having chosen to accompany his boy to school today.

Alafair was mildly surprised that Shaw wasn't in the barn, or around the nearby outbuildings, as far as she could see. His favorite riding horse, Hannah, whom he had naughtily named after his fussy sister, was not in her stall, and his saddle was gone. He had more than likely ridden out to the pasture.

She stood thoughtfully watching the sow and her eight frantic pigs feed, unable to keep her mind off the problem with Phoebe. Before she knew what was happening, she found herself walking out of the barn toward the trail behind the house, heading back to the creek, back to where John Lee had taken her that morning. She didn't have a plan. She didn't know why she was going, even. She wasn't at all sure she could find the still again. In fact, she was fairly certain that she couldn't. And yet, for some reason, she had to try. She had to stand there again and see if she could garner even the merest clue to this mystery.

She was able to follow the path along the creek bank with little difficulty. She crawled through the barbed wire fence that separated the Tucker farm from the Day farm and walked beside the creek for a few minutes, past the overhung willow, until things began to look less familiar to her. She stopped walking, turned around to face the way she had come, and scanned the path and the woods for the subtle scuffs and broken twigs that would show her where to head into the brush.

As she stood silent, studying the path, Alafair heard a noise in the woods. At first, she thought it was a breeze rustling the dead leaves in the trees, but there was no breeze. Just dead calm and an oppressive cold silence. She could barely hear the gurgle of an eddy under the thin skin of ice next to the bank. She didn't move for a few minutes, listening patiently.

There it was again. Alafair definitely heard a scuffle, like a small animal, then another brief silence. The next sound was the crunch of boots on leaves and twigs off to her left in the brush. Alafair squatted down quickly, still in the path, but now no longer readily visible in her brown coat among the bushes. The crunching became a crashing as whoever it was made his way out of the brush and toward the footpath. He was not worried about being discreet, this big-footed person. Alafair had pretty much decided that it was going to be John Lee or one of the other Days, so she was startled when a tall, scrawny, middle-aged man burst out onto the path so close that he nearly stepped on her. Alafair popped to her feet with a yelp, which was echoed by the man. His arms were full of earthenware jugs, and he came close to losing his footing and plunging headlong into the creek. Without thinking, Alafair reached out and grabbed his arm to save him a chilly dip.

"Lord have mercy!" the man exclaimed. "What the blue blazes? Who is that? Is that Alafair Tucker?"

Alafair dropped the man's arm quickly and stepped back away from him, her heart pounding. "Jim Leonard," she observed.

"What are you doing here on the Day farm?"

Leonard blinked his rheumy eyes at her, still reeling a bit from the fright, but apparently mostly sober. "I could ask you the same question," he said.

There was a moment of silence as they eyed one another. Leonard knew he was caught with the goods and Alafair knew she had caught him. The question was now how to proceed.

"John Lee said he thought somebody was using his late father's still," Alafair opened.

Leonard glanced at the jug under his arm and shrugged. "Weren't nobody else using it," he noted. "Seemed like a waste."

Alafair declined to comment. "If I was you, I think I would have moved the still off the Day property," she said. "If John Lee catches you, he's got a right to shoot you."

"I doubt if'n John Lee would shoot me," Leonard opined. "Such a mild boy."

Alafair almost smiled. "I don't know. He's been in a real bad mood."

Leonard gazed at her without comment for just a moment before replying. "I'd love to stay and jaw, Miz Tucker, but I got business."

Alafair nodded and turned to leave, anxious to get away from him, but he quickly stepped into her path.

"Before you go," he added, "I'd appreciate your word that you'll keep this here little meetin' to your own self."

Alafair arranged her face to be the picture of calm, but her heart began beating wildly. "I don't see as how it will come up," she told him. "Especially if you was to dismantle this still and take it off the Day property."

Leonard smiled unpleasantly. "Reckon I'll just have to do that, now."

Alafair brushed past him before he could consider some alternative action. "Good. I'm off then," she said.

Leonard stooped to set the stone jugs down, stood up, and grabbed Alafair by the arm as she passed. She turned toward him, really alarmed now, and tried to tug away. "Mr. Leonard," she exclaimed, "what are you doing?"

"I want to know what you're really doing out here in the woods, now," he growled. "Was you looking for the still? Was you looking to steal from me, Miz Tucker?"

"No, certainly not," she assured him, aghast at the suggestion.

"Then what?" he insisted.

She blinked. "I don't know, I don't know, really. You know Harley Day's wife got arrested for his murder. I just don't think she done it. I came down here by the creek because she said she threw the gun away down here, and I was thinking maybe I'd find it." She was talking fast, only half aware of what she was saying, concerned only with persuading Jim Leonard to let go of her arm.

Leonard's eyebrows disappeared under the dirty blond mess of hair on his forehead. "Is that so?" he wondered, sounding amused. "Day's wife, you say. Well, well, she had cause, I'm thinking. But it's a fool's errand you're on, Miz Tucker. A pack of bloodhounds couldn't find no little pop gun in this tangle of woods. So if I was you, I'd get gone from here and not come back no more." With that, he let go of Alafair's arm. She had been straining against him so hard that she nearly fell over, but she recovered and took off down the path at a run. She could hear Leonard laughing at her almost all the way to her own property.

⌒⌒⌒

Her hands were still shaking when she was standing in her own kitchen, unwinding the scarf from around her head, muttering epithets at herself for being so foolish. She was halfway across the kitchen floor when it struck her, and she stopped dead in her tracks.

"*...no little pop gun...* " he had said.

She turned around and retrieved her coat and scarf on the fly as she headed back out the door.

꧁꧂

I should get Shaw, Alafair kept telling herself, as she headed back toward the still. She knew she should wait a few hours to make sure that Leonard was long gone before she did this, but she didn't have a few hours, and she was practically quaking with excitement over the possibilities that this new information raised. I shouldn't be wishing that Jim Leonard is a murderer, she admonished herself. But truth be told, if she had to choose between Phoebe, John Lee, Mrs. Day, the Langs, junior and senior, or Jim Leonard as Harley's killer, well, she guessed she'd choose Jim Leonard.

As she neared the clearing, she slowed down to a tip-toeing walk, listening intently. She was sweating with anxiety, in spite of the bitter cold. She crouched down low and peered through the brush for several minutes before she crawled into the open place where the little distillery was set up. There was no sign of Jim Leonard, but she expected that he would be back as soon as he had deposited the jugs he had been carrying at his own place. He was afoot when she saw him, and unless he had left a mount up by the road, it would take him close to an hour to walk home, drop his goods, and get back here.

Still, no point in dallying.

Why she thought the pistol might be hidden here, she couldn't say. Mrs. Day had said she had thrown it into the creek, and throwing it into the creek would be the smart thing to do. However, Alafair's derringer was a fine little gun, worth a lot of money, and it seemed to her that a person like Jim Leonard would be loathe to throw it away. And if he had shot Harley with it, Leonard would be disinclined to hide the gun on his own property when he had a perfectly good hiding place right here. And so, following her intuition with her customary faith, she launched into a search.

Alafair peered into the big tin tub, hoping she wasn't going to have to sift through gallons of fermenting mash, but it was empty, and she sighed a sigh of relief. She squatted down and removed one mitten, then reached under the pot into the fire hole and pulled out a handful of ash, crumbling it between her fingers. She studied the pile of charcoal and ash that had been raked out of the fire pit, then stuck her hand down through the top of it, carefully brushing and crumbling. When she had sifted down to the bare earth and come up empty-handed, she sat back on her heels and puffed a foggy breath, thinking. Her gaze swept the clearing, searching for anything of significance. She paused to eye a long branch, which was leaning at an unnatural angle against the trunk of an oak. Then she saw a similar branch, and another, covered over with twigs and dead leaves—a small lean-to at the perimeter of the clearing, so cunningly constructed that had she not been squatting just where she was, she'd have never seen it.

Alafair fell forward onto her hands and knees and crawled around the side of the lean-to, where she found a neat opening. She peering cautiously into the dim interior, checking for hidden dangers, before poking her head in. The little shelter was larger than it appeared from the outside. A makeshift bed of blankets stretched down the side, under the leaning roof of branches. The blankets were cold, but relatively clear of detritus. Someone had been sleeping rough.

Alafair felt around and under the blankets and came up with nothing. She felt more hopeful about a makeshift shelf of old brick and a few rocks, which had been constructed at the foot of the pallet, but was disappointed to find only a tightly sealed jar of jerky, a tin cup and a small lantern. A little cloth-wrapped bundle which held two pieces of quartz and a turkey feather piqued her interest, and she wondered in passing whether it had been Harley or Jim who possessed the sensibility to appreciate such pretty things.

She put the bundle aside and turned her attention to the neat pyramid of empty stone pint jars laying on their sides next to the trees, under a loose pile of leaf litter. One by one she lifted the jars, turning each one over and shaking it out, then running her fingers inside just for good measure. As soon as she lifted the fifth jar, she could tell by the weight that there was something in it, and her heart leaped. She backed out of the lean-to with the jar in her hand, into the better light of the clearing. She turned the jar over, and an object fell out into her hand. It looked at first like a large lump of charcoal, but when she shook the ash off of it, Alafair could see that it was a small packet wrapped in an old flour sack. She unwrapped the dirty cloth, and there it lay in her hand—a silver-plated derringer with an ebony handle.

She actually gasped. "I declare," she exclaimed. "I declare!"

Alafair rewrapped the gun with shaking fingers and redeposited it in the jar, then carefully replaced the jars where she found them, all the while praying her thanks for the inspiration. She was smoothing the disturbed leaves at the entrance to the lean-to, when she heard the tiniest rustle of branches behind her. She leaped to her feet and turned to face Jim Leonard, now infinitely more inebriated than when he had accosted her an hour before. They gazed at one another in silence for an instant, both equally taken aback.

"I knew you was coming to steal from me," Leonard suddenly roared.

"Now, Jim…" Alafair began, but before she could finish the sentence, Jim Leonard drew back his fist and punched her right in the jaw.

Chapter Thirteen

Alafair came up slowly to a feathery touch on her cheek. She raised her hand and brushed it away. Her head ached like sin, and her jaw hurt. Her hand traveled up to the top of her head, and she could feel something wet on her scarf. She half-opened her eyes, but all she could see were the dead leaves and branches her head was cradled on.

Something touched her cheek again, and she opened her eyes all the way. It was hard to focus, but she could see what she thought was a small shoe close to her face. With a groan, she rolled over onto her back and found herself looking into a child's face.

Well, maybe. She blinked. His curly black-haired head was silhouetted against the dim light through the trees. His little hand patted her face solicitously. Alafair's first thought was to wonder what a little boy was doing out here in the cold all by himself.

"Hello, young'un," she managed hoarsely. " I don't know you. Where's your mama?"

He didn't answer, but grinned at her with two brand-new front teeth and a hole where a canine tooth should be. She took his hand and let him help her sit up. She moaned and touched the back of her head again, and came away with a bit of bright blood on her fingers. She could see the rock that she had struck her head on, lying on the ground close to where she had fallen, a cylindrical hunk as big as her fist. If she hadn't had the long wool scarf wrapped around her head a few times, the rock probably would have killed her.

"He whacked me a good one," she observed to the boy. She could see him more clearly now. He was about eight years old, she figured, big green eyes and a freckled nose, dressed only in knickers with one strap hanging off his shoulder, and a white linen shirt. His once-white stockings were falling down, one of them actually balled up over his scuffed high-top shoes. A wool cap over his untrimmed curls seemed to be his only sartorial concession to the cold. He looked like any young fellow after a day of serious play. She was sure she didn't know him, but he was incredibly familiar. "Where did you come from, child?" she asked again, concerned.

The boy still had nothing to say, but took her arm and helped her to her feet. She steadied herself against his slight frame and tried to orient herself. She had to ponder for a moment before she could remember what had happened to her.

"Jim Leonard," she said to the boy. "We'd better get on out of here before he takes a notion to come back and clobber the both of us."

She tried to take a step and reeled a bit, and the boy leaned into her side. She looked down at him. "I'm a mite unsteady," she acknowledged. "I sure am lucky you came along, or I don't know what would have happened to me."

He grinned up at her. He was a sturdy youngster, but a little small for his age.

Alafair's forehead wrinkled. "I'm Miz Tucker," she said. "What's your name?"

He kept smiling at her, but didn't answer. He took a step toward the path, urging her to move.

She obediently let him lead her through the brush. "You're a quiet one," she observed. "Can't you talk?"

They emerged onto the path. The boy let go of her and stood holding her hand until she felt more steady. Alafair looked anxiously up and down, but there was no sign of anyone else. "I guess he knocked me stupid," she told the boy. "I can't rightly tell which way to go."

The boy patted her hand a couple of times, then pointed to the west.

She nodded. "I expect you'd better come on back home with me until we can figure out where you belong," she said to him.

The boy smiled again, then gestured for her to bend down, as though he wanted to whisper to her. Still too unsteady to bend, she crouched at the knees until she and the child were face-to-face. She could smell peppermint candy on his breath. She turned her ear toward him, and he leaned in, but instead of whispering, he brushed a kiss against her cheek, giggled a silvery giggle, and disappeared into the brush.

Alafair straightened so quickly that she almost fell. "Boy!" she called. She heard his running footfalls in the woods for just a few seconds, then nothing but wintery silence. She seriously considered following him, but realized that she was in no condition, and turned for home.

It was a long, cold walk. What would normally have taken twenty minutes took Alafair the better part of an hour, since she kept having to stop and rest. The bleeding from her head wound had stopped, and had dried on her scarf, making it stiff and scratchy. She didn't think she was really seriously hurt, but she had a terrible headache that periodically made her nauseated with the pain. Then she would have to find some likely stump or rock or hillock and sit down with her head in her hand until her stomach settled. She was nearly frozen through. She had lost one of her mittens, and her bare hand was getting numb in spite of her efforts to keep it in her pocket or under her armpit as she walked. She had stopped feeling her toes long ago. The sky was lowering and gray. She had no idea how long she had been gone from the house. Had she been unconscious for hours, or only a few minutes? It was still daylight, but since she couldn't see the sun, it could have been two o'clock or six, as far as she was concerned. Her stiff fingers could feel a lump rising on her head.

She was back on her own property now, trudging grimly on, still not in sight of the house. Another wave of nausea hit her, and she sank to her knees, sure she was going to be sick right then and there. Her gorge rose, and she gagged, but it subsided, and she sighed and sat back on her heels, crossing her arms over her chest and chaffing her hands under her armpits. She was feeling sleepy. Her thinking was slow and confused, but she was sufficiently aware to realize that her problem was swiftly becoming less the bump on her head and more the frigid weather.

"Got to move," she told herself. But she didn't move. She just sat there, chaffing her hands, thinking, "got to move." It dawned on her that she was looking at a horseman coming over the hill. As he neared, Alafair's bleary eyes made out a black horse with a white blaze on its face, followed by two black and tan hounds. It was Shaw. He had seen her. His heels dug into the horse's side and he was riding toward her at a canter.

Oh, good, she thought, I can go to sleep now. She closed her eyes and slipped into unconsciousness, dropping with slow grace onto the bare ground.

＊＊＊

When she came around, she was lying on her own bed, still fully clothed except for her outerwear and shoes. She was wrapped in quilts like a mummy, with hot water bottles and towel-wrapped hot bricks nestling against every edge and extremity of her body.

"Mmmm," she said, savoring the warmth.

Suddenly three faces appeared from nowhere to hover above her. Dr. Addison looked glad to see her. Scott looked relieved and concerned. Shaw looked like he couldn't decide whether to cry, kiss her or explode into a million pieces. Alafair almost laughed.

"Alafair, honey," Shaw breathed. "Thank the Lord. What in the cat hair happened?"

Doc Addison's arm appeared and grabbed Shaw's shoulder. "Time for questions later, Shaw," he admonished. "How are you feeling, sugar?" he asked Alafair.

Alafair didn't answer immediately, before she took a quick inner inventory of all her parts. "Not too bad," she admitted, in a hoarse whisper. "Headachy, is all."

The doctor nodded. "You got yourself a nasty little bump on the head and a pretty black and purple bruise on your jaw. I don't think it's too serious. A small cut that bled a little. You have a big goose egg, but that'll go down soon enough. I'm going to give you a powder right now. That should help your headache."

When the doctor left to get some water for her powder, Scott, now sitting in a chair beside the bed, reached out and put his hand on her arm. "What happened, Alafair?" he wondered. "Did you take a spill?"

She turned her head to look at Shaw, who was standing on the other side of her. "What were you doing out in the pasture?" he asked. "When I came back to the house and you were gone, I couldn't figure out for the life of me where you were. I hunted for you for most of an hour. It's a good thing I thought of that path going to the Day place, or I'd have never found you."

"Where's the kids?" she responded. First things first.

"Still in town," Shaw told her. "I saw Martha for a minute at the bank when I rode for the doc. I told her to gather the kids at Jack and Josie's and I'd pick them up there."

"Did you tell her I was hurt?" Alafair asked, alarmed.

"No, I told her that I had some errands and would be late. Didn't want to scare them if I didn't have to."

"Y'all can play catch up later," Scott interrupted. "Did you hit your head on something, Alafair?"

Alafair looked over at Scott, but gathered her thoughts before she answered. The cat was pretty much going to be out of the bag after this. "Well, truth is, somebody hit it for me," she admitted. At her side, she felt Shaw stiffen, but Scott didn't bat an eye.

"Any idea who?" he wondered mildly.

"I'm afraid it was Jim Leonard."

"Jim Leonard!" Shaw exclaimed.

Scott looked interested. He sat back in his chair. "Well," he said.

"Why on this green earth would Jim Leonard whack you on the head out in the middle of the pasture?" Shaw asked.

Somebody had covered Alafair's forehead with a damp cloth, and she reached up to adjust it, peering at her husband from under her hand. "It was on the Day property," she confessed, "down by the creek. John Lee told me that his daddy and Jim Leonard had had a scrap about that still of Harley's a few days before the killing. I asked John Lee to show me the still, and he did. We saw that somebody had been using the still recently, and I had just seen Jim Leonard on the path down there. I got to thinking that if by some chance it had been him killed Harley, that hidden place where the still is would be a good place to hide the derringer."

"So you went down there looking," Scott finished for her.

"I did."

"Why, that seems unlikely, Alafair," Shaw protested. "Anybody thinking to get away with murder would be smarter to bury the gun, or throw it in the creek, like Miz Day said."

Alafair shrugged under her blankets. She didn't want to say that she knew that the gun was an expensive one. They would find out soon enough. "I had a hunch," she said.

"And you think Leonard came upon you down there while you were looking for the pistol," Scott interjected.

"Well, I found the derringer, Scott. Then Jim busted in like a bull and boxed my jaw for me. I must have hit my head on a rock when I fell. Probably scared Jim silly and he ran off. He had been enjoying his own brew for a while, it seemed."

Shaw leaped to his feet, red faced. "That hell-blasted skunk! I'll bash his damn head in for him."

Alafair clapped her hands over her ears, shocked. "Shaw! That language!"

Shaw balled up his fists, bit his lip, and sat back down grumbling, still angry, but embarrassed to have forgotten himself so in front of his lady wife.

Now Scott was really interested. "You don't say! You actually found a two-shot derringer hid in the still?"

"It was in one of the stone jars, under a little lean-to, to the side. I put it back, thinking to come and get you, but I got knocked cold instead."

"You could have got yourself killed," Shaw remonstrated. "Merciful heavens, if you hadn't managed to get back to the house you might have lain there until you froze to death and we might not have found you until spring."

"Well, I didn't think I was in any danger, or I sure wouldn't have gone," she assured him. "But that reminds me, I did have help getting home. Some little ragamuffin of a boy came along and woke me, helped me up and set me to going in the right direction. I've never seen him before. Scott, did we have any new families move in around here recently? Maybe I should have recognized him, but I was kind of knocked stupid for a while. He sure looked familiar. He just ran off then, and I managed to get to where I got before Shaw found me."

Scott dismissed the strange boy problem with a wave of his hand. "We can worry about that later. Do you suppose that you could take me to where this still is?"

"No, she can not," Doc Addison interjected. He was standing in the doorway with a glass of water in one hand and his bag in the other. Who knows how long he had been standing there? They had pretty much forgotten about him. "Alafair, you're probably not hurt very badly. He didn't hit you hard enough to do too much damage, but that could change unless you lay right there in that bed for a day or two."

Alafair started to protest, but Shaw reached out and put his hand over her mouth. "She will obey, Doc," he assured the doctor.

"Alafair, you say John Lee knows where this still is?" Scott asked.

Alafair removed Shaw's hand from her mouth with her thumb and forefinger. "He does. But I imagine the gun's gone by now, and maybe even the still."

"And even if the gun was still there," Shaw added, "how could you be sure Jim Leonard is the one who put it there in the first place?"

Scott stood up and picked his hat up off the night table. "I can't," he admitted. "Not yet. But when I went to talk to Russell Lang, and he told me his story about going into the ditch on Wednesday evening, I asked him if he saw anyone who might back up his story. He said he only saw one other person on the road that evening. It was Jim Leonard, just drunk enough to be profane, Lang said, riding a mule toward his own place."

"A mule," Shaw repeated.

Scott smiled. "I didn't think anything of it at the time. There's mules galore. But now—now I'm thinking that two and two just might make four."

"Here's another two for you, if you want to make six," Shaw told him. "Charlie-boy told us he saw Jim Leonard cutting across our property on that same Wednesday. Said he was on a mule and loaded down with saddlebags."

"Well," Scott said, and stood up.

"Are you going back into town?" Shaw asked his cousin, as he headed out the door.

"First I'm stopping by John Lee's place to see if he'll show me that still. Then I expect I'm over to the Leonards' to arrest Jim."

Alafair started to sit up, but Doc Addison pushed her back down and sat in the chair that Scott had vacated. "Oh, you think he's the one who killed Harley?" she wondered. "Are you going to let Miz Day go?"

Scott shook his head. "Not so fast, Alafair. I'm suspicious of Jim Leonard, now, but I'm going to arrest him for assault, and moonshining while I'm at it. And Miz Day hasn't unconfessed yet." He set his hat back on his head.

"I'll walk you out," Shaw said. "I've got to drive in and pick up all those kids before they wonder what happened to me."

"What are you going to tell them?" Alafair pressed him. "I don't want them scared on my behalf."

Shaw blinked and shrugged. "I'll just tell them that you bumped your head a bit, I reckon."

"Tell them that a jar fell off the shelf in the pantry and smacked me. Then I fell and struck my jaw. That sounds reasonable."

"I'll do it," Shaw said with a laugh. "Doc, can you stay with Alafair until we get back?"

"Be glad to," the doctor assured him.

After the men had left, Alafair looked over at the doctor, who was sitting with his arms folded across the chest of his neatly pressed black wool suit, gazing at her with a wry look in his blue eyes.

"He'll be gone at least an hour, Doc," Alafair told him. "You don't have to baby-sit me."

"Oh, I think I do," Doc Addison assured her. "Otherwise who knows what mischief you'll be getting into next."

Alafair emitted an exasperated puff, and shifted a little in the bed. "Well, then, you might as well help yourself to a glass of buttermilk and a chunk of bread. There's pie in the cabinet."

"I'm fine. Do you need something to nibble on, yourself?"

"I couldn't eat a thing. Stomach's still unsteady."

Dr. Addison helped her take the headache powder, and a companionable silence fell for some minutes. The doctor reached into his bag and pulled out a book, and Alafair stared at the ceiling.

"How's Miz Doc?" she asked, at length.

"Ann is fine. Busy as a bee."

Alafair made an interested noise, and then asked the question she really had in mind. "Doc, I'm worried about that child I saw in the woods. It's colder than all get-out, and he wasn't hardly dressed to speak of. He looked familiar to me, but I'd swear I haven't seen him before."

Doc Addison lowered the book into his lap. "Did he seem ragged or ill-cared for?"

"No, not a bit of it," she confessed.

"Well, he probably belongs around here somewhere. You know youngsters hardly feel the cold. He may have been running home when he came across you. What did he look like?"

"Eight or nine years old, I'm guessing. Smallish for his age, but healthy. Had a head full of black curls. Rosy-fair cheeks and freckles on his nose. Big green eyes."

"But for the green eyes, he sounds like Gee Dub when he was that age," Addison observed.

Alafair considered this. "Why, yes, he does! That's probably why he looked familiar to me. There was something about him. I wish I knew who he was. I wish I knew he was home safe."

"I wish you'd stop worrying," Doc Addison admonished. "It doesn't sound to me like he was in any distress. He's probably just some boy from around here whom you haven't seen since he was a baby. You have children enough of your own without worrying about some young stray."

Alafair didn't reply, chastened. But she wondered about him still.

☙☙☙

The four older girls took turns staying home to run the house while Alafair recuperated none too graciously from her bump on the head. The inactivity galled her, so she kept as busy as she could with sewing and mending. The girls knew her routine as well as she did, and they were all meticulously well-trained, and even talented, cooks and housekeepers. No direction was necessary. Alafair was proud of her daughters, and gratified to see what competent women they had become. Alafair had graduated from her bed to a rocker in the parlor, and was watching through the kitchen door as Mary cooked dinner.

Mary was an inspired cook, a deft hand with herbs and spices and a canny creator of sauces, always willing to go to some trouble to create a dish.

Today, though, on the third morning, before dinner, Mary was making a pie from the pecans that Alafair had cracked earlier in the week, and she seemed to have no desire to deviate from her mother's recipe. Why mess with perfection, after all?

Alafair watched her with interest as she beat the eggs until they were lemony yellow, then stirred in the dark corn syrup, sugar, butter, a bit of vanilla, a dash of salt, and a cup of the prettiest pecan halves she could find in Alafair's batch. She poured the mix into her pie shells and slid the pies into the oven, then turned to slicing the meat loaf that she had left to cool a little on the back of the stove.

"I wish you girls were home all the time," Alafair observed to Mary. "I wouldn't have to lift a finger."

Mary wiped her hands on a dishcloth and shot her mother an ironic glance. "Well, Ma, I thought you said we were all the laziest girls ever born," she said.

"I may have to revise my opinion," she admitted. "I suppose you'll do in a pinch."

Mary slid a pan full of biscuits into the oven. "You mean to say you think we're no longer lazier than Uncle Ed?"

Alafair puffed a laugh. The legendary Uncle Ed—which grandparent's uncle he had been wasn't entirely clear—was the family paragon of laziness to which all laziness aspired. "The one time his mama ever asked Uncle Ed to do dishes, he tried to drown himself in the dishwater. Y'all do better than that."

"High praise indeed," Mary conceded. She straightened to peer out the kitchen window. "Here comes Daddy," she told her mother, "and John Lee Day is with him."

"I'll swan!" Alafair stood up and walked over to open the front door. "Just in time for dinner, John Lee," she called, as the two men walked onto the porch and into the house.

"Thank you, Miz Tucker," John Lee responded. "I'd admire some dinner, if you've enough."

"Always enough for company," Alafair said. "Isn't that so, Mary?"

"Always enough for an army, Ma," Mary assured her.

⌒⌒⌒

After grace was said and they were passing around the meat loaf, Alafair asked John Lee for an update on the murder investigation.

"Well, since the sheriff found the gun at the still and arrested Jim Leonard," John Lee told her, "he's finally gotten my ma to take back her confession."

"That's good news," Alafair said. "Did he get the judge to drop the charges?"

"It don't seem to be that easy," Shaw interjected. "Scott's got to submit some kind of evidence that she couldn't have done it in spite of her recant, which he will. Seems he told her he found the gun, and in spite of her insisting that she had stashed it and lied about throwing it in the creek, she wasn't able to tell him where it was hidden. Once he told her that John Lee was no longer the likeliest suspect, she admitted that she had confessed to protect him." He paused to ladle an enormous spoonful of gravy over the mashed potatoes on his plate. "Scott thinks she's still pretty chary, and might withdraw her withdrawal at the drop of a hat."

"Did he tell her that he's looking at Jim Leonard now?" Alafair wondered.

"No," said John Lee, "nor did he ever tell her where he found the gun."

"I'm thinking he's really suspicious of Jim Leonard, now," Shaw went on. "He told me that Jim admitted that he had had a fight with Harley on Wednesday afternoon. Seems Harley caught Jim stealing hooch from him, and they got into it down there by the creek, rolling around on the ground and whomping on each other for a spell. Jim says he went on home then, and that night Harley showed up at his place on his mule, still looking to fight. His story is that Harley was so drunk he couldn't stand, so Jim poked him in the eye, and Harley staggered on home. Forgot all about the mule, he says, so Jim just commandeered it to haul a load of jugs back to his place. That's when Lang saw him. I'm guessing that's around when Charlie saw him on the creek path back of the house, too. Jim told Scott he kept the mule in his barn for a spell, but then let it go on the road on Sunday. Seems he got afraid of being accused of rustling."

"Now he's like to be accused of murder," Mary noted.

"Looks suspicious," Shaw agreed.

"What does Jim say about the gun?" Alafair wondered.

John Lee shrugged. "He says he don't know nothing about it."

"I expect he would say that," Alafair said. "Seems odd to me, though, that he didn't at least move that gun from where I had found it."

"How would he know that you had found it?" Mary wondered.

Alafair looked over at Mary, struck dumb for an instant. She had forgotten that the kids didn't know the whole story of her misadventure by the creek. As far as they were concerned, her bump on the head came from a jar of canned tomatoes. "Well, as I told your daddy," she finally improvised, "I could have sworn I saw him peeking at me through the trees after I put the gun back in the jar."

Shaw bit his lip to keep from laughing at Alafair's close call, but Mary's suspicions weren't raised. "If that's so," Mary offered, "maybe he got scared when he saw you and ran away. Could be he planned to come back, but the sheriff beat him to it."

"That sounds logical," Shaw said. "Also, I think we have to agree that Jim Leonard isn't much in the genius department."

Alafair laughed. "Maybe not. My goodness, Mary, look at all this food you made. We're going to have a bushel of leftovers. John Lee, I guess you'll have to do us a favor and tote all this back home to Naomi. Maybe she can put it to some use."

Out of the corner of her eye, she could see a stricken look pass over Shaw's face. He loved meat loaf sandwiches. She made a mental note to cook another meat loaf for supper.

Chapter Fourteen

Later that very afternoon, Mary drove Alafair into town for an outing. The weather had improved immeasurably in the previous few days, becoming fresh and chilly, breezily promising a change of season. Alafair's inactivity was becoming tedious, and she accepted with alacrity when Mary suggested a trip to the mercantile. The fine, crisp weather was so refreshing that Mary steered the horse and rig on a long, looping detour around to the north of town, passing almost within sight of the Francis Brickworks. They could smell the dry adobe scent of the kilns as they crossed the railroad tracks and the narrow bridge across Cloud Creek. They were passing a small farm with a straight, shrub-lined drive.

"Ain't that the Millar farm?" Alafair asked Mary.

The unexpected question caused Mary to peer sidelong at her mother. "I don't know," Mary told her. "The only Millars I know are a couple of little kids in Miss Trompler's elementary class at school."

"This is their farm," Alafair informed her. "Turn up the drive, sugar. Let's make a call on Miz Millar. No need to look at me like I've gone tetched in the head," she added with a laugh. "Zorah Millar is John Lee's aunt. John Lee came up here the day they found Harley dead and got his aunt to drive over to their farm and pick up his brothers and sisters and keep them a while. I remember that he said his aunt didn't seem very surprised. I met her at the Day place when I went to call on Miz Day after Harley died. I haven't spoken to her about this business since then. I wonder what she thinks about all these goings on?"

Mary's mouth quirked ironically, but she didn't argue and turned the horse up the drive. Alafair wasn't quite sure herself why she felt the need to speak to Mrs. Millar again. What the woman could tell her that might be of interest, Alafair didn't know. She was simply curious to hear what Mrs. Millar had to say about the way things were turning out.

The Millar farm was as small as the Day farm, but otherwise bore no resemblance to that pathetic scrap. The house was well-kept. At the side of the yard, a large, fallow truck garden lay encircled by a white fence.

As was polite, when they grew near, Mary called out, "Hello the house!"

Zorah Millar came out on the porch to greet them. She looked pleasant enough as she came down the steps. Curious.

"Morning, Miz Tucker," she opened. "What brings you hereabouts on a chilly day like today?"

Alafair was a little surprised that the woman remembered her name. But then it was hard to be incognito in Boynton.

"Hello, Miz Millar," Alafair responded. "This here is my daughter Mary. Forgive us for busting in on you all unannounced. I hope you're not in the middle of something."

"Nothing I wouldn't rather put off 'til later," Zorah assured her. "Come on in out of the blow."

The small house was warm and smelled of bacon and bread. Zorah ensconced them on a cozy, quilt-covered settee. "I was just making myself some coffee," she said, as she untied her apron. "Will y'all take a cup with me?"

"We can't stay but a tick," Alafair told her. "Don't want to put you out."

"Now, Miz Tucker," Zorah chided, "it ain't a bit of trouble. Besides, this girl looks froze."

Mary laughed. Her fair skin flushed easily, and at the moment, her cheeks were an alarming red from the brisk trot in the chilly wind. "I wouldn't mind a cup, Miz Millar," she admitted.

Zorah scuttled into the kitchen, but was still in plain sight through the door as she poured the mugs full of hot coffee. "Y'all take cream? Sugar?"

"Cream," the two women said in unison, and Mary added, "two sugars."

Zorah brought out the coffee on a wooden tray and Alafair took a mug. She had to admit that the creamy hot liquid sliding down her throat was entirely welcome.

"This is mighty good of you, Miz Millar," Alafair said, "considering my bad manners dropping in like this. It's just that I felt the need to commiserate with you about the investigation into the death of your brother...."

She had intended to say more, but the sudden change of expression on Zorah's face when she mentioned Harley gave her pause.

Zorah noted her surprise and gave a cynical snort. "There ain't no need to commiserate about Harley on my part, Miz Tucker," Zorah stated. "I made my feelings about Harley clear enough, I think, when you and me first met. He may have been my own flesh and blood, but if there was any critter on earth that deserved to get shot and die, it was Harley. And I ain't going to apologize for thinking so, neither."

Alafair and Mary exchanged a glance. "I'm not inclined to disagree with you," Alafair resumed. "I just expected that you have been troubled of late that the sheriff threw both John Lee and his mother in jail on suspicion of killing the reprobate."

Zorah nodded and took a sip of her coffee. "That surely did fret me at the time, but I hear now that Sheriff Tucker has arrested Jim Leonard. I'm expecting he'll let my sister-in-law go directly. I don't know what she was thinking, confessing to killing Harley, when I know she didn't do it. Stupid to ruin what's left of her life for the likes of him." Her sharp blue-green eyes examined Alafair's bruises critically for a second before she continued. "My sister-in-law says y'all have been good to her through all this. I heard what happened to you over by Harley's still," she acknowledged. "I was sorry for it."

"Turned out to be nothing serious," Alafair said. "I'm getting a long layabout while my girls take good care of me." She patted Mary's knee. "It was worth it, though, if it helps clear John Lee and Miz Day. We've taken quite a shine to the Days, especially John Lee."

"And you're wondering if I know anything else that could prove beyond doubt that he's innocent of the deed," Zorah added, at last enlightened as to the reason for Alafair's unexpected visit.

"That's the nail on the head," Alafair confessed.

Zorah put her mug down on the side table and leaned back in her chair. She crossed her arms over her chest and regarded Alafair thoughtfully before she answered. "It's kind of you to be concerned about John Lee," she noted. "I don't think he done it, and I don't think his ma done it, but I can't give you any facts to prove it either way. Sheriff Tucker already asked me about the morning John Lee showed up out here to ask me to get the kids, and I told him all I know. John Lee seemed pretty flibber-flobbered, but who wouldn't be? He just said his daddy had froze to death. I didn't know 'til later that Harley was shot. John Lee has always been a good boy—he's the only reason that family has been able to keep body and soul together, to my thinking. I can't imagine that he did it, but even if he did I wouldn't blame him at all. Harley was worthless."

"Is any life so worthless that it deserves snuffing out just like that?" Alafair wondered.

"Oh, yes," Zorah said. "Harley's was. I'm shocking y'all, I can tell." She stood up, fussed around a little bit with the cream and sugar on the side table, and sat down again. "Yes, I'd have done him in myself, if the opportunity had ariz, and gone on about my business without blinking an eye. Did the sheriff ever tell you how Harley harassed me and J.D. after he lost out on Daddy's will, and put my kids in danger?"

"Why, no, he never did. You said a while back that Harley had threatened to do you harm. Did he actually try to do it?"

"Yes, he did. It was bad at first. Mean things kept happening around here. Rat poison got in the cow's feed. Made her dreadful sick. Her milk was off for days. The barn door and the gate to the corral or the chicken coop kept getting opened in the middle of the night, and animals would wander all over and we never found some of them again. A dead dog got throwed down the well. One of our plow mules got hamstrung—that was real bad. We kept calling the sheriff, and he kept going out to Harley's to talk to him; threaten him, finally, I think. But we couldn't really prove it was Harley doing it, and he denied it. Finally, my boy Doyle come running home from school one day white as a sheet, telling me that somebody tried to grab him in the woods.

"That was about all we could take, Miz Tucker. J.D. grabbed up his shotgun and rode over there black as a tornado. I was scared out of my wits that he'd shoot Harley, not that I'd have cared about Harley, but I didn't want J.D. to get in trouble. I begged him not to go, but he wasn't in any mood to hear. Finally, he came back home in a much better state, and said that he'd told Harley he'd shoot him if anything else happened on our property. That was the end of it, then. Harley started drinking too much of his own liquor not too long after that, and probably couldn't think straight enough to do mischief, anyway. The last time I ever saw Harley was about a week or so before they found him dead. He showed up here one night about supper time, drunk as a lord, pounding on the front door and cussing at us. J.D. just shooed him off like a stray dog, and he went staggering back toward home."

She paused in her narrative and heaved a sigh. "How does somebody get like that, I wonder," she continued thoughtfully. "Harley just had to blame everybody in the world but himself for his troubles. How he tortured his poor wife! He never beat on the kids much, that I know of, anyway, but he made their lives miserable. Why, my niece Maggie Ellen was so scared of him that I give her the means to protect herself. She asked me for money to get away from him, and I gave her what little money I could. She wanted to take some of the kids with her, or at least Naomi, and I didn't give her enough for that. So I guess she got out while she could. I hear she's in Okmulgee now. Maybe I'll go look her up, now that Harley is out of the way."

"Well, I never thought much of Harley, either," Alafair told her, "but I didn't know he was that horrible, or we'd have done more to help the family."

"I blame the drink. He liked to make his own brew even before Oklahoma went into the Union as a dry state. Harley wasn't always a devil, though it's hard to remember that after all these years. He was always full of blow and bluster and had a kind of a mean sense of humor, but he was a good enough brother. He seemed besotted with my sister-in-law, and he was a good provider at first. He asked her pa for her, and her pa let him take her, though I surely thought she was too young. She didn't seem to mind. Harley had the bluest eyes. She liked that."

Alafair smiled. She thought those were the first good words she had ever heard anyone utter about the unfortunate Harley Day.

—⁓⁓—

As they drove back out onto the road to resume their trip to Boynton, Alafair broke the thoughtful silence. "I heard that Harley and J.D. was feuding, but I never realized how bad it was. Did you notice that Miz Millar said that the last time she saw Harley was a week before he was found?"

"He showed up drunk," Mary remembered.

"A week before he was found is about the time he was shot, you know. Miz Millar did say her husband had threatened to kill Harley if he ever showed up at their place again." She paused, thinking, then resumed. "If I remember right, her husband was supposed to be home from a business trip the next day, but never made it until a day later."

"Ma, it looks like Jim Leonard killed Mr. Day," Mary pointed out. "Why is that not good enough for you?"

"Something just ain't right, honey. It just ain't right."

"What did Miz Millar mean when she said she heard what happened to you at Harley's still?" Mary asked, out of the blue. "Is there something you didn't tell us about that shiner?"

Caught. Alafair shot Mary a glance and sighed. "Well, I guess I've got to 'fess up," she said. "Jim Leonard caught me snooping around the still and socked me in the jaw. I fell and bumped my head and Jim run off, probably scared, like you thought. But I didn't want to scare you kids so I concocted a story. I'm sorry I lied to you, and I hope you won't take my lapse as permission to do your own lying in the future."

Mary pondered this information for a moment before commenting. "Well, Ma, I don't know whether to be amused or insulted, but I think I'm leaning toward insulted. Do you think we're so tender we can't be told the unpleasant truth?"

"I'm well chastised," Alafair admitted. "It's not so much that I think you older kids need protecting, but I don't want the young ones alarmed for no good reason. The ugliness of the world will make itself known to them soon enough."

"I'm glad Jim Leonard is in jail," Mary observed.

"You won't tell the young'uns what happened?" Alafair hoped.

Mary snapped the reins and gave an exasperated laugh. "No, Ma," she said.

~~~

Though her bumped head was mostly healed by now, Alafair used it as an excuse not to go with Mary to the Boynton Mercantile Company to shop for the few supplies that she needed. "Drop me off at Josie's," she instructed.

Josie saw her coming and was standing in the open door when Alafair reached the bottom of the porch steps. "Come on in here, girl," Josie invited. "You're just in time. I just this minute took four loaves of bread out of the oven. I'll make a pot of tea and we can test a loaf."

By the time she had hung up her coat and sat down at the kitchen table, Josie had sliced a still-steaming loaf and set out a slab of butter and a pot of sorghum.

"I've got a jar of those pear preserves from last fall that I opened yesterday, if you'd like some of that," Josie told her.

Alafair considered this seriously. "I think I'm partial to the sorghum today, thank you," she decided.

Josie put the steeping teapot on the table and sat herself down opposite Alafair. "You've got a dandy bruise on your jaw, but it looks like your head is none the worse for wear," she observed.

Alafair sliced off a chunk of the pale winter butter and was pouring sorghum over it in her plate. "Oh, I got over that in a day," she admitted. "I just enjoy letting the girls take care of me, though I'm getting a case of cabin fever."

"Scott says you found the gun that killed Harley Day."

Alafair looked up from dicing the cold butter into the sorghum with a table knife. "That I did." She spooned the chunky butter and sorghum onto the hot bread and watched it melt into a glorious golden amalgam. "I had told Jim Leonard that I was looking for the gun by the creek, and he said something about a 'little pop gun.' I didn't think anybody had told him that the gun was a derringer, and it made me suspicious."

Josie nodded. "Seems it made Scott pretty suspicious, too, because Hattie just told me this morning that he's asked to press charges against Jim for killing Harley."

Alafair nearly choked on her bite of bread, which was too bad, because it was delicious. "You don't say!" she managed, at length.

"I do say," Josie informed her. "Seems that Scott got Jim to admit that he had found the little gun in the woods back of Harley's place and picked it up and hid it. Scott found it right where you said it would be. He told Hattie that it was a nice, expensive little gun, and it had one bullet of the type that killed Harley still in it. So, Jim had motive and opportunity enough, Scott thinks. Hattie told me that the charges against Miz Day have been dropped, anyway. I think John Lee is picking her up from the jailhouse in Muskogee right this minute."

Alafair put her elbow on the table and shook her head. "Well, I'll be."

Josie patted the table conspiratorially. "What's this I hear about John Lee Day and Phoebe?" she asked.

Alafair opened her mouth to answer before a thought struck her. "Wait a minute," she said. "Did you say that the derringer still had one bullet in it?"

Josie nodded, perplexed. "Yes, one empty chamber and one chamber loaded with a .22 caliber bullet. Why?"

Alafair's heart suddenly plummeted to her boots. One bullet in Harley's head, and one bullet in the blackjack tree, and one bullet in the gun. Three bullets in a two-shot derringer. She had twisted herself in knots to keep Phoebe's involvement in all this a secret. She should have known that the truth always comes out. Where did that third bullet come from? Did somebody reload? Or was there a second gun? She leaned back in her chair and covered her eyes with her hands.

"What is it, child?" Josie asked, alarmed.

Alafair dropped her hands into her lap and prepared to tell Josie all.

⌁⌁⌁

"I'll be switched from here to Dallas!" Josie exclaimed, after Alafair had finished her tale. "No wonder you've been so interested in finding out who killed Harley Day! Well, I'm glad you finally told me, Alafair. This is quite a burden to bear all by yourself."

"So you can see the dilemma, now, Josie," Alafair said. "Phoebe and I found one bullet in a blackjack, which lines up with John Lee's story about shooting at Harley and missing. There was one .22 slug in Harley's head. Then Jim Leonard says there was still a bullet in the gun when he found it."

"You didn't notice if the gun was loaded when you found it at the still?"

"I didn't think to look. I just expected it was empty."

"Scott has the gun, and it has one bullet in it, now," Josie pointed out. "He has to be thinking the same thing we are. Three bullets, two-shot derringer. Somebody reloaded. It's the most likely thing."

"Or that derringer isn't the one that killed Harley," Alafair speculated.

"Another gun?"

"Maybe."

Josie crossed her arms over her chest and frowned. "Well, then, we're back where we started. Anybody could have done it."

Alafair's forehead crinkled, and she sat back in her chair, trying to quiet the frantic noise in her brain. In the few moments of dead silence that followed, a thought floated up from the depths of her mind, ephemeral as a butterfly. She leaned forward, trying to grasp it. "I stopped by Zorah Millar's just before Mary dropped me off here," she said.

Josie blinked at this incongruous comment. "Yes?" she urged.

"She told me that before Maggie Ellen Day ran away from home, she gave the girl the means to protect herself."

"You reckon that means she gave her a gun?"

Alafair clicked her tongue, exasperated. "That comment went right by me. I could kick myself!"

Josie waved away this superfluous comment with a flick of her fingers in the air, and got back to the point. "You're thinking that Maggie Ellen Day might have done it. But how? She ran away a long time ago."

"So everybody says. But did she come back? Both John Lee and Naomi told me that she planned to come back eventually to get the kids away from Harley. Maybe she did just that."

"In the middle of the night?"

"Well, it makes sense. If she was afraid of Harley, she might want to do it on the sly."

Josie nodded. "All right, then. She sneaks back onto the farm in the middle of a snowy night, intending to spirit away some or all of the kids, and maybe her mother, too. She has her gun that her aunt gave her for protection. Then, as she gets near the house, she sees the object of her hatred lying by the house in a filthy, reeking heap, freezing to death. It's dark, it's cold, there's nobody around...."

"It's the first time she's clapped eyes on him in a year," Alafair continued. "All of a sudden it all comes back to her like a thunderburst, all the misery, all the humiliation. And she does it."

"Maybe she feels real good at first," Josie finished the tale, "but then it dawns on her what she's done, and she runs like a turkey."

"It makes sense," Alafair said, excited. "It makes sense!"

"Now, don't go getting all het up," Josie cautioned. "I admit it fits with what we know, but we're just guessing, here. Maybe Maggie Ellen did it, and maybe she didn't. Where has she been keeping herself all this time, and where is she now?"

Alafair immediately thought of the lean-to shelter in the woods, and the little bundle of quartz and a feather.

"She can't have been hiding in the woods for a year, especially not right up next to her father's moonshining setup," Josie protested, when Alafair told her about it.

"Well, no, but maybe just for a night or two, while she got ready to carry out her plans."

"How did she plan to get away in the middle of the night with a bunch of kids? She'd have had to have help."

"I don't expect that would have been a problem," Alafair assured her. "I can think of lots of folks who would have been happy to help her, maybe to be waiting up the road with a wagon."

"Like her aunt?"

"Or Dan Lang. Or Dan's daddy! He was known to be about with a buggy that evening."

"Could be that some of the Days were in on the plan, as well," Josie said. "I wouldn't be surprised if John Lee or his ma were expecting to smuggle the kids out to her."

"Or Naomi," Alafair surmised. "Naomi told me herself that Maggie Ellen had promised to come back for them. And I know that little gal hoarded food. I saw it with my own eyes. I thought at the time she was just hungry, but now I wonder if she was smuggling vittles to her sister."

"We've got to tell Scott about this, Alafair," Josie said.

"We will, we will," Alafair promised. "But let's be sure we know what we're talking about, first. Will you take me out to the Day place right now? Let's talk to John Lee."

After instructing a reluctant Mary to stay in town to pick up the kids, Josie and Alafair hitched up Josie's shay and headed out to the Day farm. As the two women drove out of town, they discussed how much they could disclose to Scott about the incident between John Lee and Harley in the woods without involving Phoebe any more than they had to. Alafair was afraid that she would have to come clean about Phoebe having given the gun to John Lee in the first place. Unless directly confronted, they didn't see why they should tell the sheriff that Phoebe was physically present when John Lee shot at his father.

As they neared the Day farm, they planned their strategy. They thought they would ask John Lee how he had gotten bullets for the derringer. Alafair knew that there were two bullets in a fancy little case that she kept in the gun box, but any other bullets would have to have been acquired elsewhere. When Josie asked her whether the bullet case was there when she saw that the gun was gone, Alafair had to admit that she hadn't noticed. Mrs. Day had told Scott that there were no twenty-two caliber firearms on their farm, but twenty-two caliber bullets were easy enough to get. Even if the bullet case was still in the box, it wouldn't mean much.

Their main interest, though, was to find Maggie Ellen Day. It never occurred to Alafair, before now, that Maggie Ellen could be involved, and Alafair had never heard Scott evince an interest in her, either. Until this moment, the girl's flight had been just one more sorry incident in the pitiful existence of the Day family, and, as far as Alafair knew, no one had ever made a concerted effort to discover where she had gone. Her family seemed to take for granted that she was better off wherever she was, and didn't really expect her to make good on her promise to return. Or, they knew more about the absent Maggie Ellen than they were telling. Josie and Alafair would press John Lee on the matter, they decided, and if that plan bore no fruit, they would approach some of the other children.

Josie reined the horse in front of the house, but before the women could disembark, Frances Day came running from the chicken coop and launched herself up the running board and into Alafair's lap.

"Well, howdy, there," Alafair greeted her, surprised. The once-shy Frances was apparently becoming more sociable since her father died.

"Howdy, Miz Tucker, Miz Cecil," Frances responded. "Are Fronie and Blanche to home?"

"No, they're in school," Alafair told her. "How come you're not in school today?"

"I'm helping out around here," Francis told them. "I been feeding chickens."

"You're a big girl," Josie acknowledged. "I'll bet you're a big help."

"I am," Frances informed her, with a grin.

"Well, we're here to see John Lee, if he's back from Muskogee," Alafair said. "Is he here?"

"No, he ain't back yet," the girl said. "He's gone to get Mama from the jail and bring her home, but John Lee told us he probably wouldn't be home 'til almost dark."

"Well, then, I expect Naomi is around here somewhere, isn't she, sugar?" Alafair pressed on.

"She was," Francis told them cheerfully, "but she walked back toward the creek a while ago, looking for the goat. That old goat runs away regular."

"Has she been gone for a long time?" Josie asked.

"I don't know. Sometimes she's gone for hours and hours. But it's all right. Jeb Stuart is in the barn, and he's watching me."

Alafair and Josie looked at one another, disappointed. "What now, Josie?" Alafair asked.

"I don't rightly know," Josie confessed. "If we go back into town, and tell Scott about the bullet in the tree, maybe he can start looking for another little gun."

"Will he be willing to think about our idea that there was a second gun and not just that somebody reloaded the first one?"

Josie shrugged. "I expect he'll decide it was a reload. That's the most likely thing. But he might decide to humor us and look to see if there could have been a second gun."

"Maybe it was a regular twenty-two rifle that did the deed," Alafair posed.

"Not likely. Scott said there were powder burns…." Josie hesitated, mindful of the little girl. It wouldn't do to say that a rifle, even a .22 caliber, fired at such close range would have made a bigger mess of Harley's head. "I'm thinking it would have had to be another small pistol like the first one."

"Are you looking for a little bitty gun?" Frances interjected.

A stunned silence as heavy as a boulder fell on the two women. "We are," Alafair admitted, at length. "What do you know about a little bitty gun, Frances?"

"Maggie Ellen had a little bitty gun," Frances said. "Aunt Zorah give it to her a long time ago. I never seen such a little gun before."

"Whatever happened to this little gun of Maggie Ellen's?" Alafair urged. Her heart was pounding. Josie gripped Alafair's arm.

"I know where it is," Frances informed her blithely. She jumped down from the buggy, and the two women followed her as she headed around the side of the house.

Frances knelt down on the ground near the back corner of the clapboard house and pulled a loose brick from the foundation. The masonry brick was almost too big for the little girl to handle, and she had to ease it out and let it drop into the moist earth that girdled the house. Frances peered into the dark hole for half a second, then reached her arm in up to her shoulder. When she withdrew, she was holding a burlap-wrapped bundle about the size of a loaf of bread. She bounced to her feet and eagerly unwrapped the package for Alafair and Josie's inspection. The two women bent over to see that lying on the dirty burlap were a variety of small odds and ends that a girl might hide as treasures. A length of ribbon, a rose stone, a pretty pine cone, a piece of quartz, like the ones Alafair had found in the lean-to, and a nickel-plated two-shot derringer that had seen better days.

Alafair's hand hovered over the gun. "May I see it?" she asked Frances, then carefully picked it up when the child nodded.

Alafair could see immediately that the gun was empty. She showed it to Josie.

"How do you expect this got under the house?" Alafair asked Frances. "Did Maggie Ellen give this to you before she left?"

"No," Frances assured her. "Mattie and me found it a while back. Maggie Ellen didn't want us playing with her nice things, but sometimes we did, and put them back real careful and she didn't know."

"Does your mama know about this cache?"

"I don't know," Frances said. "Me and Mattie never said nothing to anybody about it."

Alafair and Josie were gazing at one another, trying to comprehend the implications of this, when Frances yelped and hastily began rewrapping the bundle. Naomi was standing at the corner of the house, half hidden in her too-big coat, gazing at them without expression. Frances shoved the bundle into Alafair's hand and took off running, disappearing around the front.

"Naomi," Josie called, "come here, honey."

Naomi walked over to them, unhurried. Her hands were in the coat pockets, and only her black eyes were visible above the collar.

"Did you know about this cache?" Josie asked her gently.

"Yes, ma'am," Naomi answered. "I should have known I couldn't keep it hid from them kids."

"It's yours?" Josie wondered, surprised.

"It is now," Naomi told her.

"Where did you get the derringer?" Alafair wondered.

Naomi gazed at the bundle thoughtfully for a second before she answered. "It was Maggie Ellen's. She told me she had hid it under the house."

Alafair gave Josie a meaningful glance. She looked back at Naomi. "Where is Maggie Ellen, honey? You've just been pretending that you don't know where she went, haven't you?"

Naomi looked surprised at the question, but didn't answer.

"It's all right," Alafair assured her. "I don't blame you for keeping your sister's secret. But it's time to tell someone, now. Do you know where Maggie Ellen is?"

"Did y'all have a plan for Maggie Ellen to come back and rescue you?" Josie asked.

The girl's black eyes were unreadable. She looked from Alafair to Josie, and back again. Alafair squatted down in front of Naomi and took her shoulders. "Sweetheart, did your sister shoot your daddy? Don't be afraid. Nobody's going to hurt Maggie Ellen. Nobody blames her for running away."

Naomi shrugged. There was quite a long pause before she replied this time. "Maggie Ellen didn't run away," she finally said.

Alafair blinked. "Well, where did she go, then?"

"She got killed," Naomi replied calmly. "Daddy killed her."

When she looked back on it later, Alafair was unable to recall how long the three of them stood there, turned to stone.

"Your daddy killed Maggie Ellen," Josie managed at length.

"He did."

"When? How did your daddy kill Maggie Ellen?" Josie fumbled.

Naomi looked up at her, still composed. "Summer before last," she said. "During harvest. Me and Maggie Ellen were in the corn crib stacking corn, and Maggie Ellen saw that there was this hole dug in the floor in the corner with a piece of board over it. She pried it up with a stick, and there was a saddle bag all full of money hid in it. Maggie Ellen figured how it was Daddy's money from selling his liquor. She decided we was going to take it and run off. She said she was going to go to her beau, Dan, and the three of us was going to move to some town far away from here and Dan was going to start his own mechanic business and we was going to be rich. We was still making plans when Daddy came in." Naomi paused. Her gaze wandered out over the yard, then back to the women. She continued, matter-of-fact.

"Daddy was mostly sober, but he got mighty angry when he saw Maggie Ellen had his money. He said she was a thief and started whipping on her. He didn't act like he knowed I was there, but when Maggie Ellen went to crying it got me scared and I hit at him. Didn't hardly faze him none and he smacked me out of the way. That's when Maggie Ellen got all riled and fought him. She called him a sot and an awful misery and a bunch of other words I didn't even know. She said he owed her that money for ruining her life. He got all red in the face and grabbed her by the neck and whomped her head against the wall a couple of times. I heard her neck snap. It was an accident that he killed her, I guess. But he shouldn't have done it."

Alafair's throat felt like a hand was strangling her, too. "Why didn't you tell anybody?" she breathed.

"He told me he'd kill me, too, and some of the other kids for good measure," Naomi informed her. "He took her and buried her out in the woods. Told Mama and the rest that she had probably run off. Everybody believed Daddy when he said that."

Josie reached out and placed her hand on the girl's head. "You must have hated him for what he did," she said.

"I reckon," Naomi agreed.

"Naomi," Alafair asked, "did you shoot your daddy with this little gun as he lay there by the house?"

"Yes, ma'am, I did. I did it for Maggie Ellen. When Daddy went after her, I should have either fought him harder or let him be, one or the other. I just made him madder. I figured it was the only thing I could do to make up for not keeping Daddy from killing her in the first place."

"Oh, honey!" Alafair choked out.

Josie put a hand on Alafair's arm. "Well, when did you manage to shoot him without anybody seeing you?" she asked Naomi.

"Middle of the night. I don't like to use the night jar, so I got up to go to the outhouse and seen him there by the house. He was laying right close to my hiding place. It wasn't hard to pull it out and load the little pistol. I only had but one bullet in the bundle, but it was easy enough. Wasn't even hardly loud enough to wake a bird."

"But your mama and John Lee both said you were all together in the parlor that night and nobody stirred that they saw," Alafair said.

Naomi shrugged and almost smiled. "I did. Nobody ever notices whether I come or go or anything."

Naomi gazed up at the two women trustingly, relieved to have it out at last. Josie was pale as a ghost, absently stroking the girl's hair. Tears of grief and rage were rolling down Alafair's cheeks.

"He had it coming," she whispered to Josie through clenched teeth. "The old buzzard had it coming."

Three hours later, a solemn group of women sat in a circle of cane-bottomed chairs around the Franklin stove in the Day parlor, waiting for Naomi and the men to return from the woods with news of Maggie Ellen Day. Alafair sat nearest the front door with Phoebe, and Phoebe's chosen support, Alice, next to her. Josie had positioned her chair close to the kitchen, holding Frances on her comfortable, well-padded lap. Mrs. Day was next, twisting her handkerchief in her lap and staring blankly at the floor. Mary was in the kitchen with the younger Day children. Martha was at home with the younger Tucker children.

There was nothing to say. This was hardly the resolution anyone expected, or wanted.

"What will happen to Naomi?" Mrs. Day wondered, out of the silence.

"I don't know, Miz Day," Alafair admitted. "But under the circumstances, I can't imagine it will be very bad."

"I expect not," Josie agreed. "Even if she weren't so aggrieved, she's only thirteen."

Mrs. Day glanced up at them from under her eyebrows. "I hope not," she said dully. "I depend on her quite a lot."

They all sat up straight at the sound of the men tramping into the yard and up the porch steps. Phoebe leaped to her feet and opened the door to admit them. Mary appeared in the kitchen door, holding Alfred Day on her hip.

The sheriff entered first, and Mrs. Day stood up. "Maggie Ellen?" she asked anxiously.

Scott glanced toward the Day children gathered around Mary's skirt, then gave Mrs. Day an almost imperceptible nod.

Mrs. Day nodded back at him. Her eyes filled and she sat back down heavily. "My baby," she said. The tears flooded down her cheeks, and she emitted a thin moan. Alafair moved over to her side and began helplessly patting the woman on the back.

Shaw had followed Scott in, shepherding Naomi by the shoulders. Close behind him were a white-faced, red-eyed John Lee, and Gee Dub. Alafair hadn't wanted Gee Dub to go on this detail, but he was fifteen now, and in his father's charge. He had held the horses while the men dug. He didn't look as though he had enjoyed it any.

Alafair signaled Mary and Alice, who relieved Josie of little Frances, and the two young women herded the children back into the kitchen and out of earshot.

"We found her right where Naomi showed us," Scott began. "Doctor Addison and Jack Cecil are still out there getting her arranged decently in a box and all. I expect we'll have to take her into town, Miz Day, for a while, so that the doctor can examine her and see if he can determine what happened. She's been in the ground a long time, ma'am, so he may not be able to tell." He looked down at Naomi. "It's just as Naomi said, I'm sure," he acknowledged.

"Miz Day wants to know what will happen to Naomi, now?" Alafair asked for the mother.

Scott placed his hand on Naomi's head. "Yes, she asked me that herself," he told her. "I'm going to talk to the city judge, Mr. Sutton, tonight, and maybe Lawyer Meriwether. Miz Day, you and Naomi may have to come back to Muskogee with me in a day or two so she can tell the county judge the story herself. But I'll be surprised if any charges are filed, under the circumstances."

⌒⌒⌒

Shaw unobtrusively slipped out the door to go back out to the woods, and he was halfway into the yard when he realized that

John Lee had followed him outside. He turned around to face the boy, but neither said anything for a minute.

"I expect you think this family is cursed," John Lee opened.

"I think your curse has been removed," Shaw told him.

"Sir, I imagine you've heard that Mama intends to sell the farm and move back to Idabel with the kids."

Shaw nodded.

"I can't get her to change her mind, and I can't say as I blame her. She wants to get out of here, and she needs the money."

"Can't say as I do, either," Shaw agreed.

"But I ain't going, sir," John Lee informed him.

Shaw raised his eyebrows, but he didn't seem surprised. "You ain't?"

"No, sir, I am not. I've already talked to Mr. Francis at the brick works about a job. Mr. Turner at the livery, too. He's going to let me sleep up in the loft for part time work when I'm not at the brick plant. I'm saving every penny I make for as long as it takes, until I have enough to set myself up. Then I'm going to ask for Phoebe's hand in marriage."

Shaw nodded. "That may take several years," he warned.

"I don't care, Mr. Tucker. Phoebe said she'd wait for me. I'll do whatever I have to in order to be deserving of her."

Shaw's mustache twitched. "We'll see how determined you are after you've worked yourself to a frazzle for a couple of years."

John Lee drew himself up tall. "Yes, sir, you will see," he assured Shaw.

Shaw turned and took a few steps toward his horse, then turned back to John Lee, as though something had just struck him. "By the way," he said, "it seems you haven't heard that I'm buying the farm from your mother."

John Lee blinked, not sure he had heard correctly. "Sir?"

"I'm buying the farm from your mother," Shaw repeated. "It's good farm land with a creek and buildings, and adjoins my farm as neat as you please. It's a good deal for me."

"You're buying this farm?" John Lee managed stupidly.

"I am," Shaw confirmed. He placed one hand on his hip and waved the other hand expansively over his new domain. "I'm planning on tearing down this poor house, if it don't fall down before I can get to it. I think I'll put in a few acres of beans the first year. Good for the soil. Might use some of that back acreage for horses."

John Lee stood gazing mutely, his eyes wide and his bottom lip caught between his teeth, wondering why on earth Mr. Tucker was going on so gleefully about his purchase.

"Yes, indeed," Shaw was saying. "I believe I'll build a little house over there in that pretty copse of oak behind the barn."

John Lee straightened. "Another house," he said. "Why? You planning to lease it out?"

"Best way to go about it," Shaw affirmed. He rubbed his chin thoughtfully. "A sharecropper, I think. I'm going to need a tenant…" he began.

Before he could finish, Phoebe burst out the front door and flew across the yard into her father's arms. "Oh, Daddy," she cried, "thank you, thank you!"

Shaw laughed as Phoebe squeezed the breath out of him and John Lee pumped his right hand maniacally. "Where'd you come from, you little busybody?" he asked his daughter wryly.

Alafair and Alice stood behind the screen at the Days' front door, watching the action in the front yard, arm in arm.

"When did Daddy offer to buy the farm?" Alice asked her mother, surprised.

"After it looked like she was going to be released, Daddy rode in to Muskogee and talked to Miz Day about it."

"That was a mighty big thing to do."

"Oh, I don't know," Alafair said. "It's really a good deal for us. It's just lucky that it kills a couple of birds with one stone."

"This is a real good thing for us, too, Miz Tucker," Mrs. Day interjected, and Alafair turned to face the woman, who was still wiping tears, but bearing up better now. "And I think a good thing for John Lee, too. He's a hard worker, you'll see. I think he'll make something of this farm. He'd take real good care of Phoebe. I'd be proud to see one of my kids happy."

"Miz Day," Alafair asked, out of the blue, "what is your Christian name?"

Mrs. Day paused, and her forehead wrinkled, as though she couldn't quite remember what her name was herself. "Why, it's Nona," she said finally.

Alafair nodded. "My name is Alafair," she informed the woman. "We've been neighbors for years, and now we may be kin before long. I think we can call each other by our first names."

"So do you expect that Phoebe and John Lee will get married now?" Alice asked.

"Not right away," Alafair assured her. "Not if I have anything to say about it."

Alice laughed. "You always do, Mama." She paused and gazed into the yard at Phoebe and John Lee for a moment. "They do look happy, don't they?" she observed. "Seems funny, after all these unhappy events. Everything all mixed up together, all this sadness and horror and joy and hope for the future."

Alafair looked over at her daughter. "Why, that's the way it always is, sugar," she said. "That's how God keeps us on our toes."

﹏﹏﹏

It was much later in the day before Alafair and Shaw and the girls began preparing for the trip home. Alafair was heading up the porch steps to take her leave of Nona Day, when Scott called her name. Alafair paused curiously and looked over at him standing at the end of the porch. He beckoned silently for her to join him.

"What's up?" she asked.

Scott was leaning against the porch rail with his ankles crossed and his arms folded comfortably across his chest. He unfolded his right arm and extended it languidly in her direction, palm up. Lying in his hand was a silver plated, ebony handled derringer. "This yours?" he asked.

Alafair could feel the blood drain from her face. She looked up at him. "What makes you think that?" she wondered.

"Besides the fact that it has the initials *AG* engraved on the stock?" he asked ironically. "Seems that I remember once about a million years ago that Hattie told me you had shown her a little ebony-handled gun your daddy gave you when you were a girl."

Blame it all, Alafair thought. It was too hard to remember who all you had told things to over the years.

"You know," Scott continued, "it sure is a good thing that Jim Leonard finally confessed that he had picked up this gun in the woods, because after you told me that you had found it hidden by the still, I sure got to suspecting John Lee had something to do with it getting there."

Alafair swallowed, mentally girding her loins to come clean. "Do you want to know how that gun got into the woods like it did?"

"No," Scott said. "I'm guessing it doesn't have anything to do with the killing of Harley Day."

"No, it doesn't," Alafair assured him.

"I'm also guessing that you had a real good reason for keeping information from me."

"Well, yes, the best of reasons, to my way of thinking."

"And I'm further guessing that those reasons may have had something to do with Phoebe."

Alafair had no answer to this. "Are you going to tell Shaw?"

Scott shrugged. "I don't see why. You'd better take this and put it back in a hiding place that the kids can't find. And I don't think we ought to consider pressing charges against Jim Leonard for stealing it. The fact that he punched you in the face will put him away for awhile."

Alafair took the gun from him and slipped it into her coat pocket, limp with relief. "You're a good man, Scott Tucker," she acknowledged.

Scott refolded his arms across his chest and gave her a sardonic smile. "Just don't press your luck, Alafair," he warned.

"Well, Scott," she asserted, "I don't know as luck had much to do with it."

Epilogue

Shaw found Alafair sitting on the stone bench he had installed next to the two little graves. The family had come to his parents' farm to celebrate his mother's birthday, and when Alafair had disappeared after the feast, Shaw knew within reason that she had made her way here. His stepfather had donated the land in this beautiful wood on the back section of his farm for a family cemetery when they had first come to Muskogee County almost fifteen years before. The first grave had been for Shaw's grandfather, who was worn out by the trip. There were a dozen graves, now, including the two enclosed by a little white fence that Alafair was sitting by now.

Shaw sat down next to her, and they sat in companionable silence for a few minutes. The breeze was fairly warm. It wouldn't be long until the wild crocuses began to bloom.

"I wish now that we hadn't just put 'Baby' on the one," Alafair observed, at length. "I know we hadn't gotten around to naming him official-like when he died, and I was just too sad to think about it at the time, but now it seems too bad that he doesn't at least have a name."

"I don't see why we can't name him right now," Shaw said, "even after fourteen years. I can carve another stone."

Alafair smiled. "Well, thank you, Shaw, I'd like that. If I remember right, we had talked about naming him James, after your father. I always think of him as Jimmy, anyway."

"James it is, then."

Alafair fell silent again for a time as she pondered the other small stone. "At least we had Bobby for two years," she said finally. "He'd be almost nine now."

"Seems hard to believe."

"I wonder what kind of a boy he'd be, what he'd look like now?"

"I always thought he resembled Gee Dub," Shaw mused, "but for them green eyes."

There was a pause before Alafair replied. "He did, didn't he?" She sighed. "I never thought I'd be able to forgive myself when he sucked in the coal oil that was in the jar behind the stove. I just couldn't run fast enough to get him to the doctor before his lungs gave out."

She recounted the tale in an unemotional voice, but she felt Shaw sag on the bench next to her when she brought it up.

"Now, Alafair," he chided. "There ain't no use to fret about it after all this time. It was an accident plain and simple. I've told you that more times than I can count."

Alafair placed her hand on his arm. "No, that ain't what I mean," she assured him. "I know now that Bobby is happy. He has no hard feelings, Shaw. He still loves us."

Shaw covered her hand with his. "I'm glad you've come to know it," he said.

She turned on the bench to look Shaw in the face. "You know, it looks like we're going to be having another little one directly."

Shaw's heart leaped so violently that he almost fell off the bench. "I'll be jigged!" he exclaimed, recovering. "When?"

"Late September, early October, I figure. What do you think? Are you pleased?"

It was a rhetorical question. Shaw's grin was blinding. "Well, yes, of course," he assured her. "I was surprised, is all. It's been a long time since we had a new one. I expected that everyone had come who was going to." He grabbed Alafair's hand. "I'll be switched. Ain't this fine?"

Alafair chuckled, happy that he was happy. "Don't get too proud of yourself," she teased him. "Some folks will probably think we're long in the tooth for a baby."

"Oh, not a bit of it. Ma was thirty-nine years old with a bunch of grandchildren when Bill came along. The kids will bust. Just think. A new young'un and a new son-in-law all before the year is out."

"What do you suppose your folks think of John Lee?" she asked, smiling.

Shaw laughed. "I think Ma and Papa are enjoying tormenting the boy way too much, but he seems to be holding up."

"Well, we probably should be getting on back before they wonder what happened to us," Alafair decided. "Why don't you go on ahead? I'll be along directly."

Shaw put his arm around her shoulder and gave her a squeeze before he stood and made his way up the path toward the house. Alafair turned back and gazed at Bobby's stone thoughtfully.

"Thanks for helping me, son," she murmured.

Alafair never had the dream again.

Alafair's Recipes

Be forewarned: These are not health foods.

JOSIE'S PEACH COBBLER

Filling:
1 quart home canned peaches in heavy syrup OR
2 cups sliced peaches and 3/4 cup sugar
2 tbs. flour
1 tbs. butter

Dough:
2 cups flour
1/2 tsp. salt
4 tsp. baking powder
1 tbs. sugar
1/3 cup shortening (lard, butter or vegetable shortening
      such as Crisco)
1 beaten egg
3/4 cup milk

To make the dough, sift together flour, salt, baking powder and sugar. Cut in the shortening until the mixture resembles coarse crumbs.

Combine the milk and egg and stir them into the flour mixture until just moistened.

Pour the peaches (or peaches and sugar) into a greased baking dish. Sprinkle with 2 tbs. of flour. Dot the peaches with butter.

With a large spoon, drop the dough in several large mounds over the peaches.

Grate cinnamon over the top of the crust.

Bake in a hot oven (425 degrees) for 30 minutes or until the crust is golden and the peaches are bubbly.

Cobbler should be very runny. Spoon it out into a bowl, making sure that everyone gets some of the dumpling-like crust.

SERVING SUGGESTIONS:
1. Place a scoop of vanilla ice cream on top of hot cobbler.

2. Dot a tablespoon or so of unsalted butter over the top of your bowl.

3. Pour about 1/3 cup of heavy cream over the cobbler.

(For an authentic experience, don't try this one unless you have a cow and can make your own cream, or you can go back to anytime before 1950 to buy the cream. Cream like Alafair used is very hard to come by in the United States these days.)

BUTTERMILK BISCUITS

2 cups flour
1/2 tsp. salt
4 tsp. baking powder
5 tbs. shortening (lard, butter or vegetable shortening)
1 cup buttermilk

Sift flour, salt and baking powder together. Cut in the shortening with a fork until the mix resembles coarse crumbs. Add buttermilk all at once and stir until dough follows the fork around the bowl.

Turn the dough onto a board and knead for 30 seconds. Roll out or pat the dough 1/2 inch thick.

Dip a drinking glass, mouth-side down, about an inch into the flour sack. Cut out the biscuits with the floured mouth of the drinking glass. Press the glass down firmly on the dough and give it a smart twist. Lift the glass, and the biscuit will come up with it. Shake the biscuits loose into your hand and place them on an ungreased baking sheet an inch or two apart.

When you've cut out as many biscuits as you can, ball up the dough and roll it out again. When there isn't enough dough remaining to cut out any more whole biscuits, shape the remainder with your hand into a mini-biscuit and stick it in some likely corner of the baking sheet. This is the "pony." The pony goes to the youngest child. (A mason jar will do for cutting dough, or a jelly glass if you want petite biscuits.)

Bake on the ungreased baking sheet in a hot oven (450 degrees) until brown on top (12-15 minutes).

Makes 12-14 large biscuits.

A POT OF BEANS

1 pound dried brown, pinto or navy beans
7-8 cups water
1 ham hock, knuckle joint or good sized piece of fatback
salt to taste

Spread the dried beans out in a single layer over the kitchen table. Pick through the beans carefully to remove all the rocks and pebbles and broken beans.

Rinse the sorted beans well, then leave to soak in clean, cool water for several hours. Discard floaters.

Pour off the soaking water, then refill the pot with 7-8 cups water. Add remaining ingredients.

Heat to boiling, then reduce heat. Cover and simmer for an hour to an hour and a half, until the beans are soft and the stock is dark and soupy.

If using ham hock or joint, scrape the meat off into the soup and remove the bone before serving.

VARIATIONS:
1. Add a bay leaf during cooking. Remove before serving.

2. For a nice kick, cook with several whole peeled cloves of garlic, or 1/4 cup of minced onion. Or, if you are among friends, do both.

3. Cooking with one whole raw carrot or one 1" piece of raw peeled ginger is purported to make the beans more digestible. Neither seems to affect the taste of the beans to any degree.

FRIED HAM AND GRAVY

HAM

1 large smoked ham on the bone, with fat

Slice six thick slabs of ham (at least 1/4") off the bone and fry over medium high heat until heated through and browning on both sides.

Remove from skillet and pile on a serving plate. There should be two or three tablespoons of drippings, along with scrapings, left in the skillet.

GRAVY

3 tbs. ham drippings and bits of ham left from frying
3 tbs. flour
2 cups milk

Blend the flour into the drippings in the skillet. Cook over low heat, stirring and scraping the bottom of the pan frequently, until smooth and bubbly.

Stir in the milk. Heat to boiling, stirring constantly, until gravy thickens, a minute or two.

NOTE: There is a lot of controversy over the correct method for making lumpless pan gravy. Conventional wisdom says to add the milk to the flour mixture all at once. Some swear by adding the milk a bit at a time, making a roux first, then thinning it gradually with a thin stream of milk.

CORNBREAD

Cornbread is beautiful thing. Three recipes are included here, any or all of which Alafair would have used, depending on the ingredients she had on hand. Please note that cornbread is bread. It is not cake. Sweet cornbread is very tasty, but it is not true cornbread.

RECIPE 1

1 1/2 cups yellow cornmeal
1 cup milk
1/2 cup flour
1 egg
3 tsp. baking powder
1 tsp. salt

Vigorously beat all ingredients together in a bowl until smooth. Pour into a greased 8" x 8" x 2" baking pan. Bake in a hot oven (425 degrees) for 20-25 minutes, until top begins to crack and a toothpick inserted in the middle comes out clean.

RECIPE 2

1 cup yellow cornmeal
1/2 cup flour
3 tsp. baking powder
1 tsp. salt
1 cup milk

Follow baking instructions above. This cornbread is heavier and more everyday than the one above, but holds up very well to being crumbled into soup or buttermilk.

RECIPE 3

1 1/2 cups yellow cornmeal
1/2 cup flour
2 tsp. baking soda
1 cup buttermilk
1 egg

Combine ingredients and bake as above. This cornbread has the inestimable flavor that only buttermilk can impart.

ALAFAIR'S MEATLOAF

1 1/2 lbs. ground beef or ground beef and pork combination
2 cups corn flakes
1 cup home canned tomatoes with juice
1 egg
1/4 cup minced onion
salt and pepper to taste

Combine all ingredients in a large bowl. Squish together with your hands until thoroughly mixed. (This is a disgusting process, unless the cook needs to deal with unresolved aggression or can delegate the task to an eight-year-old assistant, who will probably enjoy it very much.) Pat into an ungreased loaf pan. Bake in a fast oven (425 degrees) for 1 hour for a drier meatloaf, or in a medium oven (350 degrees) for 1 1/2 hours for a juicier one.

VARIATION: Substitute 1 cup milk for tomatoes and 1 cup dry bread cubes for corn flakes.

SHAW'S FAVORITE MEATLOAF SANDWICH

2 thick slices of leftover meatloaf
2 pieces of white bread
2 slices of red onion
mustard and ketchup to taste

Assemble sandwich thus: On one slice of bread spread one or two tablespoons of yellow mustard. Arrange slabs of meatloaf on top of mustard. Press the onion into the meatloaf so it won't fall off. Pour two or three glugs of ketchup over all. Top with a final slice of bread, pressing it down firmly with the heel of your hand to glue into place. For best results, eat over a bucket to catch the drips.

MOLASSES PIE

Filling for One Pie:
2 cups light molasses
1 cup sugar
3 eggs
1 tbs. melted butter
juice of one lemon
nutmeg to taste

Beat all ingredients together in a large bowl. Pour into a partially baked pie shell and bake in a medium oven (350 degrees) until set (30-45 minutes).

PECAN PIE

3 eggs
2 tsp. butter
1 1/2 cups dark corn syrup
1 tsp. vanilla
1 cup sugar
¼ tsp. salt
1 cup pecan halves

Beat the eggs in a large bowl. Stir in the rest of the ingredients. Pour into an unbaked 9-inch pie shell and bake for 45 minutes in a 400-degree oven. Miraculously, the pecans will rise to the top to form a spectacular crunchy layer. Don't even ask about calories.

ALAFAIR'S NEVER-FAIL PIE CRUST

3/4 cup shortening
1/4 cup boiling water
pinch salt
2 cups flour
1 tbs. milk

Pour the boiling water over the shortening and mix until melted and creamy. Sift together flour and salt. Add dry ingredients to the creamed shortening and mix together to form dough. The dough will be rather crumbly. Add the milk and knead briefly to make the dough easier to handle.

Flour the counter top and your rolling pin well before rolling out the dough. This recipe makes enough dough for two crusts. If you are making a single-crust pie such as the molasses pie above, the remaining dough can be frozen and will still be easy to work with when thawed. Of course, Alafair would have had no way to freeze the remaining dough unless it were the middle of winter, but then with nine children she wouldn't have had any remaining crust to worry about.

This particular recipe makes what Alafair would have called a very short (flaky) crust.

The Drippings Jar

Alafair and all her female relations would have been unable to cook without the drippings jar, which was kept within arm's reach of the stove. Into this jar was poured the grease that was left in the skillet after frying any piece of meat. Bacon grease was especially desirable for both its quantity and taste.

This grease, which was semiliquid in summer and semisolid in winter, was used to fry anything that needed to be fried, such as vegetables, eggs, pancakes, and johnnycakes. It was also used as a tasty flavoring when cooking savory dishes. Alafair could tell by the smell if the fat was going rancid, which it sometimes did in hot weather. She would then throw it out and start over. It never took too long to collect another jar full.

Alafair and other farm wives had no idea about calories or cholesterol, so they never put them in their cooking. One could tell this was true just by seeing how thin these farm people were. They only knew that they craved fat after carrying yearling calves, buckets of milk and small children around under their arms all day long.

Coffee

Alafair made coffee by putting 1/4 cup of ground coffee in the bottom of a tin coffee pot, filling the pot with water, and boiling it furiously for ten or fifteen minutes. She knew the coffee was ready when a spoon stood up in the cup. Coffee was usually drunk with two or three spoonfuls of sugar. Cream was a matter of taste. After drinking a cup of Alafair's coffee, one could go out and happily plow the south forty. Sometimes one didn't even need a horse.

To receive a free catalog of Poisoned Pen Press titles, please contact us in one of the following ways:

Phone: 1-800-421-3976
Facsimile: 1-480-949-1707
Email: info@poisonedpenpress.com
Website: www.poisonedpenpress.com

Poisoned Pen Press
6962 E. First Ave. Ste. 103
Scottsdale, AZ 85251